The Dragonfly Door

By Margaret A. Millmore

Author's Note:

It is important to note that the characters and events reflected in this story are purely fictional and the imagination of the author. No employee, volunteer, or patient of the United States Department of Veterans Affairs (and specifically the San Francisco VA Medical Center) would have the unauthorized access to personal and/or medical records of any patient at the center; records are kept in the strictest confidence in accordance with the law. It is also important to note that the SFVAMC does not have a rec room or a secured ward.

Acknowledgments:

The author wishes to acknowledge and thank the following people for their invaluable knowledge and assistance: Susan Prudhomme, author; Chief of Police Douglas P. Millmore (retired); individual staff members (who wish to remain anonymous) at the San Francisco VA Medical Center; Marie Stanley and Thomas Stanley.

Chapter 1

Sometimes the confines of Bio-1 could be so claustrophobic. Although it was huge—the size of a large city to be exact—just knowing you could not leave, could not venture into the vastness beyond could feel so confining. Clarisse walked the catwalk that ran around the perimeter of the main compound, sixty feet up from the vastness below, which allowed one to see the great fields, orchards, and even jungle-like greenery that blanketed the compound floor. Lazy rivers and small lakes fed the lush vegetation, and here and there a building could be seen. Some housed the equipment that made it all run; some gave them shelter when it rained and privacy when they needed it. But still she longed to leave.

Turning away from the beauty below, she stared out at the beauty beyond the compound walls; the gentle plains, the rolling hills, and in the distance, the soaring mountains, all covered in nothing but white. An occasional breeze sent ghostly sheets of snow whipping across the plains; it was beautiful and mesmerizing all at once. However, she knew that to venture into the land outside of the compound was the one thing she could never do. To do so could change everything, and one thing she did not want was to find that her home was no longer her home when she finally returned there.

A quiet buzzing sound penetrated her reverie. She turned to the source and saw three dragonflies hovering close by, and then, as if they were ghosts of her imagination, they quickly dispersed and disappeared. The facility was full of all kinds of insects, so the sighting of a dragonfly wasn't unusual, but they didn't usually venture up this high. She dismissed it; maybe they, too, were feeling claustrophobic, and soared to the top of the dome for relief.

Footsteps interrupted her thoughts again, and she turned to see Dr. Christian Blare coming her way, smiling at her. As usual, it was a confident smile that was as full of white teeth as it was of ego and self-love. She didn't care for him. Yes, he was brilliant and remarkably handsome; and yes, without him the project wouldn't be a success. However, he was only one component of many, not the all-powerful driving force that he so arrogantly thought he was. He was also a womanizer, and she cared for that even less than his ego.

"Ah, Clarisse, you look wonderful today. Am I interrupting?" he asked, flashing those brilliant teeth and winking one sparkling blue eye at her. She smiled back, but not with much sincerity, trying to exude only a professional interest toward him.

"No, just taking a walk, enjoying the scenery; heading back to work now." She was deliberately vague; she didn't want to give Christian any openings for social conversation. He smiled again. He made her feel as if gaining her affections was a game, and he was determined to win.

"Would you care to join me later for dinner?" he asked.

Clarisse responded, trying to keep the loathing from her voice. "I'm afraid I have too much work to do, especially since Jorge isn't here."

It was just an excuse. Clarisse's job was to monitor the timeline, to make sure that what they were doing did not interfere with or change things. And Jorge was her only real concern in that regard. What they were doing at Bio-1 was relatively harmless as long as they stayed within the confines of the compound, but Jorge was not at the compound...Jorge was in 2013.

It was obvious that Christian didn't like Jorge. Clarisse thought it was because Christian believed he should have been the one to execute Jorge's current assignment, which was by far one of the most important to the success of the project. She had heard Christian complain about the audacity of the scientific and world leaders' decision to bypass him for Jorge, and it was clear that he was appalled by this, but it was also clear that his ego was bruised.

She turned to leave and he reached out, gently grasping her arm and turning her back toward him. "You know Clarisse, we should have dinner together, I think it would be enjoyable, and I think the others would resent you less if they saw that you and I were friends."

Like the majority of the staff on Bio-1, Clarisse was a scientist. However, her specialty had little to do with botany and everything to do with computer sciences. Her aptitude for this field had started early in life, and by the age of eighteen she had mastered the theory of computation, algorithms and data structures, programming methodology and languages, and computer elements and architecture. She furthered her studies by obtaining degrees in software engineering, computer networking and communication, system analysis, database systems, operating systems, and numerical and symbolic computation. In a nutshell, Clarisse was brilliant. In an effort to diversify, she had minored in botanical sciences. Her botanical knowledge also allowed her to do supplemental time as an assistant to one of the biologists.

Clarisse didn't think the staff actually resented her; however she did know that some didn't understand the importance of her primary job at Bio-1. There were three timelines involved. The 22nd century was her time, Jorge's time, and the time for the occupants of the bio compounds. But the bio compounds themselves were all located in the past, a past that was ten thousand years before her time.

Finally, there was 2013, which was the time that Jorge was sent to in order to complete their mission. The only way to detect a change to her time would be to monitor a fixed version from the earliest time they occupied…thus she needed to be at Bio-1. If a change were to occur while she occupied her own time, her data would change without her even knowing it had happened.

"Dr. Blare, I'm flattered, but there is someone else." She left it at that, shrugged loose of his grip, and walked away.

God, she missed Jorge. She had hoped coming to Bio-1 would allow her to spend more time with him. It was selfish, but it was the truth and she knew it. Although he was away from the compound most of the time, she was usually able to see him every few days when he checked in. Otherwise, if she stayed in the 22nd century, which had limited access to the compound's timeline, it would be months. Of course, her job was important and necessary as well, but it was really Jorge that had convinced her to come. She knew that his success could be the only possible way to save everything and everyone, and she knew he could do it. Jorge was brilliant in ways that Christian Blare never could be. He was also kind and generous, and she missed him terribly. Lately, though, she'd had a foreboding; he'd been out of contact for well over a week. That wasn't unexpected considering where he was, but she just felt very uneasy; the sooner Jorge returned, the better.

Chapter 2

It was the mother of all hangovers, and it was peaking. I thought to myself, "Frankie, you need to get a grip on yourself." I'd been lying in bed for a while, waiting for the pounding in my head to subside. My alcohol-poisoned body wanted…needed…aspirin, but I knew my stomach would revolt. As I rolled over, hoping to go back to sleep, it did just that, and I barely made it to the bathroom in time. Sitting on the bathroom floor, gasping for breath, the after-taste of cheap whiskey and God only knew how many beers made me want to retch again. After several minutes of painful dry-heaving, I wanted water, Gatorade, and maybe some food. But I knew what I'd find in the fridge, and when I finally made it to the kitchen and opened it I was assaulted by the smell of sour milk and rotten leftovers. Slamming the door quickly, I leaned against the counter, steadying myself against another possible onslaught of barfing.

After a few more minutes I decided there was nothing to it; I had to go out. My body needed food or this would just get worse. After putting on a pair of dingy jeans, a sweatshirt, and a San Francisco Giants ball cap, I glanced at my face in the hall mirror. My eyes were so red I could have lit up a dark room with them. I rubbed my hand over the stubble on my chin and wondered if it would make any difference to my appearance if I shaved or not. Deciding I didn't care, I grabbed my sunglasses and went out.

The day was bright and post-card-beautiful. Under different circumstances, it would have lifted my spirits and I would have smiled and appreciated it. Today I just wanted to get the task at hand done quickly. The market was only a block away, but it was an uphill block and I was beginning to sweat profusely, a cold sweat that stank of stale alcohol. I kept my head low, hands shoved in my pockets, and silently willed myself up and forward. After reaching the market and filling my basket with a variety of frozen foods and some Gatorade, I paid and started back home, relieved that the journey was more than half over.

The sidewalks were empty of people, and there were no cars moving on the street. The neighborhood was uncharacteristically silent, except for the dragonflies, and there were hundreds of them. At first I didn't notice them, but the constant movement in my peripheral vision was getting hard to miss and I stopped and looked around. I was surrounded by them. They swooped and dodged and played in the warm, bright sunshine, and they were beautiful. I smiled slowly. I'd never seen anything like this; I could even feel the air move as they buzzed my face. I wasn't sure if it was the sheer number of them or the spectacular colors, but it was an amazing sight to see.

Their wings were an intricate, transparent, lace-like design that looked like carefully filigreed silver, every flap reflecting the colors surrounding them. The elongated bodies that ranged from an inch in length to almost three inches were infused with rich greens, blues, golds, reds, and just about every other color in the rainbow. I stood still, just watching them; they came closer, as if they were attracted to me. I wondered if it was the sweet smell of alcohol-based sugar seeping from my pores or something else.

This went on for what seemed like forever, and in my awe-inspired mind I completely forgot about my hangover. I don't know how long I stood there, but eventually my weakened state made me move forward. As I did the swarm slowly dissipated. I started to walk again, realizing at once that the silence was gone and the sounds and movements of a normal weekday in a quiet San Francisco neighborhood were all around me. Where had those things been a minute ago?

By the time I got home, burned a frozen pizza, and downed a bottle of Gatorade, I'd completely forgotten about the dragonflies and their amazing performance. I hit the couch and turned on ESPN. My goal was to go back to sleep, but the events of the previous night were slowly coming back to me and the memories were not pleasant.

The *bitch* had shown up (that would be Joel's nickname for her, not mine) arm in arm with a big guy easily twice my size. She was hanging all over him and shooting looks at me from the table they'd taken on the other side of the bar. The two of us had dated...nothing serious, but I guess I thought things were still at least warm between us. We'd had a small fight a week or so before. She wanted a commitment and I didn't, but I thought we were still…together. Joel, the bartender, and the old man who was my regular companion at the bar encouraged me to ignore her. As they'd said before, she was a tramp (and a bitch) and not worth my time. Joel handed me a whiskey on the house and we left it at that. Unfortunately, it didn't stay that way.

After I'd had another whiskey and two more beers, she sidled up to the bar next me and ordered a few drinks. She was so close I could smell her cheap perfume, something acidic with a lavender overtone. I turned away from her and continued a conversation with the old man about the Giants. Were we gonna win the World Series again? You bet. Before Joel could fill her order she turned to me, laid her hand on my arm, and said, "How are you, Frank?" I looked at the old man; he arched his eyebrows slightly and shrugged. So I turned toward her and said, "Fine." Nothing else…I was determined to have the upper hand.

Joel brought her the drinks and nodded his head, indicating she should go back to the big brute she'd come in with. She did, but it didn't take long for her new boy toy to approach me. I tried to ignore him too, but he grabbed me by the shoulder and turned me around to face him. I held up my hands and I think I said something like, "Listen, I don't want any trouble. Obviously she's done with me, she's all yours." I remember trying to turn back to the bar, but he held me tight. I wasn't really sure what happened after that. I vaguely remembered a fight, then Joel and some other guys tossing the bitch and the brute out of the bar, and then a lot more whiskey.

With full knowledge of last night having returned, my head began to throb at an unbearable pace. I located some aspirin and returned to the couch, and soon I was in la-la land. When I woke again it was dark out; I figured I'd slept the day away, which was fine by me...I was still too out of it to care much. I took a shower, ate some canned chili, and went out for a little of the hair of the dog that bit me.

As I approached the bar, I noticed the absence of the usual smoking crowd at the curb; in fact, the absence of pedestrians in general. Although it was a quiet little neighborhood in the western part of San Francisco, it was still a big city and people were generally out and about until at least nine or ten p.m. The quiet was eerie. The bar was dark, no lit-up neon signs or sounds of music. I tried the door and it was locked. Joel opened at eleven a.m. and closed at two a.m. It didn't matter if it was a holiday, if he was sick, or if the world was coming to an end, he was never closed during the assigned operating hours.

I briefly looked around, feeling a little uncomfortable in the silent and deserted streets and sidewalks. This was a city with almost a million people in it...it was never silent. A shadow passed above me, momentarily blocking the street light, and I looked up. There were several dragonflies swarming just beneath the light, flitting around like moths to a flame, and again I got that eerie feeling. I shrugged and headed to the liquor store, where I purchased a six-pack of beer and went back home.

Chapter 3

I don't have a job. I'm what they call a "trust fund baby." When I was five my mother married a very wealthy, much older man. My mother was a gold digger, no doubt about it, but she was also a grifter of sorts and she had the old man conned...or so she thought. You see, my stepfather had always wanted a son, and she provided that via me, so the deal was set in stone.

In general, my mother was a mean-spirited, manipulative woman, and I was often the victim of her bad moods. My step-dad, Marcus, whom my mother considered a doddering old fool, knew all of this. In fact, I'm convinced he tolerated her because of me, for which I am forever grateful. She did us all a favor and died of cancer when I was fourteen. I know that sounds cruel, but like I said, she was mean. Then it was just me and Marcus, and they were the greatest teenage years a kid could ask for; he loved me and I loved him. Marcus had a heart attack when I was twenty-five. I mourned for months; he was the only parent I ever truly loved.

Aside from all the amazing memories and things that Marcus taught me while growing up, he also left me well taken care of; a large trust fund with one contingency...that I receive $250,000 a year for the rest of my life, no more, no less. Since I lived a relatively modest and simple existence, this worked out very well for me. I stayed under the radar and kept my nose clean. When someone asked what I did, I usually shrugged and said "this or that." Most people were only making conversation and really didn't care for much of an answer, so mine sufficed. For the more inquisitive, I said that I managed an apartment building, which was mostly true. I did manage an apartment building—I just happened to own it too. If pressed for additional details, I said that I did odd handyman jobs, which was also true. I did them for the elderly and invalid in our neighborhood, and I didn't charge them a dime for the work.

I spent quite a few evenings at Joel's bar. I loved to play pool, something Marcus and I used to do in our game room almost every night. The old man at the bar was my surrogate Marcus in these games, and we could go at it for hours. I had few friends, and considered Joel and the old man to be two of the good ones. I knew Joel's last name because that was the name of the bar, but I just call it "Joel's." I never asked the old man his last name and he never asked mine, but we were still friends and it worked out for both of us.

After I downed three beers I began to feel normal again, which was a bad thing. I'd been drinking way too much lately; I knew I needed to get a grip, and I also knew why. It was a stupid excuse, but I grabbed onto it and couldn't seem to let go; it was a woman, of course. I had met her five years ago, right before my thirtieth birthday, and I was sure it was love at first sight. In fact, Sarah was the only person, besides my best friend Clint, that I ever told the truth about my financial situation and my life with Mother. But I guess after four-plus years of dating and no sign of my being anything more than what I was, she was done with me. She said I had no ambition…I could do great things, but I was too lazy. We began to fight daily and then she was gone.

A few weeks after we broke up, I decided that we needed to try again. I loved Sarah deeply, and if she wanted me to change, I thought I could do that. When I went to her apartment and her roommate told me she'd moved back to Boston, I considered getting on a plane right then and there. Two days later her old roommate called me to say that Sarah had been killed in a car accident. I was devastated, and I smothered my sorrows in booze and a series of women who were simply no good for me…the girl at the bar last night being the most recent of them. Maybe Sarah was right…I could do better. I needed to make a plan, to do something more with my life…but not tonight. I downed the rest of the six-pack and fell asleep on the couch, waking early the next morning.

Chapter 4

Selena fingered the small pin while she thought about all the reasons that this was pure madness. The story he'd told her was ridiculous and simply impossible. She stared across the sand into the distance, watching the ocean but not really seeing it. As she held the pin lightly in her hand, running her finger over its delicate and intricate silver design imbedded with the smooth mother of pearl center, she thought it had to be true. The pin was her mother's, and the only thing she had left of her. She'd never shown it to anyone; she'd kept it in her jewelry box, looking at it occasionally, but never wearing it.

The pin had been a gift to her mother from her father upon the announcement of her mother's pregnancy. Selena had never met her father. He had been a police officer, killed in the line of duty shortly after learning of his impending fatherhood. Her mother died of an aneurysm twelve years later. Selena remembered her kindness and love and the struggles she'd had raising a fatherless daughter, but she never remembered the pin. The day of her college graduation, her aunt, who had taken her in and raised her, gave it to her. Her aunt had been holding onto it, waiting for the right moment to give it to her. It was the first time Selena had ever seen it. She had never worn it; it was too delicate and valuable in her mind, like a special little secret between her and her parents.

The man, younger than she was by at least ten years, maybe more, had come to her five days ago. He was sick too, physically, and although he seemed mostly clear-minded and coherent, she wondered what the physical ailment was doing to his mental health. He had described the pin to her as if he was holding it in his hand. Then he told her the most outrageous story she'd ever heard.

She could somehow rationalize his knowing about the pin, but there was no way to rationalize the simple fact that, by his features, he could be her twin. Even though he was younger, his hair and skin just a bit lighter, he had her face; the eyes, the nose, the shape of her mouth, even the tiny dimple to the left of her mouth. And there was no way to rationalize that they were definitely related in some way, but his explanation of that relationship was impossible, wasn't it?

The man scared her, too, with the things he'd said...not just about where he'd come from, but that he himself was in danger. He'd asked her to hold onto something for him; a small metal case with an odd-looking lock on it, begging her not to open it, just to put it someplace safe and tell no one about it. He promised that he'd be back for it, or at the very least he'd send someone for it. And that was it. He'd left her with a strange but compelling story and a little box.

She had wanted to take him to a hospital, but he'd refused adamantly, saying it would be too dangerous for him. He told her he had come to her because he had no other choice, no one else he could turn to. The things he knew about her lent him credibility. With a deep sigh, she wondered if the danger he was afraid of had found him.

Now she sat on the beach, watching the ocean pull out and come rushing back in a ferocious white fury of waves and foam, and she wasn't sure what to do. She glanced to the left; hang gliders were swooping through the air, having taken off from Fort Funston. To her right, sea birds of every kind were swooping around the Cliff House, hoping for a tourist to drop their hot dog or pretzel. She wished she could just float on the ocean breeze like the birds and the hang gliders.

Chapter 5

Dyse had managed to follow Jorge from the bio-compound to 2013 without detection. But something had gone wrong, and he had no idea what it was. Jorge had disappeared, and the last time he saw him, Jorge was sick, very sick. Dyse wondered if it had something to do with the door, and his own access to it.

The other problem, of course, was the virus. He needed it, and he believed Jorge had it, but he had to find him. Jorge's cover was simple. When he arrived in 2013 he would enlist in the Army and get assigned to the base in Kansas, where the virus was created. He would gain access to the virus and steal enough to bring back. Unfortunately, the military protected its own. Jorge was sick, and they made sure he was being treated. Jorge's commanding officer had him admitted into the base hospital, and no one had seen him since.

Finding out what had happened after Jorge's admittance was proving to be quite a challenge; for such a selfish society, they sure as hell knew how to guard and protect their own. If he was a more sentimental man, one who cared more about humanity, he'd be touched. He wasn't, though, and his only real concern was finding Jorge, obtaining the sample, and bringing them both back to their timeline. What his superiors planned on doing with Jorge after that wasn't his concern.

Chapter 6

Hugo was not trained to think...he was trained to be a ghost—or shadow if you prefer—and of course a killer if needed, the latter being his favorite. His current assignment was to follow the scientist that his employers had tasked with stealing the virus sample from Dr. Jorge Mendoza. To Hugo it was obvious that his *benefactors*, to use the term loosely, were not completely confident in the scientist, and he had to agree. The man was arrogant, and to some extent careless. Hugo hoped that he would be asked to use his most perfected skill once the sample was obtained.

Hugo had been adopted at the age of five by a seemingly nice rural farmer and his wife. This was simply a front—they too were employees of his benefactors, and it was their job to raise and train Hugo for his future. His "mother" home-schooled him in the basics, while his "father" trained him endlessly in the arts of disguise and assassination. He could blend into any crowd in any situation. No one noticed him, ever. He was of average height, build, and coloring. His clothes were fashionable but plain, and he never spoke sternly or impolitely. And because of this, he simply went through life without recognition.

He'd also perfected the art of killing, and it always looked like an accident. It had to, since murder was very rare in the 22nd century; unlike 2013, when it seemed more a form of entertainment than anything else. He liked it in

2013...people killed without compunction. Every time he read a news headline, it was full of murder...spouses killing each other, robberies gone wrong, drive-by shootings, murder for monetary gain, wars across the globe—it was endless. He thought maybe he was born in the wrong century.

Chapter 7

With last night's thoughts of self-improvement still lingering, I decided to start with my apartment, which was a mess. I spent most of the day scrubbing every surface, washing the windows, and doing laundry. By mid-afternoon everything was spotless, and I felt pretty darn good.

I made my way to Joel's…I deserved a drink for my efforts. The neon bar signs were flickering a bit and the usual smoking crowd was at the curb in front of the door. I nodded to them as I entered the bar, breathing in that familiar smell of stale beer and old cigarette smoke, hearing a Steve Miller song on the CD jukebox. I went straight to my seat at the bar, next to the old man.

Joel came over from the other end of the bar and looked at me skeptically. I smiled and nodded my greeting, which was also the signal to bring me a beer. He placed it in front of me and said, "So, we gonna repeat the other day?" He was smirking and I knew it was just a joke at my expense. I tipped the beer to my lips and smiled back, shaking my head in the universal "no."

After a few more sips I asked Joel what had happened to him the previous day. Was he sick? Why was the place closed? He exchanged an odd look with the old man and then said, "Dude, we never close; what the hell are you talking about?"

Now I was the one with the odd look. I told him about my pilgrimage to the bar the previous day and how the place was locked up tight. He shook his head and said it was open, and the old man confirmed this. I let it go. After all, I was hung-over pretty badly that day. Had I just imagined the place was closed? That eerie feeling I'd had the night before came back...the quiet and empty streets, the dragonflies. I shook it off and had a few more beers, played a game of pool with the old man, and then decided to call it a night.

As I left Joel's, the lingering feeling that something wasn't right stuck with me. I knew the bar was closed, damn it. Then the uneasy feeling from the night before came over me again as I spotted a dragonfly sitting on the parking meter just outside the bar. It was the largest one I'd ever seen. Its wings were silver and its body a luminescent blue-green, and the light was hitting it in a way that made it seem almost metallic. And I could swear on a stack of bibles that it was looking right at me.

I stared at the dragonfly for another second and then turned and began to walk home. A clear memory of the day and night before struck me; the utter silence of the streets, with no cars coming along...I didn't even remember hearing any in the distance. It had been a mild night and people would have been out, their windows open to let in the night air. I should have heard them...I should have heard something.

I shivered, but not just from the previous night's memories; it suddenly felt like I was being followed. I turned around. No one was there, but hovering just above me and out of reach was the dragonfly. I shook my head and laughed at myself, but I also picked up the pace and got myself home.

I spent the next day doing odd jobs around the apartment building, then spent the afternoon at Mrs. Dimensky's down the street. Her microwave, toaster, and coffee maker were all coincidentally broken. In actuality, she was lonely and I knew it. I took my time carefully fixing the perfectly working appliances and chatting idly with her. I was pretty tired by the time I got home and decided to stay in for the night.

The next afternoon I made my way to Joel's, feeling a little guilty. I'd made a promise that I'd slow down on the drinking, but there I was again. I shrugged and went in.

The old man was sitting in his usual spot, and I sidled up to the bar and took the seat next to him. Without looking at me, he nodded his head and grunted in greeting. I said hello back and nodded toward Joel, who was at the other end of the bar. He said, "The usual"— a statement, not a question.

While Joel was getting my beer I noticed something out of the corner of my eye. Perched on the very top of the bar-back was a dragonfly…not as big as the one on the parking meter that I'd seen the night before, but with the same vibrant colors. As I stared at it, wondering how and why it was in the bar, it lazily fluttered down toward me. Before it reached me something like a vision, or a dream, or—I don't know—something, filled my head.

I was suddenly in a lush and beautiful place, like a garden, but big, really big. I couldn't see an end to it anywhere. The smells were so powerful they were almost overwhelming, but at the same time they were so clean and natural that I instinctively inhaled deeply. The smell of rich, damp soil and flowers, whose fragrances I couldn't identify but could certainly enjoy, filled my head. It was overpowering and cleansing at the same time. I looked up; the sky was a crystal clear color. I'd never seen anything like it; it was as if it had never been touched by pollutants of any kind. The clarity was hypnotizing, a light blue so clear and bright that it was almost white, and beyond that a cobalt blue that seemed to fade to black. You could almost see the stars starting to peek through. It was amazing; the clear blue of a summer day in one layer, the night sky in the next.

Somewhere far beyond the landscape of the garden I could see mountains…or maybe they were hills; it was difficult to tell because everything was white, as if covered in snow. How could a Garden of Eden like this be surrounded by snow-covered mountains? I reached out and touched the leaf of a small bush. It was cool to the touch, slightly moist with condensation, and it was real, not like a dream. I was actually touching it.

Then as quickly as the images came to me they disappeared, and I was looking at the same spot on the bar-back, but the dragonfly was gone. I looked down at my fingers, the ones that had touched the leaf. There were tiny beads of water on them. I brought them up to my nose, and that wonderful clean smell was there.

I looked down at the bar to find a full beer bottle in front of me. I glanced at the old man, who was looking at me in the weirdest way, and I said, "What?"

"What? Where the hell did you go?" he said sharply.

"Go? What d'ya mean?" I asked.

"You were here, and then you weren't. You go to the head or something? How'd you do that so fast...get back, I mean? You got Superman powers all the sudden?" His annoyance was replaced by confusion and seriousness.

"Bathroom? I haven't moved...what are you talking about?" I asked. Now I was the one confused, but scared too, because what I'd just experienced was so real. I rubbed my fingers together, feeling the moisture from the leaf, and knew deep down inside that I had gone somewhere...just for a second or two, but I was there.

Joel was watching and listening, and he said, "Yeah, what's up? That was the quickest thing I've ever seen. It was like you disappeared from your seat, then just reappeared."

Were they serious? I looked at them both, hoping they wouldn't see the fear I felt. Finally I said, "Quit messing with me."

I spent another hour at Joel's and then went home, but I couldn't get the dragonfly or the garden out of my mind. Why was I all of a sudden seeing them everywhere, and what was the deal with that little mind trip in the bar?

Chapter 8

The next morning I went to the VA Medical Center on Clement. It was a huge compound that didn't look that big from the street, but spanned over twenty-five acres in the heart of the Richmond District of San Francisco. I volunteered there at least once a week, often more than that if they wanted me. I'd do just about anything they needed, from delivering hospitality beverages, comfort articles, or books and magazines, to escorting patients to the various buildings that spanned the center. But my favorite thing was companionship…spending time with the vets, talking, playing board games, whatever they needed.

I was sort of the "jack of all trades," and Betty, the Chief of Voluntary Services, loved it…and I loved her. She was a stout woman in her late fifties of undeterminable ancestry; she once told me that she had a little bit of everything in her. Her skin was a rich mahogany color that I'd never seen before, and her hair was a salt-and-pepper mix that she kept short. Her eyes were a deep, dark brown and could emit utter kindness or put the fear of God into you, depending on what she needed that day.

I'd known Betty for so long I lost track, which was probably why I got to do all sorts of jobs; she considered me part of the regular staff. I started going to the VA as a kid. Marcus was huge on helping vets, being one himself, and I tagged along when he went. When I got old enough, I started volunteering on my own. Marcus always said the best way to give back was to help those in need. He was a huge patriot, and the VA was his cause.

Betty was sitting at her desk scowling at a paper in her hands. Her reading glasses were perched on the edge of her long nose and her eyes were narrowed to slits. I could tell she was pissed off about whatever she was reading. I knocked softly on the open door and smiled. She looked up over her reading glasses and glared at me for a few seconds. Her expression said, "I'm gonna bite your head off," but once she realized it was me, she smiled and waved me to the chair in front of her desk.

I sat and then tentatively asked, "Everything okay, Betty?"

She dropped the paper, then slapped her hand down on it and said, "Damn budget cuts again! How do they expect us to help these people without any damn money?" She trailed off in exasperation…it was a complaint I'd heard from her often. She leaned back in her chair, removed her glasses, and rubbed her nose for a second, then looked up at me and smiled.

"How are you, Frank? You look like hell." There was humor in her voice, but also concern.

I smiled back meekly. Should I tell her the truth…that I was in self-destruct mode and couldn't seem to pull myself out of it? Oh yeah, and I was seeing dragonflies everywhere I went. I laughed at the last thought. This lady dealt with some seriously sick people, sick of body and mind. She didn't need my problems, too.

I shrugged and tried to look sheepish, and said, "Just a little too much night life lately."

Before coming to the VA and becoming the CVA, Betty was a psychiatric nurse at General Hospital. She did the same at the VA for many years, and then decided to try her hand in the voluntary services department, eventually becoming the Chief of Voluntary Services. But she maintained her connections to the medical side of the center, and over her long career she'd developed a vast network of friends. Although it was against the rules, this allowed her to keep her finger in the pie and on the pulse of everything that happened at the center. It also meant she'd seen just about every form of mental and physical disarray and disorder, including those who drowned their sorrows in booze.

She leaned forward and said, "Well, quit it, Frank! You have way too much to live for and we need you here, so just stop!" Betty knew about Sarah, how hard I fell when Sarah left me, and how devastated I was when she died. She had given me the motherly comfort I'd never had and talked me through the really bad parts. She'd been around the block in the relationship department and knew all about death and getting dumped.

Her first husband had killed himself after a long bout of depression spurred by a car accident in which he hit a family crossing at a dark intersection, killing two small children in the process. It wasn't his fault; they hadn't checked for traffic and the parents were distracted in an argument, but Bill never got over it. Her second and third husbands couldn't take her dedication to her work, and eventually left her for younger, more attentive wives. She wasn't sour about it; she knew who and what she was and that she was better off single, because she wasn't going to stop doing what she loved…taking care of people.

I smiled, gave her a little salute, and said, "What we got going today?"

She leaned forward, clasped her hands together on her desk, and said, "Well, I have someone new here; a young fella, real bad off, like he's checked out mentally. They're calling it PTSD. But the thing is, he never saw combat, so the docs think he's faking it to avoid deployment. I don't think he is."

She sighed, then continued. "He said *they* sent him here to get something, but he won't tell us who or what. He just kept saying he wanted to go back there—he was actually begging at one point." She shrugged, as if she couldn't really describe what this guy was telling them.

She was also talking in past tense and I wondered out loud what that meant. "Isn't he talking anymore? You're describing him in past tense."

She smiled, happy that I caught that, and said, "Nope, hasn't said more than two words since his second day here; just clammed right up."

"Uh, Betty, I appreciate your confidence in me, but I'm not a shrink. What exactly do you think I can do with this guy?" I was perplexed at her request. She'd never asked me to try and get in someone's head before. Why would she? I was not qualified for that sort of thing.

She sighed loudly and said, "I know, darling, but here's the thing; no one seems to be able to get through to this kid...he's keeping it all bottled up." She shrugged. "You just got a way with these guys; they seem to relax around you, tell you stuff they won't tell us. I just thought it was worth a try. Remember that guy last year? Tory, I think his name was. If it wasn't for your visits we would have never had the breakthrough with him."

She was talking about a young vet named Torrance Holiday, a former high school football star with a partial college scholarship and potential that went sky-high. He had decided to enlist and get his education paid in full via the Army. What he ended up with was one less arm, and the bloody memories of his fellow soldiers and several civilians (women and children included) being blown to bits by a suicide car bomber in a little village on the outskirts of Baghdad.

The kid couldn't close his eyes without seeing blood, guts, and mangled body parts everywhere. He shook constantly, hardly ate more than a few bites at meal time, and more often than not, never slept more than an hour at a time. He was a wreck, a classic PTSD case, and there was no sign of improvement no matter how hard the doctors and staff tried.

I saw him sitting in the corner of the rec room one day and decided to go over and talk to him. After an hour or so of useless chatter on my part, I finally found something he could talk about without memories of death coming to mind. It seemed that every subject under the sun brought him back to that fateful day…except football. That was one subject he could talk about that actually brought him to life.

So we talked football. I came to see him often; I even brought him a book on football that was full of facts and statistics, and we'd take turns asking each other questions out of it. We made a game of it, keeping score on who got the most questions right. Eventually other vets joined in too. After several weeks, Tory was interacting with his fellow vets, starting to eat regular meals, and sleeping more than he had in the past year.

After a while I asked permission to take him on little trips to the high schools in the area so he could watch the kids play football. Eventually he was asked by one coach (a vet himself) to help out as an unofficial assistant coach with the team. That was the real turning point for him; he now had a purpose. Last I heard he was at City College, studying for his teaching and coaching credentials and working part-time for the high school.

However, that was an unusual situation, and I got lucky hitting on the one thing he could talk about that wouldn't haunt him. From what Betty had said so far about this other kid, he was no Tory, and his problems didn't seem to relate in any way to what I'd managed to do for Tory.

What the hell? I thought, and shrugged. I could give it a try, so I asked, "What's his story?"

She reached across her desk for a plain manila folder, opening it as she replaced her reading glasses on the tip of her nose. She scanned the file contents for a minute and then said, "Well, he enlisted when he was twenty-two, trained at a fort in Kansas as a medic. He was supposed to deploy to Iraq after his training, but things got weird. He would disappear occasionally, an hour here, an hour there. Then one day he started talking about wanting to 'go back.' He was adamant about being sent back. They admitted him to the base psych ward for evaluation. One day he disappeared altogether, and they were ready to list him AWOL when he showed up in San Francisco. He'd been picked up by the police, who found him wandering around the Tenderloin, disoriented, dirty, and hungry, and unable to tell anyone who he was. The police found his military ID and tags on him and brought him to us."

She scanned the file some more, and then continued. "His psych review is pretty vague," she shrugged. "Vague isn't the right word. You know I don't have authority or access to their complete files," she winked at me. I knew if she really wanted that access that she'd get it. I smiled back and she continued. "Who knows what their actual assessment is? But the bottom line here," she tapped the file lightly with her finger while looking at me over her glasses, "is that he's delusional…seems to be living in a world that isn't this one."

She closed the file, placed it on the blotter in front of her, and just stared at me. What was she expecting, my non-expert diagnosis? I stared back, a game we played when she wanted me to "figure it out," as she often liked to tell me when I came upon a challenge.

"Okay, well, that wasn't enlightening, but what the heck? Let's meet this guy," I said, smiling as I began to get up from the chair.

"Thanks, Frank." She picked up the phone and dialed an extension. She asked the person on the other end if the topic of our conversation was in the rec room, then made some grunting noises that I knew meant "yes" and hung up.

"He's in the rec room. Nancy said he was sitting by the window staring out at nothing. Go work your magic," she said, winking at me, and then she waved her hand at me in a gesture of dismissal.

Chapter 9

A person from the future wouldn't survive well in 2013 if they didn't have credible credentials and a background. Since 22nd century technology was so much further advanced, this wasn't very hard, and technicians were tasked with creating a program that would infiltrate all pertinent computer databases of that time. When Jorge arrived in 2013, his first order of business was to find a computer that was Internet-enabled. He did so by going to the public library; then he simply inserted the drive and let it run. Their program was designed to seek out the necessary databases and input Jorge's false identity with a full background, and generate the corresponding identification, which was then mailed to "general delivery" at the local post office…all very simple.

Dyse used the same program for himself, but instead of creating someone new, he hijacked a few existing identities. He had to; Clarisse's job was to monitor the timeline, and she was good at it. She had created an algorithm that would use everything they knew about 2013 and continuously compare the data to what their own time was reporting, thus making sure they did not affect anything. If he had created a new identity, she would detect it. If that happened he would fail, and that he could not do.

Today, his credentials said he was a lawyer. He knew this society both revered and hated them, but he also knew that lawyers got things done, and he needed to find Jorge. He approached the corporal manning the desk at the main hospital entrance at the base in Kansas. He presented his credentials and told the young man that he was an attorney, sent there by the family of Jorge Mendoza, a young private who'd been admitted earlier last week.

It took him three days to find out that Jorge had been admitted to the hospital for a psychological evaluation. Dyse couldn't be in this timeline full time like Jorge, so he had to do his work there when he wasn't expected to be elsewhere. This left little time to keep track of Jorge and his activities. He had to go back and study this military society and how they worked; it was different from the civilian society, more closely guarded. But he was a quick study, and soon he discovered what they called "human resources." He used another set of fake credentials, this time as a captain in the army, to gain access to the base, and from there he went to the administrative offices. However, they wouldn't tell him anything, either. What he did discover was a lovely young lady working there, so he followed her when she left the base.

She went to her off-base apartment, changed her clothes, and then headed to a bar frequented by the servicemen and women on their time off. He didn't think she had gotten a good look at him when he was in her office, and he didn't think she'd recognize him in civilian clothes, and he was right.

When he entered the bar he took a table in the back. Three young women were seated at the table next to him, and they smiled in his direction. As he watched his prey, trying to decide how he would approach her, he listened to the women at the next table. They were obviously also military personnel, and were complaining about their choices of men. Most of the men at the base just wanted a quick fling before deployment. The civilian men that lived and worked near the base were of even less desirable stock. The women were exasperated at these options, but he now knew what he would do. He'd always done very well with women of all ages. His extraordinary good looks and charm (when he chose to display them) allowed him to pick and choose, and he was rarely rejected.

Before following her, he had changed into jeans, a collared shirt, and a simple but expensive leather jacket. He knew he looked attractive but humble in this attire. He approached her while she was ordering a drink at the bar. Smiling demurely, he asked if they served food. She smiled back and said they did, and then asked if he was from out of town. He said he was, that he was considering moving there for employment and didn't know the area. After a few minutes of talking with her she agreed to have dinner with him; they would eat at a booth in a quiet corner of the bar.

By the end of the night she wanted to take him home. He humbly obliged her and they spent a pleasant and sensual night together. The following day they met again. He mentioned that he had a friend on the base, but was unable to contact him. She willingly volunteered to find this friend, and that was how he discovered that Jorge was in the base hospital.

His attorney credentials certainly had the desired effect on the corporal at the main desk, but not on the doctor who was summoned to deal with him. She was a severe looking woman; her skin was clear, but lined around the eyes and mouth, her hair pulled back in a tight chignon, and he supposed she was somewhere between fifty and sixty. Her eyes were dark brown and suspicious. This woman was obviously intelligent, and he treaded carefully.

In a no-nonsense tone and without personal introduction, she immediately asked why he was there. He told her he had been sent by the family, that they hadn't heard from Private Mendoza in several days and were concerned. She cocked her head to the side suspiciously and told him that he should have contacted Mendoza's commanding officer. She nodded to the corporal at the desk, who said he would get that information for him. Then she turned and walked away. He was shocked; he was sure that by presenting himself as an attorney that he would get the information he needed.

Obviously he'd underestimated some of these people and this bothered him a little, but he didn't have time to ponder it; maybe later, when it was all over, he'd come back and study them more closely. He turned to the corporal and smiled. The young man handed him a slip of paper with a sergeant's name and number on it, and told him to call to inquire about Private Mendoza.

Chapter 10

I entered the rec room and stood at the doorway looking around, recognizing several men and women that I'd spent time with before. When I went there I generally made the rounds, saying hello, asking how they were, how their families were, etc. This time I was greeted by a vet named Kyle. He was in his mid-sixties and had served in Viet Nam. His right leg was missing but he generally opted out of using his prosthetic, saying it was just easier to hop around using the forearm crutches, which were custom made with sheepskin-lined cuffs and leather grips. He really didn't need the VA services; he was a retired lawyer with a big bank account, but he came to help out, like I did.

Kyle was also an old friend of Marcus's. In fact, he was the administrator of Marcus's estate and handled the various charitable trusts that Marcus had set up in his will. Although Marcus didn't specifically include me in the administration of these trusts, he did say that if I wanted to be part of the decision-making Kyle and I should work out an arrangement. I was not really that adept in legal matters, but Kyle liked to keep me in the loop, so we met every four to six weeks to discuss the various applications for funds through the trusts.

"Frankie, my boy, how the hell are you?" he asked with a smile and good humor. He knew he was lucky to be alive, and he relished every day he spent on this planet. I smiled back and we chatted for a few minutes, mostly about needing to get together in the next few weeks to discuss the new trust applicants. He said he had a very interesting applicant and wanted my take on it.

Nancy, the nurse that Betty had spoken with on the phone, was across the room when I entered, and now she made her way over to us. She was a petite woman in her mid-thirties with light brown hair with a scattering of gray, and pale green eyes that always looked tired but determined. She smiled wanly at us as she approached; as usual, she'd probably pulled a double shift and was too tired for small talk or congenial greetings.

She jerked her thumb behind her and said, "He's over there. But Frank, you need to know, the guy is gone. He checked out way before he came here, and no one has been able to get more than 'send me back' out of him."

Kyle glanced in the direction of the bank of windows that lined the far wall of the rec room, and asked, "You talking about Jorge over there?" She nodded and was about to say something else when Kyle said, "That's who you're here for today, Frank?"

I nodded that I was and he said, "Well I sure as hell hope you can help. Kid's in deep brain shit." He patted me on the back and hobbled away toward some guys playing cards.

I turned to Nancy and said, "Tell me about him." She shrugged again. Damn, I thought, she sure looked tired and irritated.

"You okay, Nancy?" I asked before she could answer my first question.

She smiled wanly again, but this time there was emotion in her eyes that said, "Yeah, I'm okay." She added, "It was a rough night, but I'm out of here in a few minutes." She cupped her hand to her ear and said, "I can hear my bed calling me, and that's all I really need—some sleep."

She sighed and pulled me into the hallway. "Kyle's right, the kid's brain is fried. From what I could find out he was stationed at a fort in Kansas for basic training; he wanted to be a medic. I have a friend there so I called her and got the low-down on him. He started disappearing for an hour here and there, then half a day, then days at a time. When the longer disappearances started, he began to talk about the 'virus,' how he had to go back or the project would fail. But he wasn't part of any project on base; he was just part of basic training, nothing unusual.

"His CO tried to be understanding, thinking the kid was just experiencing the jitters about deployment, and had him sent to the base hospital for evaluation. When they brought him here we contacted the CO. He said to keep him. Some of the doctors both here and there are trying to call it PTSD, but without having seen combat that's as inaccurate a diagnosis as you can come by. Anyway, he's here now...." She shrugged. "I think it's more to get him out of their hair than anything else. Our doctors haven't been able to make any progress with him. He eats when he's told to, doesn't cause any trouble, and doesn't talk to anyone...just sits there." Again she jerked her thumb over her shoulder toward Jorge and finished with, "By that window, staring out at nothing."

I gently put my hand on her shoulder and said, "Thanks, Nancy; hope you're going home soon." She nodded and walked away, hopefully to her locker, then her car, then home. I took a deep breath and re-entered the rec room. As I made my way to the windows and Jorge, I stopped off and said hello to the other vets I knew. It took me about ten minutes to finally get to Jorge, and he hadn't moved the whole time I'd been in the room.

He was of average build, but looked thin, like he could use ten or twenty more pounds on him. His head was shaved and his skin was an even, light olive tone. His facial features were handsome; straight nose, evenly spaced eyes. He had the slightest dimple to the left of his mouth and he was clean shaven. Betty had told me he was twenty-two, but he looked younger, fragile and innocent. His eyes were a light brown color and as vacant as a spring day in Chernobyl. There just wasn't anyone home. I sat down in the chair next to him and said hello. No reaction from Jorge.

I leaned back in my chair and got comfortable, and began talking. First I told him about myself, where I lived, what I did, what my dreams were. Since I was a pretty simple guy this didn't take very long. There was no reaction from Jorge; for all I could tell he didn't even know I was there. I leaned over, gently touched his hand, and said, "So Jorge, tell me about you."

Jorge moved his head very slowly in my direction, but the vacant stare was still there. He was only reacting to having been touched, but I took that as a good sign anyway. I got up and walked over to the bookshelves on the far wall of the room and selected a Scrabble game. I'd read somewhere that people often spelled out their thoughts when playing the game, and thought it was worth a try. When I got back to my chair, Jorge was back to staring out the window. I pulled a little side table between us and started setting up the game, all the while talking aimlessly and explaining how the game was played.

I started the game and tried to engage Jorge. Still nothing—just that blank stare. I leaned a little closer to him, trying to see what was in his line of sight, assuming he was actually seeing anything. The window looked out onto the center's grounds—trees, grass, and flowers in the foreground, people and cars moving around in the parking lot. Beyond that, a bus out on Clement Street was slowly turning into the compound. Technically, his line of sight was directly into the branches of a cypress tree. He twitched, then moved a little forward and twitched again, as if seeing out the window for the first time. I followed his gaze. Two butterflies were frolicking in and around thick green cypress branches. He sighed, as if disappointed by what he saw.

I said, "They're pretty, the butterflies."

He mumbled something in response and I asked what he'd said, moving closer to him in case he mumbled again. He did. "I thought it was the dragonflies," he said almost inaudibly.

The mention of dragonflies caught me off guard and I wasn't sure how to respond. Finally I said, "What about the dragonflies, Jorge?"

This time I got no response, but I was still a little shocked—the continued occurrences of these damn bugs were beginning to *bug* me. I spent another half-hour trying to get him to talk, but no luck. I decided to spend some time playing cards with some of the other vets and then I headed home.

Chapter 11

Since I lived in the same general neighborhood as the VA, I usually walked there and back. Today was no different. I left the compound and headed south on 42nd Avenue toward Balboa Street and my neighborhood. The day was a typical San Francisco day. Fog had blanketed most of the western part of the city overnight, and since the Richmond District was at the north-western end of the city and flanked by the Pacific Ocean on the west and the bay on the north, the fog hadn't completely receded yet. A lot of those kind of days, the fog turned to overcast skies and there was no sign of the sun. Today it was like that; overcast, slightly foggy with a light ocean breeze, sort of damp and depressing.

People who lived in the city long enough became accustomed to the weather; those post-card sunny days didn't come nearly as often as the tourist board would like people to think. The city was full of micro-climates; while downtown could be enjoying a beautiful clear sky, the Richmond and Sunset Districts would be grey and overcast. The Mission and Potrero Hill Districts seem to see more sunny days than most. My general rule of thumb was, never leave the house without a jacket and sunglasses. Depending on where you were in the city that day, you'd most likely need both.

I wasn't really paying any attention to my surroundings though, mostly because I'd made the trek so many times I was on autopilot, but also because I couldn't stop thinking about Jorge and his dragonfly comment. Generally these solitary walks led me to thoughts about Sarah, and that was never a good thing. She was gone, and was never coming back; I really needed to accept that. When we were together she often accompanied me to the VA. She thought it was the most wonderful thing. The vets loved her, and so did Betty. She wasn't just beautiful on the outside (although that certainly helped when it came to the men); she was amazingly beautiful on the inside. When we broke up and she stopped coming, the vets harangued me for months, berating and faulting me for her absence. Of course, that absence was due to her moving and subsequently dying, information that only Betty, Kyle, and my best friend Clint knew. The vets had enough people dying around them, and I wasn't going to add to their never-ending list of casualties. However, they were right…it was my fault, but it was hers too; she could have stayed in San Francisco, where she wouldn't have been killed by some asshole drunk driver.

Today, however, my thoughts of Sarah were specifically related to Jorge's comment. Back when Sarah and I were still happy, we once were walking through Golden Gate Park on a beautiful day and we came upon the Conservatory of Flowers. The conservatory was a marvel of Victorian architecture and the oldest glass and wood conservatory in North America, not to mention the oldest building in the park. It had a center dome and wings spanning on each side, and was divided up inside to accommodate a variety of plant species. Although the building had been constantly maintained and repaired since its completion in 1878, it received a major rehabilitation from 1999 to 2003, resulting in historical status and making it yet again a favorite of tourists and locals alike.

As we approached, we saw a sign for a butterfly exhibit in one of the greenhouse rooms and Sarah made a beeline for it. It was a wondrous sight; more than twenty-five species of butterflies were free-flying around the large room from flower to colorful flower, sometimes even landing on people.

Jorge's mention of the dragonflies while looking at the butterflies brought back the memory, and from there I connected it to the garden experience I'd had at Joel's, although the similarities ended there. The gardens were vastly different, and of course my sightings were of dragonflies, not butterflies. But the sensation was the same…being surrounded by such beautiful creatures, the smell of the plants and damp soil of the conservatory, and the similar smells of the "other" place. I tried to remember if I'd seen dragonflies in the "other" place. I didn't think so, but I definitely saw one before I went there. All I could really be sure of was that they were somehow connected—the dragonflies and the other place—and that logic dictated that I didn't actually go anywhere, that maybe I was having a very lucid daydream of some sort.

I was approaching Geary Street, a busy thoroughfare running east and west through the city, two and three lanes going each way. As I waited for my opportunity to get across, it happened again. I was no longer on the corner...I was on a footpath of gravel, surrounded by lush greenery. The shock of it caused me to stumble, and I fell to one knee before catching myself. But it was undeniable; I was no longer in San Francisco. I could feel the gravel embedded in my palm where I'd caught myself. I could smell scents so sweet and fragrant that they almost gagged me, and I could smell the damp earth and fresh dew on the plants and flowers around me. I looked up, and there it was again...a sky so clear, so clean, that it would be impossible for it to exist in the world I lived in.

I slowly got up, moved to the edge of the path, and gently touched a large leaf, feeling its glassy smoothness, my fingers dampening in the dew that dripped off its edges. In an almost fugue state I moved down the path, listening to my feet crunch lightly on the gravel.

Remembering the dragonflies, I looked around. It was then I realized that there was other wildlife there. Birds flitted here and there, butterflies too, but not a dragonfly in sight, so I kept walking. Then I heard another sound...voices...not too far away, and I stopped and listened. They were talking too quietly for me to understand their words, so I moved closer, this time moving into the damp soil so that my feet wouldn't make noise.

I saw a man and a woman, both wearing white tailored coveralls. He was tall, over six feet at least, with light blond-brown hair that was thick and unkempt and beginning to cover his ears. His skin was lightly tanned and he had on thick black-rimmed glasses that he was constantly pushing up on his nose. He had sharp features, and could have been a good looking guy if he ditched the glasses and combed his hair.

Her figure was petite, but she was at least five-eight in height; her hair was jet black with reddish-gold streaks through it, and her skin was creamy and smooth. I couldn't see her entire face, but she looked younger than the man, and her voice had a soft lilting accent, possibly British.

He seemed to be agitated and was waving his hands around as he talked. She was calm and composed, and it was obvious she was trying to get him into the same frame of mind. As they came closer, I could understand what they were saying. She said, "We haven't heard from him yet, but we will."

He pushed his glasses back up and said in that agitated tone, "When? If he doesn't get back we're in big trouble; we need that sample, without it…." He trailed off.

The agitation was rising in his voice to the point of panic. She turned slightly, laying her hand gently on his arm and saying, "Jonathan, it's not just us that would be destroyed if we don't get him back here. He'll probably die, too; the device isn't meant to allow him to be gone this long."

The man, Jonathan, didn't seem to care about "him." He said, "Yeah, yeah, that too, but what about"—he waved his arms around the garden—"this? It would all be for nothing if we don't get that sample. This is the only thing keeping the planet from utter destruction, and it's not enough. If we don't succeed, then neither does the human race."

Now that I could see her face, I realized she was probably in her early-to mid-twenties. She was pretty and her eyes were an astonishing color of green. Even though she was young, her eyes held an impression of knowledge, intelligence, compassion, and determination, all at the same time. I wanted to move closer, to see her better, but I couldn't because a second later I wasn't there anymore.

A horn honked loudly and I again stumbled to the ground, this time hitting hard concrete and knocking my head against a telephone pole. I stood up and looked around. I was across Geary on the opposite corner; cars were zooming by in the street. Had I crossed the street without knowing it? This was crazy, dangerous…I could have been killed.

I was shaking now and I took a deep breath and looked around. What the hell was going on; was I day-dreaming? Three metal newspaper stands were a few feet from me, and as I looked at them, I saw the dragonflies, several on each stand. All appeared to be staring at me. Some were large like I'd seen a few days before; others were average in size. Their wings were still, and as I stared back at them they began to take flight, at first one at a time, then all of them in a swirling cloud. They flew over my head and disappeared into the sky. I didn't remember seeing them when I was on the other side of the street, but I had been in deep thought and not paying that much attention.

I looked down at my hand. Embedded in my palm were small tan pieces of gravel, gravel like the footpath in my daydream. I started checking the ground around me. There had to be gravel like that somewhere here, where I'd fallen on the concrete, but there was nothing. In fact, the sidewalk was oddly clean, except for the occasional blob of dried-up gum. It was spotless.

I was a logical guy. I didn't believe in ghosts, alternate universes, aliens, or the supernatural. I knew that religions and governments alike had strange secrets, and I was fine with that as long as they stayed out of my business and didn't hurt anyone. But this was something else entirely. I could not deny that what I'd seen and felt was real. The proof was in the gravel on my hands, the wetness of the dew, and the smells of the foliage and damp earth still lingering in my nose.

Working at the VA, I'd heard stories about vets that had flashbacks and nightmares so real that they couldn't distinguish them from reality. I once heard a story about a freed WWII POW who was having such vivid nightmares about an enemy guard who'd tormented him, that in one nightmare he was strangling the guard, only to wake up and find he was strangling his wife, who had been sleeping next to him.

I also knew these flashbacks could be triggered by the simplest thing; a car backfiring, a horn honking, the smell and sight of food that was specific to the region they served in for the military. But I didn't have those problems because I'd never served, and the worst thing that had ever happened to me was my mother's lack of parenting skills and the deaths of the people I loved most. So was this some sort of government conspiracy or secret experiment? I didn't think so.

I started to walk home again, confused and frankly scared out of my mind, a mind I was sure I was slowly losing. I thought about going to Joel's. It was now four in the afternoon and a suitable time to start drinking, but I changed my mind. If I went there, they'd know something was wrong, and I didn't know if I'd have the presence of mind to *not* tell them what was happening. They'd probably call the men in white coats to take me away. If Joel didn't do it, the old man certainly would.

When I got home I poured myself a healthy glass of Bushmills and sat on the couch to ponder the situation. I could talk to Betty; I *should* talk to Betty. She'd been a psych nurse for so long she'd probably forgotten more than most of the doctors ever learned. But how would I approach her? "Hey, Betty, I'm having these really vivid hallucinations about bugs and gardens. I can smell it and feel it; what do you think?" Yeah, that wouldn't really work, would it? I pulled my laptop from the coffee table onto my lap and fired it up. I thought maybe a little research on the Internet would be in order at this point.

I started with Wikipedia and *hallucinations* and moved on from there. Sadly, nothing I read told me anything useful, aside from the fact that I was almost definitely hallucinating. However, the cause was still elusive. I wasn't showing signs of schizophrenia, epilepsy, or Parkinson's, I didn't do drugs now or ever, and aside from my recent drinking habits, I was a pretty healthy guy. The connection to drinking was something to think about, but after careful consideration I realized that probably wasn't it, either. For most of my encounters with both the dragonflies and the "other" place, like the one today, I was totally sober. Although I was pretty damn hung-over the first day I saw the huge swarm.

I shoved the laptop aside and flicked the TV on, finding a *Law & Order* marathon to keep my mind busy. I must have fallen asleep, because when I woke up it was pitch black outside and the clock said one a.m. I made my way to my bedroom and flopped into bed, quickly falling back asleep.

I dreamed of Sarah. We were happily walking hand in hand through the conservatory, the humid air and smells of lush greenery and exotic flowers enveloping us as we made our way to the Butterfly Zone. As we entered the outer vestibule of the greenhouse room housing the butterfly exhibit, I noticed a sign that warned the visitor to be sure no butterflies had hitched a ride on their bodies as they exited. I laughed lightly and pointed it out to Sarah. She turned to me and said, "It doesn't say butterflies." I turned to her in that slow dreamlike way to protest, but it wasn't Sarah anymore; it was the pretty girl from the "other" place.

When I turned back to the sign, it read *dragonfly,* not butterfly. The girl led me into the main greenhouse room and suddenly we were surrounded by dragonflies, some perched on leaves, some darting around here and there, some hovering around us. As I looked around in amazement, I realized that there were far more of them than I'd ever seen before, even on that fateful day of my first encounter with them.

She led me further into the room and more began to swarm around us. I started to get scared; there were just too many of them. She sensed my fear and said, "Frank, they're here for you; you're the only one that can open the dragonfly door. Please help us." I startled awake, sweating and shaking as if it had been some horrible nightmare, which to some extent it had.

I stumbled out of bed and to the kitchen. I wasn't going back to sleep, so I might as well have some coffee. The clock on the wall said it was five-forty-four in the morning. While I was making the coffee I assessed the dream. The fact that Sarah and the conservatory were in it didn't surprise me…after all, I'd just thought of that memory yesterday. Then there was the girl and the dragonflies. Again I wasn't surprised…those things had occurred yesterday too. But it was what she said that worried me, about being the only one who could open the "dragonfly door," and that they needed my help. But who were "they" and where the hell were they? Were they in that other place?

I leaned my head against the upper cabinet, sighed in exasperation, and repeated to myself, "This cannot be real." Unfortunately, those logical thoughts did not account for the dew on my finger tips and the gravel embedded in my hand. I was wound up tighter than an arachnophobe in a room full of spiders. I needed to blow off some steam, so I put on my jogging clothes and hit the pavement.

I jogged…well, it was more like a full-blown sprint…to Ocean Beach, and followed the shoreline down as far as I could go, then turned back and ran up to the Sutro Baths. I was so exhausted from the run and upward climb that I had to sit on the retaining wall overlooking the baths and the Pacific to catch my breath. I felt a lot better after a few minutes rest, and I jogged at a reasonable pace until I reached home.

Chapter 12

I had a string of things to do around the building and some requests from the elderly in the neighborhood, so my day was pretty full. My elderly neighbors tended to be pretty lonely. I tried to encourage them to get out and do things, but it was not easy for most of them at their age, so a lot of them stayed inside most days. Today that was a blessing. The constant chatter and storytelling kept my mind from the dream and the events of the past week. I listened with vigor and even asked a ton of questions instead of my standard head nodding and smiling.

When I was done for the day I headed to Joel's. The old man was in his usual seat and I moved to the stool next to him, mumbling a hello and nodding at Joel for a beer. The bar was virtually empty, but it was early and would probably do a fairly good business as the working crowds finished their dinners and made the pilgrimage for their evening libations.

I looked around the bar suspiciously for the dragonfly or multiple dragonflies, whatever the case may be. I didn't see any, but that didn't mean they weren't lurking somewhere.

The old man noticed my uneasy demeanor and said, "What's wrong with you, boy?"

What could I say? "Hallucinations old man, driving me nuts." Thinking that comment wasn't a good idea, I settled with, "Just not sleeping too good these days, that's all."

Joel slid a beer in front of me and I drank most of it in one long gulp. He was looking at me with the same concern as the old man, and said, "Yeah, you been acting weird; what's up?" He narrowed his eyes at me, then continued. "It ain't that girl from the other night, is it?" I laughed; how I wished that was the problem. Life would be much easier if getting jilted by a woman you really didn't want a relationship with in the first place could trump a slow slide into insanity.

"You guys notice all the dragonflies around these days?" I asked, not really meaning to change the subject, but hoping to deflect them away from my odd behavior. At least I thought I was.

"Dragonflies? What in the hell are you talking about?" the old man asked irritably. He wasn't one for idle conversation unless it involved baseball.

"Dragonflies,…you know, colorful multi-winged bugs that fly around?" I said sarcastically, fluttering my hand around in simulated flight.

The old man shrugged and said, "We get swarms once in awhile. Why, you seeing 'em? That why you're acting so weird, having visions of dragonflies?" He snorted a chuckle and went back to his beer.

I laughed back. Yeah, I was seeing them everywhere. And every time I did, I seemed to slip away to places unknown.

"I saw a swarm the other day, then again yesterday," I said, shrugging. "Just thought it was weird. I thought they were warm weather creatures," I finished, trying not to seem too interested in them, just pretending to make conversation.

"Well, let's see…." The old man had a serious look on his face, one I'd never seen before. "Seem to remember reading somewhere that they symbolize new life, or birth, or something like that, and it is springtime. Think I also read that they got some superstitious-type meaning as well." The old man shrugged again, the serious expression changing to disinterest.

I decided to change the subject again and said, "Play you a game, old man?"

We played pool for over an hour, not talking too much, just hitting those colorful balls and trading one dollar bills back and forth to the winner. Joel was eyeing me suspiciously from the bar. He knew something was up with me, but I sure as hell wasn't going to admit to him what it was. When I left the bar I looked around anxiously and cautiously. Of course, I was looking for my new multi-winged stalkers, but I didn't see any.

Chapter 13

Jorge was on my mind when I woke up, so I decided to go see him. When I got to the VA, I went straight to Betty's office, thinking maybe I'd feel her out on this little mind trip thing. She was on the phone and her expression screamed bad mood. I waited a minute or two and then left, deciding I'd stop by on my way out.

The rec room was filled with the usual suspects, but no Nancy or Kyle today. The nurse on duty saw me at the door and began to slowly stroll over. He was a big fella, six-six at least, with skin so black that the whites of his eyes and the pinkness of his lips practically glowed. It seemed like it took him forever to walk over, which was a strange thing to me since his legs were twice as long as mine, and for every step he took, it would take me three steps to keep up. He was smiling broadly by the time he got to me and extended one of his humongous hands in greeting. I shook it and was again (for what must be the umpteenth time) shocked at just how big those hands were; how they swallowed mine like my own hands would swallow a fly.

Clinton was a good-natured guy. He was thirty-five, the same age as me, and we were as different as could be, but we were also best friends. He had short-cropped hair that didn't have a grey strand in it, and a smile as big as the rest of him. He had grown up in the not-so-good area of Hunters Point, a run-down, poverty-stricken neighborhood in the south part of the city near the stadium previously known as Candlestick Park. He wasn't a bad kid—in fact he was pretty smart—but you didn't make many friends in that area by being smart, and he fell in with the wrong crowd. He was busted for robbery when he was fifteen, but he was damn lucky, too. He pulled a public defender that actually cared, and since this was a first offense and he was a minor, the judge went easy, giving him probation and community service. Where he wasn't lucky (or maybe it was luck, hard to say) was getting a probation officer and a community service worker who were both hardasses and could see his potential if he straightened out. After his probation and community service was completed, his PO talked him into continuing his good works and got him a volunteer position at the VA. That was how we met.

Somehow and some way, that was the turning point for Clint. I'm not sure if it was because his idle hands no longer had idle time to hang out with the bad element or if it was our friendship, but Clint finished high school, went on to college to get his nursing degree, and then got a permanent job at the VA, where he'd worked ever since. He did a lot of volunteering and mentoring outside of the VA, but the VA was his passion.

When I first met Clint he scared the hell out of me. I knew he'd been in jail for some crime he'd committed, but I didn't know what it was. What I did know was that he was a huge and imposing guy, even at the ripe old age of fifteen. To everyone's surprise, we became immediate friends. Betty liked to call us "Mutt and Jeff" from the comic strip that originated in the San Francisco Chronicle in 1907. She made this association because of our striking differences in appearance, not any similarities to their personalities, although these days I was beginning to feel like I should be in an insane asylum like Jeff.

Since Clint's volunteer work as a teen brought him out to the VA several days a week and on most weekends, he'd more often than not come to my house for dinner afterwards. Sometimes he'd spend the entire weekend with us. Marcus loved him. Clint was a funny guy and he kept Marcus in tears with his jokes and humorous discourse. Marcus even offered to pay for Clint's college education, but Clint declined. He said he was a poor black kid and that would get him all the funding he needed, that and his good looks and good grades, of course. Like I said, Clint was a smart guy. He may have been joking when he told Marcus that, but he also knew that the combination of those things and his volunteer work would indeed get him a scholarship, and it did.

So the poor kid from Hunters Point and the rich kid from Presidio Heights became, and remained, best friends. We didn't seem to socialize as much as we used to, but we saw each other a lot at the VA and talked on the phone at least twice a week. His wife, Kathleen, a six-foot tall lanky brunette with pale light blue eyes, was a high school teacher. When you saw the two of them together, ebony and ivory would come to mind, really tall towers of ebony and ivory. When Sarah and I were together we'd often catch dinner with them. Sarah and Kathleen got along great, but they came from different worlds, and sometimes that caused uncomfortable tension. You couldn't help but admire Clint and Kathleen. Although Kathleen didn't come from Hunters Point, her beginnings were impoverished and humble, and like Clint, she pulled herself up by her bootstraps and made something of her life.

They didn't have kids, much to their dismay. They'd been trying for years, but no luck. Last I heard adoption was being discussed, and sadly it was harder to adopt an American orphan than it was to get one from another country, but they were determined to do it.

"How's tricks, Clint?" I asked, smiling. Seeing him always put me in a good mood; he just invoked that in people.

He smiled and said, "It's a beautiful day, my friend…always a beautiful day when you got health and happiness; am I right or am I right?" This was Clint's signature response; the day it didn't come would be the day I knew the world was really going to hell in a hand-basket.

I smiled again and said, while nodding my head toward the rec room occupants, "Always good to hear, my friend. So how are the troops?"

"Doing good; got us some Texas Hold 'Em going on over there, a marathon of Wild Wild West over there," he said while waving his huge hand around the room. I followed it as he did; a group watching the flat screen TV, another at a card table. Then I spotted Jorge in the same corner as before, and as before, he was staring vacantly out the window.

"How's Jorge doing today, Clint?"

His expression turned serious and he shook his head in dismay. "That kid's got it bad. He doesn't talk, doesn't do anything, just sits there and stares out that window. His roommate says he talks in his sleep…never shuts up, just talks all night long."

I looked up at Clint and asked, "What's he say?"

Clint shook his head. "Not sure; you'd have to ask his roommate. Why?" he asked, frowning a little at the question.

"Betty asked me to see what I could do for him; she thinks after what happened with Tory that I've got some sort of magic touch."

Clint chuckled a little and said, "Sure can't hurt. He's over there…his roommate, that is." He pointed to a guy in a terrycloth robe and flannel pajamas reading a Dean Koontz story; one of my favorites, the first in the Odd Thomas series. I thanked Clint and meandered over to him.

"Hi, I'm Frank; you're Jorge's roommate, right?"

The guy looked up from his book and nodded without any expression crossing his face.

"Mind if I sit?" I asked, pointing to an ottoman nearby. The guy nodded his head and placed a scrap of paper in the book and closed it. As I pulled the ottoman over to sit down, I said, "Great book. Do you have access to the others in the series? I could loan them to you if you don't."

He looked down at the book, then up at me and said, "Thanks, didn't know there were others." His expression said, "What do you want?" so I jumped right in.

"I'm a volunteer here and I've had some success with guys like Jorge. I heard he's pretty vocal in the wee hours of the night; wanted to know if you could tell me what he's been saying."

He looked at me with suspicion. These guys were protective, of themselves and others like them. They were fighting not just their own demons, but the demons of the system that was put in place to help them.

"You a shrink or something?" he asked.

I smiled, hoping it would disarm him. "No, just a volunteer. Like I said, I've had some success in helping some of these guys open up, talk about stuff."

He looked at me for what seemed like forever, then said, "Yeah, I seen you around, but you can't," he jerked his thumb in Jorge's direction, "help him. He's way too far gone."

I sighed. That seemed to be the running theme for Jorge. "What can you tell me? Anything will help. I mean, it can't hurt, right?"

He shook his head, then looked me in the eyes and said, "He talks about a door a lot. Every night, in fact, he says he needs to get back through it, that it's stuck or something. It's weird...he's pretty coherent—in his dream talk, that is—but when he's awake, he just ain't there."

I didn't know what to make of that, so I asked, "What else does he say?"

The roommate thought about it for a minute, then said, "The other night he was going on about flies...no, that ain't right, it was dragonflies. Kept saying something about the door and the dragonflies. I was just falling to sleep so I didn't catch it all, but I think that was it."

I was startled for a second and it must have shown. The roommate said, "You okay man? You seem like you seen a ghost."

I collected myself and asked, "What's your name?"

"Alex."

I stuck my hand out to him and said, "Thanks, Alex. How long you in for?"

Alex shook my hand listlessly and said, "Oh, not too much longer." I couldn't see any visible wounds on the guy, but that didn't mean much.

"Well, I hope not; thanks again for the info."

I started to get up and Alex said, "You won't be able to help him, but hey, good luck."

I walked over to where Jorge was sitting and pulled a chair up next to him. He was still staring out the window; that vacant look in his eyes was scary, like he was gone and this was just a body without a soul sitting next to me.

"Hey Jorge, remember me? I'm Frank, I was here the other day. We saw butterflies by that tree." I pointed toward the window, but Jorge wasn't looking at me anyway, so it was a useless gesture.

He didn't react to my voice either, and I decided to go for it. "So Jorge, I heard you like dragonflies. You know, I like them, too…well I think I do. They've been sort of hounding me lately. I see them everywhere I go."

At first he didn't respond, then his eye twitched and he slowly turned his head toward me and said in a low tone, "Did they take you to the door?"

"They? You mean the dragonflies?" I asked cautiously as I leaned closer to him. He was staring at me now; the vacant stare was still there, but not as evident as before, and something else, too. Something like desperation.

He nodded his head slowly and whispered urgently. "The door. I need to go back through the door." Just then his hand shot out and grabbed my arm, startling me, and he said, "Can you take me to them?"

I was sure now that the look on his face *was* desperation, but there was pleading and outright fear in it, too.

"Jorge, where does the door go?" I asked. Deep down inside I knew the answer, but the answer made no sense.

He dug his nails into my arm and looked at me, the vacancy I'd seen before completely gone. I was now looking into the eyes of an intelligent and coherent, but desperate, man. He looked around, his eyes narrowing into slits as he did, then he turned back to me and whispered urgently, "I must be taken back to the bio-compound. I cannot stay here…the longer I am here, the worse my condition becomes. They need me there. Please, can you take me through the door? Do you know how to open it?"

The bio-compound? Was he talking about the garden in the "other" place? "Jorge, what is the bio-compound? Does it have something to do with the dragonflies?"

Loud laughter from the other side of the room startled us both. I looked up to see a few guys at the card table guffawing and pointing at one of their companions; the fella was laughing too. When I turned back to Jorge, I could tell the moment was gone. His grip was loosening on my arm and the vacant stare was seeping back into his eyes.

I grabbed his hand before he let go of my arm, held it tight, and asked, "Jorge, what is it, tell me, please?" But he was gone; his hand slipped loose from mine and he slowly turned his head back to the window. I leaned back in my chair, rubbed my eyes, and sighed.

Somehow he was connected to these hallucinations I was having. I was sure of it now, but I still had no idea what the dragonflies meant, or what he meant, for that matter. I got up slowly and patted Jorge on the shoulder, and said I'd come back to see him tomorrow. As I was leaving the room Clint approached me, this time moving quickly. It only took him a few long strides to reach me from the opposite side of the room. He'd been watching us and had caught Jorge's lucid moment.

"He talked? I mean, it looked like he was talking to you?" he said in amazement.

I tried to smile, but I knew it came off fake. "Yeah, he said a few words...nothing meaningful." I shrugged as if to confirm that.

Clint patted me on the back. "That's great; I mean, it doesn't sound like much, but it's better than anyone else has gotten out of him. What did he say?" Clint's eyes were full of hope. He lived and breathed these people, and with every positive step they took, he took it as a personal accomplishment.

"He said something about dragonflies and a door. I don't know what it means. I guess he talks about it in his sleep, too." I nodded my head toward Alex, who was still sitting comfortably reading his book. "That's what his roommate says."

Clint looked a little dejected, but not much. He was used to these baby steps, but I think he was hoping for a little more. "Great, Frank, that's great. Betty was right…you're the man for the job." He smiled that huge smile and I relaxed a little. "Everything else okay, my man? You look a little haggard." A glint of concern showed in his eyes.

I nodded my head. "Yeah, I'm fine, just not sleeping too good lately." That was becoming my signature excuse since this dragonfly hallucination thing had started.

"Hey, I'm meeting Kath at Bill's Place on Clement Street for dinner tonight, wanna join us? She'd love to see you." I wanted to beg off, but I knew he'd never take "no" for an answer. Besides, I hadn't seen Kathleen in a while, and dinner with two of the happiest people I knew would certainly cheer me up.

"Yeah, Clint, I'd love that; sure Kathleen won't mind?"

He chuckled and said, "Meet us there at 6:30." Then he strolled away to check on his patients.

Chapter 14

Clarisse was becoming frantic. Jorge had first travelled through the door two months ago, but he'd always checked back in with them every few days. It had been almost two weeks since they'd heard from him, and she was worried something had happened.

Upon his last return he'd been in a hurry, so his briefing had been quick. He had figured out how to access the original virus and thought it would only be a matter of a day or two before he returned with it. However, he didn't look well. She asked him about it and he said he was fine, but she knew better.

Before he left he took Clarisse aside and asked if anything odd had been happening. She told him that she hadn't noticed anything and asked why he wanted to know. Jorge seemed nervous, which was nothing like his usual casual confidence. He said that he thought he was being followed, not here, but on the other side of the door, in 2013. Before they could finish their conversation, Dr. Blare approached. Jorge squeezed her hand gently and smiled, then said it was okay, things would be fine and he'd be back soon. Jorge didn't like Christian; it was obvious and mutual. He said his goodbyes and went back through the door.

Clarisse had been monitoring the timeline with more diligence than normal. If someone was following Jorge, perhaps they would do something that would alter the timeline, at least enough for her to determine who they were. She had detected some small variants, but these things had happened on her side and they appeared to be normal updates to information that was readily available to everyone, so she dismissed them.

Chapter 15

I left the VA, completely forgetting that I meant to stop by and see Betty. I decided I needed some fresh air and a walk, so I took the back way out of the center. The center was located just west of the California Palace of the Legion of Honor, one of the city's many fine art museums. The building itself was a smaller version of its namesake, Palais de la Légion d'Honneur in Paris, and it boasted an impressive collection that included artists and sculptors such as Monet, Rodin, El Greco, Rubens, and Degas. I thought about walking toward it and around the grounds of the golf course that surrounded it, but changed my mind. Instead, I headed to the trail that led out of the VA and down a path past the back side of the museum. Following it west for a short while would lead to the Coastal Trail, and by walking the whole trail, one would end up at the Sutro Baths and the Cliff House, another San Francisco icon. The trail soared high above the rocky and wild coast that was the city's westernmost promontory, known as Land's End. It was a popular haunt for locals and tourists alike, but many were surprised by its rugged, overgrown paths that often soared upward at impossible inclines or plunged downward at neck-breaking angles. The roar of the ocean slamming into the cliffs below was so powerful and hypnotizing that I thought it was the best place in the world to think. The sounds and beauty of it all drowned out civilization completely.

I'd walked this trail so many times that I could do it in my sleep. As I made my way at a moderately fast clip, I thought about what Jorge had said. When I mentioned dragonflies, he asked about a door, and there was no doubt that every time I had the hallucination, there were dragonflies around. Was he trying to say that they somehow opened a door to this other place, this "bio-compound?" Was he trying to say he wasn't from here? That by being here his brain was deteriorating? There was no doubt that for a moment he had been perfectly coherent, perfectly in control of his mind.

All these strange and impossible thoughts were swirling through my head, when suddenly I realized that the overpowering sound of waves crashing below me was gone, and that I was suddenly no longer on the trail. I stopped and looked around…I was in the other place again; the now-familiar sounds of the garden were all around me, and I started to panic. Last time this happened I walked along the path of the garden, and when I came back out of the hallucination I was on the other side of a busy street. If I moved from this spot, I could very easily find myself plunging off the cliffs of Land's End when I snapped out of it. I stood frozen, listening for the sounds of the people I'd seen in my earlier hallucination. I could hear voices in the distance, and I couldn't tell what direction they were coming from, but they were definitely getting closer to me.

The path was only about three feet wide. Thick, tall shrubbery was on either side of me. I wanted to move into it, to hide from the coming voices. I tried to remember exactly where I'd been on the coastal trail. I'd been moving south, which meant the ocean should be on my right. I darted left into the bushes, managing to just cover myself before I saw them come around a bend in the path.

It was the young woman from before. This time her companion was another woman, and they were talking in low, desperate tones. The other woman was older—she appeared to be in her mid-fifties—and taller, with short, spiky, jet-black hair with a smattering of grey and a smooth complexion. She was wearing the same type of coveralls as the younger woman.

They were getting closer now and I could almost hear what they were saying when the younger woman looked away from her companion toward the spot on the path I'd just been occupying. I looked to where her eyes were fixed and saw them, tons of them…a swarm of dragonflies. They weren't darting around aimlessly as before; they were hovering, right where I'd been standing. She cocked her head to the side and started to say something, slowly raising her arm and pointing toward the swarm.

The other woman looked up, saw the swarm, and turned to her companion. I heard her say, "Oh my God, is that the door?"

Just as she spoke, the dragonflies moved quickly to where I was hiding, and right before I snapped back to my own world I saw the younger woman looking in my direction, right at me. I stumbled over a small outcrop of rocks and landed hard on my back side. I was panting, sweating, and sure that she'd seen me. But more than anything, I was relieved, because right across the path from me was a cliff. It was cordoned off with a rope looped through four-by-four posts, and a warning sign showing a stick figure falling off a cliff was posted for all to see.

Sitting on top of the sign was a single dragonfly, a really big one. I stood up and walked over to a bench that had been placed on the east side of the path, a bench that overlooked the cliff and the ocean beyond. I lowered my head into my hands and tried not to cry. This was getting ridiculous. These hallucinations could kill me. I had to stop them, but I had no idea how.

My thoughts were broken by a snorting sound, and I looked up to see a fat beagle sniffing around the bench, undoubtedly picking up the scent of one of the many critters that called these trails and the surrounding flora home. A couple was walking hand in hand toward me and I heard them call the dog. The dog took one more sniff and proceeded up the path.

The couple slowed and looked at me, asking if I was all right. I must have looked pretty bad, and I smiled weakly and said that I was fine. They moved north on the path, and when they were out of sight I headed south, staying as far to the left as I could in case I had another hallucination. I made it home without any further incidents and poured myself a stiff whiskey.

I must have fallen asleep and woke with a start, the sun beaming in through my western windows. The day's earlier overcast sky had cleared, allowing the sun to warm the western part of the city for those final daylight hours. I glanced at the clock—it was a quarter to six in the evening. I made my way to the shower and got ready to meet Clint and Kathleen for dinner.

Normally, I would have walked. It was only about three-quarters of a mile from my house, but today I decided to drive. It took me ten minutes to find parking, so I was late. As usual, the windows of Bill's Place were steamed up and I couldn't see in. I walked through the painted red door and glanced around. The woman behind the diner-style counter smiled at me and said to sit anywhere, but when I glanced back to the seating area, I saw a huge hand waving at me from the back of the restaurant. Clint and Kathleen were sitting near the sliding doors that led to the garden seating, and I walked over and smiled. Clint's arm was around Kathleen's shoulder, and I leaned past him to kiss her cheek, then patted Clint on the back and sat in one of the chairs opposite them.

Kathleen was looking at me in an odd way, and I knew my expression revealed the events of earlier in the day. "You look horrible, sweetie, what's wrong?" she asked in her usual blunt but kind manner.

What could I say? Certainly not the truth, so I shrugged and said, "It's nothing, just not sleeping too good lately."

She cocked her head to the side and said, "Liar."

Before I could respond, the waitress came over and placed menus in front of us and asked for our drink orders. Kathleen and Clint both ordered a Corona and I ordered a Miller Light. When she left us to get our drinks I opened my menu and pretended to read, hoping Kathleen would do the same and not pursue her earlier concern.

When I looked up from the menu she was staring at me, a hard stare that said she wasn't dropping it, and I knew my choices were limited. Kathleen could sniff out a lie from a mile away—she was a school teacher, and years of working with teenagers had honed her skills. I wasn't going to fool her. All right, I thought, what the hell, these two were my closest friends. If I couldn't tell them, who could I tell?

"I seem to be having a little problem lately. I'm hallucinating—I think. One minute I'm doing normal stuff, the next I'm not here anymore. I'm…well, I'm in a sort of Garden of Eden, and every time this happens it's accompanied by dragonflies." There…I'd said it out loud, and damn if it didn't feel good to get it off my chest.

Clint had looked up and now he was staring at me, looking scared. He'd seen enough mental illness to know this could be a real problem.

"Of course, that's not the worst of it. While I'm having these little mind trips I'm also walking, which has proved to be a little dangerous; almost got killed crossing Geary the other day without any idea I was doing it." Before they could respond, the waitress appeared with our drinks and took our food orders. After she left we resumed the conversation.

"Dragonflies; you mean like Jorge's dragonflies?" Clint asked, ignoring the implication that I was a danger to myself.

I shook my head and said, "I don't know. It started before I met Jorge, but I can't discount that there's a connection in there somewhere."

Clint was a continuing education kind of guy. He didn't do it because he aspired to be more than the awesome nurse he was; he did it because he wanted to understand and help the people he worked with. He'd taken his fair share of psych classes and knew a little bit more than the average guy about the mind and its workings, or lack thereof.

"Okay, is it possible that you heard about Jorge's problems before you actually met him? I mean, maybe you overheard a snatch of conversation at the VA or something and it sunk into your subconscious."

I shook my head again and said, "I don't think so, but what's got me really perplexed is what Jorge said today, about the dragonflies and a door of some sort, and a 'bio-compound.' This place I go to, this 'other' place, it's like a nursery, I guess. I mean, it's so huge I can't see an end to it, so there could be farm land, too, but it's luscious and so full of plants that it would boggle the mind. The other thing is…well, I'm not sure how to describe this…the sky beyond isn't right. I mean, there's this strange clarity to it, like it's never seen pollution. It's so clean, so blue, and you can almost…well, you can actually see the night sky beyond the day sky." Now I knew I sounded crazy and I just stopped talking, letting them make what they could of it.

"So you see the dragonflies, then you just blank out?" Kathleen asked.

"No…well, yes…." I blew out my breath in frustration. "Sometimes I see them and I go to the other place. Sometimes, like the other day and today, I don't see them until I come back."

"What happened today?" they asked in unison. I told them about the trail and what had happened. Clint whistled out his breath in a deep relieved sigh and said, "Frankie, man, this is bad; you could have gone right over that cliff."

I nodded my head and said, "I get that now. I just have to remember where I was before…before I snapped over. That way I know which way to go, or not to move at all."

Kathleen raised her eyebrows and asked, "So you expect this to happen again?"

I shrugged and said, "Well, yeah, I guess I do."

Just then the waitress showed up with our food and we began to eat in silence. After a few minutes Clint asked, "You talk to Betty about this?"

I didn't look up from my plate when I responded. I didn't want to bring Betty into this and I said, "No, and I don't intend to." No one talked for a few minutes, and when I had my fill of food I leaned back in my chair and said, "So Kathleen, how's school going?"

She looked up from her plate and smiled and shrugged. "The usual," she said.

Kathleen was not a fan of unions; she firmly believed that they had gone from protectors and representatives of the employees to greedy political machines. She also was not a fan of the way the public school system seemed to have more bureaucrats that knew nothing about actual teaching and a lot about wasting money and time. She was fed up and constantly talked about switching to a private school. The money and benefits weren't as good, but they let you teach without the hassles of the public system.

"I interviewed with that private school," she said, smiling.

I noticed Clint was smiling, too, and I was instantly reminded that these two were truly the most beautiful couple I'd ever seen. It wasn't just the stark contrast of her creamy white skin to his ebony complexion, or the fact that they were both very tall and almost statuesque. It was the unconditional love and understanding they had for each other. Seeing them walking down the street hand in hand, you just knew something perfect was going on there.

I arched an eyebrow and smiled. I knew what this meant. They had been trying to adopt, but they both had to work and didn't want someone else raising their child; nor could they afford the cost of daycare or a nanny. The school she'd been considering had a full-time day care center, and it was available to the employees, which meant their new addition could be near her all day long.

"So," I said, "what happened?"

Her smile was huge, so big it actually dwarfed Clint's smile, and that was no small feat. She said, "I have the job if I want it."

I reached across the table and squeezed her hand, then I high-fived Clint and said, "When's the kid coming?"

She laughed and so did Clint. "Well, I won't start until next term, but we've told the agency we're ready to proceed, so as soon as a child is available." She shrugged. "I guess we're next in line." There were no two people on this planet more worthy of adopting a child than

Kathleen and Clint, and this was quite possibly the best news I'd heard in forever.

"Well, put me on the babysitting roster!" I said with honest delight.

We each had another beer and chatted about the pending adoption some more, then decided to call it a night. We all walked out together, and as we were saying our goodbyes under the big red awning, Kathleen's expression turned serious and she grabbed my hand. She said, "Frank, I'm worried about what you told us in there. Would you consider seeing a doctor? Please?"

I looked down at the sidewalk and shuffled my feet. It was clear they didn't actually believe I was going somewhere. I decided I should drop the bomb on them. "Uh, there's something else. The first couple of times it happened...I touched stuff; a leaf that was covered in dew, and the second time I fell and hit the gravel path." I stopped to watch their expressions; they weren't getting it, so I continued. "When I got back here, my fingertips were wet, and the second time my hands were embedded with gravel. I checked around...there wasn't any gravel near where I was standing...on this side, that is."

They exchanged looks with each other and then looked back at me. Clint said, "Frank, are you saying you actually went somewhere?"

Well, yeah...wasn't that what I'd been trying to tell them? I slowly nodded my head.

"Uh uh," Clint said, shaking his head, "there's another explanation." But he didn't have one any more than I did.

"Don't worry, okay? I'll be really careful. I'll be by the center tomorrow…maybe I can get more out of Jorge," I said.

I left them standing there. There wasn't any more we could say on the topic, and as usual, I needed time to think. Something occurred to me on the drive home. The first time I hadn't moved around in the other place. The next two times I had, and ended up in a different spot when I got back to my time and place. So I really needed to be careful—I could end up anywhere—someone's house, a bathroom full of school girls. God, the possibilities were endless and downright scary! Then I thought, what if I made it back to the original spot before I returned? Would I land in the spot I'd previously vacated? I sighed. This was everything I didn't believe in; I didn't believe in time travel, other dimensions, or the fricken *Twilight Zone* for God's sake.

For the remainder of the drive home, Rod Serling's monotone voice played in my head. *"You're traveling through another dimension—a dimension not only of sight and sound but of mind. A journey into a wondrous land whose boundaries are that of imagination…."* The images from the show's intro were playing along with Rod's famous words; a door flipping around through outer-space, opening onto another dimension. Yeah, this was like that; only this wasn't TV, this was real, and it was happening to me.

Chapter 16

I dreamed of the conservatory again…Sarah and I strolling toward the butterfly exhibit, happy, holding hands and laughing. When we entered she pulled away from me and I wandered around on my own. As I moved through the exhibit the dragonflies began to come near me, to swarm around me, and I panicked; I tried to run, to find Sarah, but I couldn't move. They just kept getting closer and closer, more and more of them.

I woke with a start, sweating and out of breath, then the dream started to slowly fade and I realized something odd. Not about this dream, but the one I'd had the other night, the first conservatory dream. That dream was before I'd had the brief conversation with Jorge, before he'd said anything about the "door." But the woman from the other place was in the dream and she had said something about the door. I rubbed my eyes and looked around the room, then at the clock. It was six-fifteen, so I decided to get up.

When I arrived at the VA later that day, I went straight to the rec room. Clint and Nancy were on duty and they both meandered over to say hello. Clint didn't bother with his signature greeting today, he just patted me on the shoulder and said hello, which really bothered me. If Nancy noticed this she didn't say anything. She looked better today, like she'd actually gotten some sleep.

"You look great, Nancy. Did you take a few days off?" I asked with a smile.

She smiled back sincerely and said, "Oh yeah, and it was wonderful. I stayed at home, ate pizza and ice cream, and caught up on my DVR shows." We made idle conversation for a few minutes and then I wandered over to Jorge; as usual, he was parked in front of the big windows, staring out vacantly.

"Hey Jorge, how are you today?" I asked, not really expecting an answer. I didn't get one, so I decided to try the one thing that seemed to bring him out of it. "Jorge, I went there again, yesterday after we talked; you know, to the bio place."

At first he didn't react, and then just as slowly as before, he turned his head toward me. I leaned in, expecting him to talk in low tones like he did the day before. He looked at me and slowly his eyes began to clarify, to focus.

"Can you take me with you next time, please? I need to go back," he pleaded.

"Jorge, I don't know how; I don't have control of it. I don't even really know what it is. Can you tell me?" Now I was the one pleading.

Jorge sighed. I wasn't sure if he could tell me...he was obviously struggling. Finally he spoke. I had to lean in even closer; his voice was very low. "It is...the way to my time."

He was silent again and I thought that was going to be it, but then he began to look around the room like he did before, eyes closing into narrow slits, as if he was trying to hide the fact that he was conscious of his surroundings.

"There are others that want to control our success. I believe they did this to me. I believe they also altered the door so that I cannot return. Without me they will fail." He leaned even closer, to the point where we were almost touching, nose to nose. He said in a whisper so low I had to strain to hear him, "I don't think they know where I am, but the dragonflies do." He smiled lightly. "I created them; they are…tuned to me." He looked me directly in the eyes and cocked his head to the side, as if he was slightly amused, but also slightly confused, and he said, "And I believe they are tuned to you as well."

I leaned away from him. What did that mean, "tuned to me"? Oh hell, what did it mean that they were tuned to him?

"Jorge, they're not real dragonflies, are they? What are they?" But he was gone again, the vacancy filling his eyes faster than before, and within a few seconds he was back to staring out the window. I slowly got up and started out of the rec room, oblivious to everyone else in the room, and Clint noticed. He caught up to me as I approached the door to the hallway.

"Hey Frankie, hold up," he said. He looked around nervously and I followed his gaze.

There were a few guys looking at me— some looking from me to Jorge, and the others just looked confused and hurt that I hadn't said hello. Damn, I thought, I'm letting this consume me. I'm ignoring the reasons I come here in the first place. I sighed loudly, smiled at Clint, and said, "Gotta hit the head, I'll be right back." I had raised my voice a little, in the hopes that the others would hear me; I didn't want them to think something was wrong.

He smiled, catching my drift, patted me on the back, and said, "Me too." Then he turned to where Nancy was and said in a raised voice, "Hey Nancy, be right back; going down the hall for a sec."

She nodded her understanding and we left the room, walking briskly to the men's room. When we got inside Clint checked each stall to be sure we were alone. "So, what did he say?" he asked in a hushed tone.

"He said it was his place, the way to his time. He also said that he created the dragonflies and that they were tuned to him and to me." I shifted on my feet. I was nervous because now I realized something else; Jorge believed he was in danger. He'd said, "They did this to me."

"Clint, he said that someone did this to him. That they altered the door so he couldn't return, that they don't know where he is, but that the dragonflies do." I sighed and dragged my hand through my hair. "Clint, I don't think he's from here…."

Now it was Clint's turn to sigh. "Frankie, listen man, you gotta realize something. Jorge is sick, he's delusional. I think somehow you're tuning into this…somehow your subconscious is producing these hallucinations you're having." I looked at Clint. He was serious, but I could also tell he needed to believe this, because there simply was no other explanation.

"Do me a favor, okay? Just keep an eye on him...keep an eye on everything and everyone that goes near him." I walked past him and out of the bathroom toward the rec room.

I spent the next hour hanging out with the vets, mostly just chatting and visiting. As I was leaving, Nancy came over and said that Betty wanted to see me, so I headed to her office. She was on the phone when I got there, so I sat and waited patiently for her to finish her call. When she finished she looked at me over her glasses, then removed them and rubbed her nose.

"How are you, Frank? You don't look much better than last time I saw you." Her forehead furrowed in a disapproving way that I knew all too well.

I just smiled the most convincing smile I could come up with and said, "Thanks, Betty. You, on the other hand, look fabulous—new hair style or new dress?" She threw a paper clip at me and shook her head, but she was smiling now.

"So, I hear you've got Jorge talking." Nothing happened at the center that Betty didn't know about. It was just how she was...with her finger always on the pulse.

I nodded my head and said, "Yep, but don't get excited…he isn't saying anything really coherent."

This time she arched just one eyebrow at me and asked, "What *is* he saying?"

I shifted in my chair. I didn't want to lie to Betty, but I was sticking to my earlier conviction…I was not going to tell her what was going on. So I shrugged and said, as nonchalantly as possible, "Well, he likes butterflies and dragonflies—he's mentioned them a couple of times now—and talks about that place he wants to go back to."

She was silent for a while, and before she could say anything I asked, "What can you tell me about him? I mean, where is he from, what about his family? I'm thinking maybe these disjointed things he says may go back to that stuff." I smiled at myself; damned if I didn't sound like one of the shrinks.

She riffled around her desk for a minute and finally located a manila file folder…probably the one she'd looked at during our first conversation about Jorge. After she'd replaced her glasses on the edge of her nose and flipped through the file, she said, "Well, says here he's from Philly, Hispanic origin, parents are dead, no siblings." She flipped through more pages and then said, "No next of kin or emergency contact listed." She shut the file and looked at me over her glasses.

"Is that normal? I mean, not having someone listed?" I asked.

She removed her glasses and placed them on top of the file, and said, "It's not abnormal; a lot of kids that are orphans will enlist. It gives them a sense of family, of belonging."

Well, that actually made sense; I very well could have done the same if it wasn't for Marcus.

"Okay, maybe I'll try that route, asking about his folks, childhood home, that sort of thing," I said, smiling.

She nodded her head, then she leaned forward and crossed her arms on her desk and said, "And you...what's going on with you? You still staying out late, drinking too much?"

I shook my head and put three fingers above my eyebrow, "Scout's honor—I'm being a good boy."

She looked at me skeptically, then asked, "You dating anyone? Not the skanks you've been dating, but anyone good?"

She'd always been careful not to judge my love life since Sarah, so this took me by surprise and I smiled broadly. "No. You offering yourself to me? We'd make a beautiful couple, you and me."

That got her; her eyes lit up with amusement and she laughed...I mean, really laughed. It was hearty and deep and brought tears to the corners of her eyes. "Get out of here," she said as she wiped her eyes with a tissue.

I blew her a kiss and headed out of her office. The encounter left me feeling good. I loved making Betty laugh. She didn't do it that often, and it was just plain fun.

Chapter 17

I headed out of the center through the front entrance, taking my usual route south on 42nd Avenue. This time I paid attention to my surroundings, looking for the dragonflies or anything else unusual. Once I'd crossed Geary Street I felt a little more relaxed; there really weren't any more big streets between there and home to cross unawares. I was almost to my apartment when I realized I needed a few things from the store, so I stopped at my neighborhood market, nodding hello to the clerk, whose name I never remembered.

I was at the back of the store by the coolers when it happened. I was staring at the items inside, trying to decide which beer I wanted—bottles or cans—when I saw something flicker in the reflection of the cooler's glass doors. I knew right away that it was a dragonfly and I braced myself, looking around quickly so that I knew exactly where I was in the store. The smell of slightly sour dairy and dusty shelves of canned goods faded quickly, and soon my senses were filled with the fresh, clean scent of the other place.

I listened closely for voices and looked around for people on the pathway. I didn't see any dragonflies, so I checked the planters around me for something to use as a marker; I wanted to be sure that when they did reappear I could find the exact spot I'd arrived on. There was a white quartz rock about the size of my fist in the dirt next to the path, and I grabbed it and placed it where I'd been standing.

The last few times I'd gone in a forward direction on the path, but this time I turned around and looked behind me. The path wound its way for about five yards, then turned sharply. I walked that way, quickly but as quietly as I could, all the while keeping my eyes open for the dragonflies. I approached a clearing with a small covered area in its center. There were several stainless steel work stations with sinks and jars of what appeared to be plant specimens on them. Someone was hunched over one of these tables wearing a lab coat that looked too big and a white cap that covered their hair. I couldn't tell if it was a man or a woman.

A moment later, I heard a sudden buzzing. I didn't bother to look around—I knew what it was and I turned and ran. By the time I made it back to the rock on the path they were everywhere. I picked up the rock and tossed it in the planter. The dragonflies seemed to wait for me to finish this task. They were scattered about, but when the rock was back in place they converged on me. It was almost pleasant, being completely surrounded by them and their melodic buzzing.

As I began to go back to where I belonged I saw something white out of the corner of my eye, but before I could tell what it was, I was back in front of the coolers again. I looked around, wondering if anyone had seen me reappear, but I was alone.

A sound brought my focus back to the coolers. It had come from inside, behind the rows of beer, in the cold storage room. I looked through the glass, past the bottles and cans to the open cold room beyond. Something moved quickly away, but it was too dark inside to get a better look. I shook my head in frustration. I was getting paranoid. I realized it was probably the stock boy who worked at the market. On more than one occasion I'd asked him to venture back there to get me a six-pack of beer.

I made my purchases and headed home. I felt good about that last encounter. I hadn't heard the buzzing before, but it had almost felt like they were communicating with me, letting me know it was time to go. I just wished I could figure out a way to stay longer, to explore the place and find out what it was.

Chapter 18

Clarisse had looked up and around when she heard the buzzing sound. This time she was sure she'd seen him. He was running away, down the path toward the same spot as the day before. She ran after him and saw him stop in the same spot as before. He'd just tossed something into the planter and was moving back toward the center of the path, the dragonflies that weren't really dragonflies surrounding him. She darted forward just in time to get caught in the swarm, and then she wasn't on Bio-1. She had no idea where she was.

She felt the cold almost immediately, but it was the semi-darkness that startled her the most. She was looking at bottles of some sort, rows and rows of them, and then something moved beyond them and she jumped back. She eased forward again and realized she was in a refrigeration unit. Through the glass she saw the man.

She looked around quickly. A sign to her right said "exit," and she headed toward it and through the door. The man was walking through an aisle full of small boxes and cans. She knew these were dry goods of food, and she also knew she couldn't lose sight of him. He stopped at a counter, presented several items to a man standing behind it, and they exchanged pleasantries and paper and coin money. That told her something, as society had done away with physical currency some time ago.

When the two men finished their exchange, the man behind the counter put the items in a bag and the other man turned to leave. She removed the lab coat and cap and shoved them behind some boxed items on the shelf nearest her. She hadn't been wearing coveralls today and she was relieved, because she thought her khaki pants and red shirt more appropriate, regardless of where or *when* she was. She took a deep breath and walked past the clerk with as much confidence as she could muster.

Outside she looked around. It took her a few minutes to realize where she was. Probably the early 21st century, but she wasn't sure of the exact date or what city she was in. And she didn't have time to ponder it; she needed to follow the man. She looked in each direction; he was moving down the street at a moderate clip, and she followed. If she lost sight of him she may not be able to get back. He was swinging the bag lightly as he walked, and didn't seem to have any idea he was being pursued. He turned a corner and walked a few more yards before entering a building. She waited for him to go in and then approached the entrance. The door was locked. There was a keypad to the left with what she assumed were a list of names, with numbers beside each name, but she had no idea what name to try. She would have to wait outside, hoping he would leave again.

Chapter 19

I called Clint as soon as I got home. I wanted him to know what had just happened, and one more thing that I'd just realized. I was sure they'd waited for me...waited for me to put the rock back and get back to the center of the path. Maybe Jorge was right, the dragonflies were tuned to me.

He couldn't talk right away. He was with a patient, but would call me later; he too had something he wanted to tell me. A half hour later he was on break. Time was short so we did away with pleasantries and I told him everything that had happened. He sighed heavily when I finished talking. He was still having trouble believing that I was actually leaving this world and going to another. Unfortunately, I thought his news was more disturbing than mine.

Jorge had had an episode. At approximately the same time that I was coming back from the other place, Jorge had jumped up from his chair in the rec room and called out. Clint wasn't sure, but he thought he'd said, "No, stay there." Clint had gone to him immediately. Jorge was breathing heavily and the vacant stare was gone; Clint said it was like looking at someone completely different, someone who was *all* there. He'd grabbed Clint's arm, looked him directly in the eye, and said, "She must go back...tell your friend to take her back." Clint didn't know what to make of it, but he knew that "your friend" could be no other than yours truly.

I hit the end button on my phone and realized there was a voicemail message. It had come in while I was on my last journey to the other place. I pushed the play button and Kyle's friendly voice said that we really needed to talk. I called him back and we made plans to meet at his home office the next day.

Chapter 20

As Clarisse waited outside the building the man had entered, she looked around. It was early evening and the sun was beginning to set. The streets were lined with automobiles and more were moving along the roadway. They were huge metal and glass things, and they stank. Of course, they had personal transportation vehicles, or PTVs, in her time, but they were not so big and so numerous, and they didn't smell or sound like this. The majority of people in her world opted for public transportation. She knew this wasn't the case in this time. Public transportation was not a priority, nor was it convenient, and more often than not it wasn't safe to use. She shook her head, wondering how these people ever survived the horrible stench they emitted.

Lights began to turn on overhead as the sun began to fall below the horizon. People were walking along the concrete footpaths; many were talking into hand-held devices, or simply looking at the devices and using their fingers to navigate the screens. That wasn't very different from her world, except many of these people also had wires attached to the devices that led up to their ears. She smiled, realizing they were ear buds, but they weren't the tiny wireless kind used in her time.

Clarisse needed to know exactly when and where she was. She looked around, trying to find something that would identify this time and place. It looked familiar, but she couldn't place it exactly. A large vehicle with many windows was coming toward her on the street, and it was full of people. There were two roof-mounted poles that led to wires running parallel to the roadway. She laughed a little when she recognized it. It was a bus...an electric bus, to be exact. However, they were used in many cities during the early 21st century, so that didn't tell her much. She recalled that they had stopped using the larger, louder vehicles sometime in the mid-21st century. In her time they were quite compact and almost silent; these were so huge that the ground shook when it passed her. The large bus stopped and many people exited. One person stopped at a small metal box and opened its glass door, pulling out something flimsy...multiple pieces of paper, she thought.

After that person left she approached the box and tried the door. It opened easily and she removed the flimsy paper. It had an odd feeling to it, not quite like the pages of the old books her grandfather had—it was thinner, and the writing smudged a little under her touch. She realized that this was a newspaper; she had seen one in a museum but had never actually held one. The top portion of the paper was written in large Old English script; the word "The," then a large eagle with its wings spread out and the word "Examiner." Under the word Examiner was "San Francisco." She laughed. She should have recognized the distinctive architecture. At least now she knew where she was, although this was certainly not the San Francisco she knew. On the far left was the date…March 9, 2013. No, definitely not the San Francisco she knew.

Chapter 21

Clint had tried to get Jorge to say more, to explain what he meant, but Jorge had fallen back into his stupor within seconds of his outburst. Clint wanted me to come to the center, to talk to Jorge, but we both knew that would be difficult and draw even more attention to the situation. It was late; they would have started serving dinner and visiting hours were over.

What really seemed strange to me was that Jorge had never shown any signs of noticing his surroundings, yet he knew Clint and I were friends. I mentioned this to Clint. He'd picked up on that, too, and there was another thing that bothered him. He said it was as if Jorge was struggling massively to get those few words out, as if his brain had allowed him a brief opening through the darkness that shrouded it. But Jorge couldn't seem to keep the connection to reality open; it slammed shut on him the moment he got his warning out.

I promised Clint I'd come over after my meeting with Kyle the following morning. After we hung up I started thinking about what he'd said. Jorge had broken through for a brief moment, but it wasn't like before…he hadn't been prompted by comments from me. So what made him shout out? I didn't know, but I did know that I wanted a beer and some idle company. Pool with the old man was what I needed. So I made myself something to eat and then headed over to Joel's.

Chapter 22

Dyse made his rounds at the compound, checking in on the various projects that he oversaw. All was going well and it didn't appear that he'd been missed. He'd made a habit of locking himself in his quarters, informing the others that he did not want to be disturbed, explaining to them that the solitude helped him work better. This allowed him to spend short periods in the other timeline without being missed. However, he'd been gone longer this time, and was concerned someone had noticed. He hadn't seen Clarisse on his rounds, and when he asked, no one seemed to know where she was. He assumed she was off somewhere pining for Jorge. His extreme dislike for Jorge was growing exponentially; he needed to reign in his emotions.

He headed back to his quarters. He'd contacted his superiors as soon as he returned last time, giving them a short synopsis of the situation and asking for more information on Jorge. He was hoping that they'd had enough time between his rounds to come up with something.

There was a communiqué waiting for him. His superiors were not happy with the current situation. They didn't say it so much as express it with the tone of their words. They said there was no record of Jorge after the base. All information about a private in the army with his name ended at the initial record of his enlistment and his time at the fort in Kansas.

Dyse sat back and thought about this. Jorge could not have simply disappeared. If he had the sample, he would have come back. If anything, the man was dedicated to the success of the project. So what happened to him? Where did he go? If Jorge had deviated from the plan, it must have had an effect on the timeline. He needed to find Clarisse, to find out if anything was popping up.

Chapter 23

Clarisse was saddened by what she observed. This was a world that no one in her time would ever see. Museums could not describe the beauty. Even though it was dark and she was slightly cold, she could appreciate it. Everything and everyone was so different— there was a definite air of individuality about it all. Not that her time was bad in the least, but so much of this world had been lost over time, and it seemed as if her people and their predecessors had opted not to recover any of it.

She knew, of course, that the beautiful buildings, the parks, even the ghastly automobiles were destroyed. As she recalled, it had been a warm Tuesday morning, just after ten. Most of the population were at their places of work, probably gazing out at the beautiful day, wondering how to escape their enclosures and enjoy the weather.

Much like the previous major earthquakes in the early and late 20th century, this one was centered on the San Andreas Fault line. However, that was where the similarities ended. This quake had lasted a great deal longer, well over two minutes, and was a magnitude of 9.8. As if that wasn't enough, several large aftershocks continued throughout that day and the days and weeks that followed, causing more damage and severely hampering the efforts of rescue teams.

The city was on fire, and buildings had collapsed into themselves. Several feet of glass covered the financial district downtown, trapping those who hadn't been flung out of the swaying buildings and exploding windows inside. Hundreds of thousands of people were buried and trapped in the rubble. The initial quake was felt as far north as Oregon and as far south as San Diego, even as far east as Nevada. It was complete chaos.

In the end it was estimated that over five hundred thousand people died related to the quake, most of them in San Francisco and its immediate neighboring cities. Many bodies were never recovered, fire consuming them along with the crumbled buildings they were trapped under.

It took them almost twenty-five years to recover, to rebuild. Arguments were made from the rebuilt capital of Sacramento to Washington, DC, about allowing them to resurrect the devastated city. What if it happened again, they asked? Can we in good conscience allow them to rebuild, for a third and fourth time? But in the end they did, and it became one of the most innovative cities in the world, using every possible technology available to build safer, stronger structures and infrastructure.

There had been quakes since then, of course, none as large or as devastating, but it allowed them to study the stability of their new city and make even more improvements. Most if not all geologists now thought the city could withstand another quake like it.

Unfortunately, the new San Francisco looked nothing like the one she currently stood in. By the time they began to rebuild, most of the old citizenry had moved on or were dead. A new generation of people had moved in, and they no longer remembered the beauty that had made the City by the Bay famous. Even its most iconic structure, the Golden Gate Bridge, had been rebuilt and resembled nothing of its previous glory. The city was now a place of modern, space-age structures, all similar to each other. Sadly, the architectural beauty that had once been one of this city's claims to fame was no longer.

She was shocked out of her reverie by a door slamming to her left. She'd been standing against the building the man had entered, and now someone had just come out. At first she wasn't sure it was him, but as he walked under a street lamp she saw enough to know, and followed.

Chapter 24

As I walked to Joel's I kept my eyes peeled for the dragonflies. It was becoming habit now and I was doing it automatically, like crossing the street, looking right and left. The usual crowd was outside smoking at the edge of the curb, the neon signs in the bar windows casting an odd glow of reds, greens, blues, and yellows that reminded me of the dragonflies' colorful bodies.

The old man was parked in his usual seat and I pulled up a stool next to him, nodding my greeting as I sat. Joel acknowledged me with a slight nod and came over a minute later with a bottle of beer. We talked for a few minutes about nothing important, when Joel suddenly snapped his fingers and said, "There was a guy here earlier, looking for you."

The old man grumbled an "uh huh," then said, "Yeah, fella seemed real anxious to find you."

I couldn't think of anyone who wanted or needed to find me, so I asked, "Did he give a name?"

They both shook their heads and I asked, "What'd he look like? What'd you tell him?"

I must have sounded paranoid. The old man gave me a sideways glance and Joel said, "He was about your height, young, like mid-twenties, Hispanic-looking, I guess, kind of nervous-acting. Told him I didn't think I knew you, but if he wanted to leave a number I could ask around and pass it on."

Before I could respond to that, the door to the bar opened. Joel instinctively looked toward it while the old man and I ignored it like always. Joel was still staring at the door when he said, "She's got to be lost." He began to move toward the end of the bar closest to the door when I turned my head to look.

At first it didn't register, and I had begun to turn back to the old man when it hit me. Standing just inside the door, looking around as if she was indeed lost, was a tall, slender woman with long jet-black hair infused with reddish-gold streaks. She had on khaki pants and a red shirt, and she looked a little cold. Our eyes met at the same instant and I knew she was looking for me. My hand was on the neck of my beer bottle and I almost tipped it over in shock.

The old man, who never missed a thing, said, "You know the girl?" I nodded my head slowly, slipped off the stool, and put a five-dollar bill on the bar, then mumbled a good-bye and started toward her, waving to Joel as I went.

When I got close enough to her I gently put my hand on her arm and said, "We need to leave." She didn't resist me in the least, just turned and walked out the door with me. We went past the smokers to the end of the block before we said anything. All the while I was keeping an eye out for the dragonflies. I wasn't sure if she got here the same way I went there, but I thought it was a pretty good bet that she did.

A million questions were swirling through my head, but I finally settled on, "Do you know Jorge?"

She gasped, then said in a pleading whisper, "Yes, where is he? Please take me to him!"

"I can't, not right now. Come on, we need to get off the street." I wasn't sure why, but I felt an urgency to get her out of sight, like someone would see us and it would be the wrong someone. My place wasn't far away, but we made it in record time. She seemed to almost know the way and I had to assume she'd followed me from my apartment to the bar. Suddenly I remembered the market from earlier in the day, the cooler, the *something* I saw in the cold storage room just after I came back. That *something* was her; somehow she had followed me through.

As soon as we were in my apartment I said, "You followed me here, from the other place…this afternoon, right?"

The woman was looking around the apartment like she'd never seen one before as she said, "Yes, I saw you before, when you were hiding in the bushes. When I saw you today I knew I had to follow. I knew you were somehow connected to him."

"How, why…?" I sighed loudly. "What the hell is going on?"

Stopping her curious inspection of my digs, she turned to look at me. "Because of the dragonflies," she said, as if that should mean something to me, which of course it did.

I sat down heavily in a chair and looked up at her. "Yeah, the dragonflies; they show up sometimes before I go there and right before I come back here." I put my head in my hands and ran them through my hair, sighing again. She was still staring at me when I looked back up. "So why are they doing this to me, the dragonflies?" I asked.

Walking over to the couch, she gently lowered herself and perched on the edge of the cushion. Her back was straight, hands clasped tightly in her lap. I could tell she was struggling with something, but I had no idea what.

"Look, I need to know what's going on. Please tell me who you are, who Jorge is, what is that place?" I pleaded. I was feeling desperate.

She smiled then. It was meek but sincere, and she said, "I cannot tell you much—to do so would jeopardize both our futures—but I will tell you what I can." She eased back a little, getting more comfortable, and began slowly. "We are not from your world," she said. I was pretty sure she wasn't an alien, so I didn't bother asking.

"Fine, where are you from?" I asked.

"We are from another time. We are scientists. We…he came here because…because there is something here we need, something we must have in order to save our world."

I'd get back to that part. I had more pressing questions. "What about the dragonflies, and Jorge?"

As if on cue, a dragonfly appeared out of nowhere and alighted on the arm of the sofa. She saw it out of the corner of her eye and slowly turned her head toward it. A panicked look began to fill her face. I got up slowly and said, "Take my hand." She did and within seconds we were back in her world.

Looking around in amazement at the sudden change, she turned to me and said, "As I cannot be seen in your world, you cannot be seen in mine. Hurry, we must go. I must hide you."

She tried to drag me, but I held fast and said, "No, wait, I can't. If I move from here I don't know where I'll end up when I go back. I need to remain here; they never let me stay long anyway."

Again, as if on cue the buzzing began and I knew I would soon be surrounded. I shoved her away gently and said, "I'll be back; try to be near here and I'll try and find you again." And then I was home again.

Chapter 25

In Clarisse's absence, Dr. Christian Blare had been on the warpath. He'd checked everywhere for her and was furious that she hadn't responded to his pages. When she caught up to him it was obvious she was in trouble. He was one of the most senior scientists there and the director of the bio facility; it was her job to report her findings, if any, every day to him, which she hadn't done yet. She was still a bit shaken from her recent experience through the dragonfly door and hadn't actually compiled today's report. She decided to wing it, which was something she had never done before.

As she was walking to the lab where she was told Christian was, she ran into Jonathan and Joe, two of their better technicians. "Blare's looking for you...where have you been?" Jonathan half-whispered.

"I wasn't feeling well, so I went to lie down. I guess I turned my comm system off," she lied.

"Well, good luck. Any word on Jorge?" Joe asked hopefully.

"Yeah, any word, Clarisse?" Jonathan echoed. His tone, however, was more desperate.

She thought about it for a second, then decided at this point she shouldn't trust anyone until she knew more. "No," she sighed.

"Okay, let us know as soon you hear anything," Jonathan said. He and Joe left, veering off onto another pathway.

She shook her head. Jonathan was a sweet and intelligent man, and he was one of the better scientists at the compound. In fact, she would rate him close to Jorge's abilities. But he allowed things to get to him so easily. And the way he looked. She laughed a little to herself. It was as if he didn't know how good-looking he was. He insisted on wearing the old-fashioned glasses. No one did that anymore. If they had a problem with their sight…well, they simply had it repaired. No one had impaired vision in their time. And his hair…always too long, always ruffled, never combed. But that was Jonathan. She liked him for it; his work was simply more important than anything else.

Joe was different, outgoing and fun to be around. He was very well liked at the compound and she felt good knowing he was her friend.

When Clarisse caught up with Dr. Blare, he was talking with another young scientist named Samantha, flirting with her, as he did with all the women. Clarisse approached, trying to show confidence in her stride, but to be humble as well. She didn't need to be on Dr. Blare's bad side.

"Ah, Clarisse, how nice of you to join us," he said sarcastically. He didn't seem to be too upset, but it was obvious he wasn't happy, either.

"I'm sorry, Dr. Blare. I wasn't feeling well and I went to my quarters to lie down. I must have turned my comm badge off," Clarisse said, trying to seem apologetic and believable at the same time. She simply wasn't used to lying.

He nodded his head in acknowledgement. "Please inform a member of the staff next time...we tried your quarters, but there was no answer," he said suspiciously.

She was positive no one had seen her go or come back, yet his statement made her nervous. "I'm sorry," she replied meekly.

She gave her report, a modified version of the one she'd given the day before. She thought she'd done a good job lying, but couldn't be sure.

She was relieved when Dr. Blare dismissed her, saying as she was leaving, in a kind, but condescending voice, "Oh, and Clarisse, please call me Christian. I've asked you many times to do that. It makes me feel as if we have a better working connection."

His smile was smarmy...she hated it. He thought he was the greatest gift to humankind. Her dislike for him was growing with every day. When Jorge was around he'd tease her about it, how she let Blare get to her. But she hadn't talked to Jorge in weeks, and the need for his friendship was taking a toll on her. She wanted to see him so badly, it was almost physically painful.

Chapter 26

Back in my apartment, I sighed heavily. I needed a drink. When I opened the fridge to grab a beer I realized that I wasn't cutting down. If anything, I was drinking even more. I slammed the door shut and got a glass of water instead. Then I paced and thought. That last trip was odd, as if the dragonflies were very much in control, as if they wanted me to get her back to her world, and me back to mine. It was interesting that only one appeared to signal that the woman should go back. But when I was in the other place, there were several. The buzzing was new as well. They didn't do that the first few times. Maybe they were communicating now, the buzzing being their way of telling it was time to go. I was still pacing when I realized I'd never even asked her name. That was pretty rude of me, but of course she hadn't asked mine, either.

What really bothered me, though, were the same old questions, and the fact that I didn't get the answers when I had the chance. How come I could go through in the first place? What was Jorge's connection? She obviously knew him, and it was clear she was desperate to see him. I wanted to call Clint, but I was hesitant, too, for the simple fact that I didn't think Clint actually believed this was happening. Why should he? The whole thing was bat-shit crazy. So I paced some more and gave in to having a beer.

After my second beer I realized a few things. One was obvious—I needed to stop drinking so much beer. That thought made me laugh out loud and relieved some of the tension. But the next few thoughts brought it all back. It didn't seem to matter where I was on my side; I always landed in the same spot in the other place. That was interesting, especially if you added in the fact that if I moved over there, I moved over here. Okay, I didn't know what to make of it, but one thing I knew for sure...I needed to see and talk to this woman some more. She had answers—that I was sure of. The next question was, how did I get enough time with her? The dragonflies seemed to control my time back and forth. I needed sleep, but I didn't think I'd be able to. I lay down on the couch and turned the TV on. My last thought as I drifted away was that I would go see Jorge first thing in the morning.

Chapter 27

Josephina and Michael Mendoza were scientists, so it wasn't farfetched that their sons would be scientists, too. Jo and Mike had a secret pet project; they'd figured out how to travel through time. However, as they neared completion and perfection of the device, they also began to realize what it could mean. No matter how far the world had come, evil still lurked, and if the device were to somehow get into the wrong hands, it would be disastrous and could destroy their world. And they were very fond of their world. So, they hid what they'd done, only telling their sons about it. They made the boys promise to never tell anyone, and more importantly, to never complete the device for fear of its possibilities.

Their eldest son, Jorge, was a scientific anomaly on his own. From the time he was a small boy, he'd shown great interest and adeptness in many fields of scientific study, earning several degrees at a very young age. His brother Felipe was also a genius, almost as brilliant as Jorge. Felipe had been born with a rare disorder and was doomed to die young. However, by their time, the 22nd century, stem cell technology had been perfected to the point that it was the common cure for most, if not all diseases. By using the stem cells of his stronger, older brother, they were able to save Felipe's life, and somehow this life-saving connection created a bond stronger than average siblings had. Jorge and Felipe were inseparable as children; as adults, they were rarely seen apart, making the first trial of the dragonfly door all the more tragic.

As teenagers, their curiosity got the better of them and they secretly worked on the device. But in order to keep their promise to their parents, they put in a failsafe. The device could only work with one person. Their modifications created a biological link to the device, a link that was tied to one individual's DNA. Therefore, it could not be used by others unless Jorge or Felipe programmed an additional device, tied to that person, which they promised they would never do. They kept their research secret, even from their parents. Actually, they never intended to let the world know about it at all.

All of that changed when the virus, which had been unleashed by a 21st century madman, took hold of the agriculture in the 22nd century and was destroying it at an alarming rate. More importantly, the scientists were unable to engineer a virucide without a sample of the original virus. The only option was to use the dragonfly door to travel back in time to the virus' origin and obtain a sample. A more pressing problem had also arisen. They needed food—theirs was dying at an exponential rate. The only solution was to travel to a time when they could grow enough food to support humanity.

When the leading scientists of the world gathered to discuss the virus, the Drs. Mendoza was among them. When it was apparent that all viable solutions were exhausted, Jorge and Felipe presented the device, and explained how they could use it. Society had changed. Greed and power were social anomalies. The leaders throughout the world accepted their terms without argument. Jorge and Felipe would lead the program with the help of others in the scientific community.

Jorge and Felipe had initially decided that Jorge would make the first test run through the door and Felipe would monitor from his side. But after much discussion and the toss of an antique coin, it was decided that Felipe would make the first journey. Everything had gone right; the door had opened, Felipe had gone through and when he was ready, he signaled from the other side that he was coming back.

But they had made a grievous error. Originally they had programmed the door with Jorge's DNA, and then with the last-minute change, the door was reprogrammed with Felipe's. The similarities of the two DNAs were either too close or they hadn't properly removed Jorge's DNA. When the dragonfly device opened the door, it encountered two DNA strands, and latched onto only one, the one that had originally been programmed. Instead of Felipe, only a microscopic amount of DNA returned...Jorge's DNA, the same DNA that had saved Felipe's life as a child. The door closed and they were never able to regain access to the location to which Felipe had travelled. He was presumed dead and lost forever.

Chapter 28

Everyone on the Bio-1 project knew about Jorge's failsafe mechanism, and the horrible accident that had killed Felipe. However, the functionality was kept highly guarded. Only the basics were released and the fact that it had a failsafe. The Drs. Mendoza had always made it quite clear that this technology would never be used again, and they would never tell anyone how it worked.

This is why Dyse was so amazed at the resourcefulness of superiors. He believed they had a mole of sorts. It really was the only way they could know so much about both the project and the door. How they had gained access to the door was something different.

Jorge had programmed two types of doors. One set went from his time, the 22nd century, to the bio-compounds, which were located in the Ice Age. Each door was specifically designed and programmed to allow bio-compound personnel and scientists to travel back and forth to their time, and to allow cargo to travel through. It also allowed them to communicate with their people in their own time. The second type of door was programmed for only Jorge's use so that he could travel to the 21st century to obtain the original virus. To Dyse's knowledge, and that of his peers, no one else could re-program any of the doors, only Jorge. If they tried, the doors from the compounds to the 22nd century would close, stranding them all in the Ice Age, and if Jorge was still in the 21st century, he would be stranded as well. Somehow his superiors had managed to re-program a door, and he had wondered earlier if that was going to cause a problem now and later. He also wondered if this interference with the original programming could have caused Jorge's disappearance.

Chapter 29

Clarisse knew that there was a connection between the man and Jorge. There had to be, otherwise the man wouldn't be travelling through the door. She had an idea that this man was related to Jorge; it had to be a genetic connection. She had used the computer in her quarters to research Jorge. His parents were famous scientists, and so was he, for that matter. She began by searching his name. One thing that had not changed since the 21st century was the Internet. It was still called that, and it still allowed you to search for information from an enormous and endless variety of databases. Although the computer systems at the compound were not continuously tied to the 22nd century, they were updated each day when the communication lines were opened to her time. This allowed the technicians in the 22nd century to update the compound's Internet information daily.

His name popped up immediately, mostly in scientific journals where he'd published articles, but it also appeared on encyclopedic websites, which she read. They described him as a prodigy, obtaining many degrees before his fifteenth birthday, and more after that. But that was all, and she found that strange. The encyclopedia sites were known for their details, but aside from his scientific accomplishments and connection to his parents and brother, Jorge's page was vague. She tried ancestral and genealogical sites as well. There was nothing, as if Jorge's history had begun with his parents.

She and Jorge had been friends for many years, but they had begun dating three years before. Their relationship was strong, and they intended to marry once they completed the project. One evening, shortly after they'd come to the compound, they were idly talking about family. She mentioned that she missed hers and he said he felt the same about his parents. The conversation had moved onto ancestry and he said that his great-great-grandmother had lived in San Francisco in 2013. He sadly reminisced about a conversation with Felipe about that time, how they would have loved to visit her. She would be famous in her own right many years later, but at the time he would be visiting, she was just an ordinary woman, living an ordinary life. Of course they both knew that was not possible. He could not see her and risk changing something. Besides, they were going to the army base in Kansas, not California. Just the same, it was a fun fantasy to entertain. Clarisse was sure she'd asked the woman's name, but it hadn't meant anything at the time and now she couldn't remember it.

The information about his great-great-grandmother should have been on his page, or his parent's page, or even Felipe's, but all of those pages were empty of any such information. The name suddenly came to her, as she knew it would eventually. Clarisse entered the name and the year 2013 in the computer and waited for the results. Then she remembered that he said she was famous later in her life, so she removed the year. The number of possibilities was overwhelming, as she had expected it would be. She scrolled through until something jumped out at her. A woman whose maiden name matched the one she remembered had been credited as the mother of modern education in 2027. Was that her?

She went to this woman's page and read. Of course, she knew about this woman. Her achievements were taught to every school-age child, and it didn't surprise her that she could be Jorge's great-great-grandmother. However, like Jorge's page, this too, was vague. It did say she lived in San Francisco until 2016, and then moved to a home in Wyoming where she raised her family and spent her free time when she wasn't travelling to work on education reform. But it said nothing of her husband or children. It had been sanitized like Jorge's page. She wondered if the man she'd seen was somehow connected to this woman. She sighed in exasperation. She would tell the man about Selena Montenegro. Maybe he knew her, and maybe he was related to her.

Chapter 30

I woke up on the couch; dim light was coming in the window and I realized it was early morning. I looked at the clock on the mantel...six-forty a.m. Well, at least I'd gotten some sleep, but my sleep was full of weird dreams and they left me feeling hung-over, as if I'd pounded a six-pack the night before. I decided to go for a jog, just to Ocean Beach and back. I needed to clear my head and kill some time before my appointment with Kyle at nine.

Kyle and his wife Trish were our neighbors when I was growing up. They had a five-bedroom Spanish-Colonial house two doors down. After their last child went off to college they decided they just didn't need the huge house. They had income properties all over the city and one of them had been recently vacated, so they decided to sell the mini-mansion in Presidio Heights and move into the home in the Marina District, an expensive and highly desirable neighborhood. The bay bordered it to the north with Crissy Field, the St. Francis Yacht Club, and the Marina Green all within walking distance.

They spent some time renovating the Marina-style home. It was built in the 1920s with the garage at street level and a rather steep staircase to the front door. Kyle made jokes during the renovation about downsizing, but with all the modern conveniences. He installed an elevator that went from the garage level to the single story above and to the roof deck. He knew that regardless of what shape he was in now, he couldn't hop one-legged up and down those stairs forever.

One of the updates they made was converting the storage area behind the tandem garage space into a home office for Kyle. They put in a street-level door that opened to a hallway that ran the length of the garage bay. Kyle knew I was there because he'd buzzed me in from the street, but I still knocked lightly when I reached the door at the end of the hall. The office was one large open space that looked out onto the garden in the back. There were french doors leading out and windows flanking it on either side, making it bright and airy. Bookshelves lined one wall, a big desk and several comfortable chairs scattered about in the center and a small but functional desk in the corner for Trish, who often lent a hand with the paperwork.

Kyle was seated at his big desk and got up to greet me when I came in. He didn't move from behind the desk, he just reached over it and shook my hand. "Good to see you Frankie. Sit," he said as he waved to a well-used but comfortable leather club chair.

He sat too, and started shuffling papers around on his desk, all the while filling me in on various charities he thought were good causes. I nodded and agreed; he knew a lot more about this than me, and it was pretty basic business as usual. Finally, after fifteen minutes of that, he leaned back in his chair and looked at me.

"What?" I asked. It seemed like there was a question in the expression on his face.

"You've been spending a lot of time with Jorge these days. I heard he's been talking a bit." It wasn't a question per se, but one was implied.

"Yeah, poor fella is really messed up. I wish I could do more," I said, hoping that would end his enquiry.

Kyle looked contemplative and I knew there was more on his mind. I decided to wait him out. After a few moments of silence and an uncomfortable staring contest, Kyle finally said, "Listen, a lady came to see me the other day. She's got some very interesting ideas about an educational program that she wants to run by us for funding." Okay, well that wasn't unusual and I said so.

Kyle sighed and said, "Well, I'd really like your input on this. Would you be willing to meet with her?"

That was unusual, and I was immediately suspicious. "Kyle, I don't meet with the applicants...why her?" He shifted in his chair and smiled—actually, it was more like a smirk—and I said, "What?"

"I just think you'd benefit from this, getting a little more involved. She's a nice lady, about your age." And there it was, a nice lady, about my age. I smelled a set-up a mile away.

I couldn't help but laugh. "Kyle, if I didn't know better, I would think you were trying to introduce me to her for more than just a discussion about trust money. Listen, I appreciate it, but I'm just not ready for that sort of thing." Before he could answer, the garden door opened and Trish came in. She smiled at me and came over and pecked me on the cheek.

"Frank, sweetheart, how are you?" she asked as she perched on the edge of the nearest chair arm.

I told her I was good and then looked suspiciously back at Kyle, who was looking at Trish. The exchange between them was almost telepathic, the kind that people who've been married for more than forty-plus years seemed to share.

"Did Kyle tell you about Selena? She's really amazing, Frank. She's smart, pretty and has her head on straight." Trish was a good judge of character, which told me right away she'd spent some time talking to this Selena woman.

I smiled at her, then at Kyle. "Listen, I appreciate the gesture, but dating isn't something I want to do right now; and besides, I don't think it's a good idea to mix trust business with pleasure." Trish snorted quietly, but didn't say anything.

Kyle said, "All right, don't want to push you into anything. I get it, you're still recovering and all, but I do want you to read her proposal. I'm serious about that part. I'll email it to you; take a look and get back to me next week."

I should have been suspicious that he was giving in so easily, but I wanted to wrap up our business and go see Jorge, so I let it go. We finished up, I promised Trish I'd come over for dinner soon, and then I headed to the VA.

Chapter 31

I got to the VA center around ten-thirty and went to the rec room first, hoping to find Clint. Nancy was there and she said he'd gone on break and I was welcome to check the employee break room. I saw Jorge sitting in his usual spot and asked Nancy about him.

"Has he said anything? Clint said he sort of freaked a little yesterday."

She glanced over her shoulder at him, then back to me. "Nothing today. I missed the episode yesterday, but some of the guys here told me about it. I asked Alex, his roommate, about it, too. Alex said it sounded a lot like the babble he says while he's sleeping." She shrugged and sighed. I could tell his condition bothered her a lot. All of the patients here were dear to her, and sometimes she let it get under her skin too much.

I put my hand on her arm gently and said, "Nancy, it's okay, he's sick. You can't save them all." She smiled and nodded her head, then turned and left to attend to her other patients. The big question was, could *I* save him? For some reason, something deep inside said I could, that I *had* to.

I made my way over to him. As usual, he was sitting in a chair, staring out the window. I pulled another one up to him and sat. "Hey, Jorge, how are you?" No response, so I said, "She followed me through, but don't worry, I got her back. Who is she?"

It was so strange, the way one word or statement could get to him, as if he was there, but had to really, really fight through the fog. It was obvious that he was doing that now. He turned slowly to face me, the vacant look in his eyes slowly dissipating, and I realized for the first time that he was much older than I'd originally thought.

"Thank you," he whispered.

"Jorge, what's her name?" I asked.

He smiled and an expression of deep affection, or maybe even love, filled his eyes. "Clarisse," he said.

Okay, great, I thought, we're making progress. I said, "Jorge, I need to talk to her, to find out how to help you, but the dragonflies, they don't let me stay long. Can you tell me how to control them?"

His brow furrowed; the struggle to stay with me was evident in his face. "I...I don't know why it's you," he said. He was losing the battle for lucidity. Whatever was wrong with his head was winning. He tried again. "Use...your...mind." And then he was gone. I wanted to scream in frustration. Instead, I pounded my fist on the arm of the chair. What the hell did that mean, "use your mind?" I dragged my hands through my hair and sighed. If I kept doing that I was going to end up bald as a baby's backside. Sitting back in my chair, I watched Jorge's eyes cloud over. He slowly turned back to the window and stared out vacantly.

I felt a soft touch on my shoulder and looked up to see Clint standing there. For such a big guy it was amazing that he could just sneak up on me like that. He nodded his head toward the double doors at the other end of the rec room and I got up and followed him.

When we were outside in the hallway he asked, "Did he say something?"

Damn, this was the second time in so many days that Clint's signature greeting was MIA. This was affecting him worse than me and that just wasn't going to fly. I had an idea and I said, "Yeah, he did; but listen, can you and Kath come to my house tonight? There's a lot of stuff I want to tell you guys…run by you."

He narrowed his eyes. When he did that he looked downright mean, but I knew he was just thinking, thinking hard. "Sure, what's going on, my man? Seems like some bad shit is going down." Yeah, he was stressed. The accent and vernacular of his youth rarely made an appearance unless he was stressed.

"I think I have some ideas; be there at seven, okay? And Clint, you need to get back to being yourself. I…well I can tell this is freaking you out. Don't let it, okay? Between the three of us, we'll figure it out. It's gonna be fine," I said, using my best and most sincere smile.

He smiled back. It wasn't his usual ear-to-ear grin, but it was something and that worked for me. He patted me on the shoulder hard enough to make me stumble a little, and I laughed and headed toward Betty's office.

Chapter 32

Clarisse hoped the man would show up soon. She so desperately wanted to see Jorge, and she knew the man could take her to him. She was lingering around the area where he'd appeared before, pretending to study the flora there, but her heart and mind weren't in it. She heard someone coming from around the corner and she tried to look busy.

It was Dr. Blare, or Christian, as he preferred. "Ah, Clarisse, how are you today? Feeling better?" he asked. That smarmy smile was on his face, but she forced herself to smile in return. She knew it wasn't sincere and before she could cover it his brow furrowed in mock concern. He said, "You don't look all right."

This time she managed the smile better and said, "I'm so worried about Jorge, Dr. Blare...I mean Christian. Have you heard anything?" She knew he didn't like Jorge, so she figured this would be the best way to get him to move along and leave her alone.

He puffed up his chest a little, the dislike showing through, and said rather gruffly, "No, I'm afraid we haven't. If he hadn't insisted on that failsafe we could send someone to investigate."

She wanted to smile. It was a little gratifying to see him squirm like that. Everyone knew that he had fought to be the one to go through, but Jorge and Felipe had invented the device and no one but Jorge could use it, especially not after what happened to Felipe.

Instead she said, "Do you think something has happened to him?" She knew he didn't have a clue, but again she was hoping to get him to go away, and since Jorge was his least favorite topic, she thought she'd pursue it until he left her alone.

She thought he flinched, as if he did know something about Jorge, something that wasn't good. But that couldn't be...no one could go there but Jorge. Then she realized that wasn't true—she'd been there, and the man had been here. Before she could finish the thought, the expression was gone and he was all arrogance and false concern again.

"We just don't know, Clarisse. We can only hope things are fine. Carry on." He finally walked away.

Chapter 33

Betty was at her desk as usual. She was on the phone when I tapped on her open door, but she waved me in and I sat and waited for her to finish.

"Well, Frank?" Huh, I thought, well what? She caught the look and said, "People have been saying that Jorge is talking. Well, sort of. What's going on?"

"Not sure, Betty, I guess he's ranting more than talking." I shook my head as if I was as frustrated as everyone else, which of course I was. "I need to know more about him. He managed to get from Kansas to San Francisco; does anyone know how? I mean, if he was so out of it, how'd he manage that?"

She shook her head and said, "I don't know, sweetie. The cops found him. He was a mess. If it wasn't for his dog tags and ID, he'd be at General Hospital right now, listed as John Doe."

"Well, don't they do background checks on these guys before they enlist? There has to be more than what you told me," I said, letting my frustration show through. Then I said, "I mean, what did he do before he enlisted? You said he was twenty-two. He had to have a job or something, right?"

She narrowed her eyes at me, then turned to her computer. It was the only thing in her office that was built in this century, although by computer standards it was a dinosaur. She tapped a few keys, glanced out her door as if worried someone would see her, and then read what had come up on the monitor. "I'm not supposed to have access to this stuff," she said, a cynical and secretive smirk on her face. I smiled. Leave it to Betty to have figured out a way to break into classified files.

"Says here that he was born in San Diego and moved to Philly. We knew most of that. Parents died when he was eighteen, car accident. There are some employment records here, mostly low-paying jobs. A stint at the local city college, that's it."

I thought about that for a moment, then asked, "Okay, what were his parents' names?" I wasn't really sure why that mattered, but it seemed important.

She said, "Selena and Richard Mendoza...hmm, that's interesting."

"What is?" I asked. The names didn't mean anything to me, but something had caught her eye.

"The mother's maiden name is the same as your last name."

My eyebrows rose involuntarily. That was interesting, but then I realized that my last name wasn't uncommon; there were probably hundreds of thousands of people with the last name Mann.

"The one my mother stiffed me with, or Marcus's?" I asked. Marcus had adopted me and I had taken his last name, so technically I had two. She cocked her head at me. As far as she was concerned, Marcus was my father and that was that. I wasn't even sure if Betty knew my mother's last name. And no one was sure if it was her real name or my birth father's name…or just one she'd made up. I decided it wasn't important and moved on.

"When he's coherent…well, he seems super-intelligent, more than just what a short stint at a local junior college would do," I said, almost to myself.

"What do you mean?" she asked, confused at the comment.

I looked up from my thoughts. "Well, I don't know. It's just that when he comes around, it's like a light bulb turns on. You know, like there's a lot in that head of his."

Neither one of us knew what to make of that; I hadn't even meant to say it out loud. I shrugged my shoulders and said, "It's probably just the difference in his facial expressions when he comes around. Sorry, I'm reading more into this guy than I should." I smiled demurely at her; sometimes that worked. This time it didn't.

She leaned forward, folding her ample arms on her desk and narrowing her eyes at me. "Frank, you telling me everything?"

Crap, I thought, lying to Betty was never a good idea. I had to really try here and I didn't think she bought it. "Yeah, I am; not much to tell anyway," I shrugged. "Besides, you know everything that goes on around here, Betty, so you probably know more than me."

This she bought, simply because it was true. She dismissed me with a wave of her hand that I knew meant "get the hell out of here." I blew her a kiss and hit the road.

Chapter 34

The man had said that the dragonflies never let him stay long, but what really perplexed Clarisse was the use of the plural. There was only supposed to be one dragonfly device per person, not several.

She didn't know the exact specifics of the device because Jorge had kept that all to himself. She did know that each device was designed specifically for individual DNA, so there would only be one per person per device. That being the case, there were approximately three thousand or so dragonflies, one for Jorge, one for each person that worked at the various compounds, and a few for security personnel that remained in the 22nd century. When the device was engaged it would materialize to take that person to the other side, and there were only two sides per device.

Clarisse wasn't sure what it all meant, but she knew that time was short...not just for her world, but she thought for Jorge, too. If Jorge's device was malfunctioning—and she was sure it was Jorge's device that was bringing the man back and forth, so it must be malfunctioning—the residual effects were most likely going to be disastrous for everyone.

She tried to walk casually to the supply building at the far end of the compound. When she entered there were two other people there, so she studied the shelves, trying not to draw their attention. When she heard the outer door close twice she figured she was alone.

Immediately, she went to the section that held the communication badges. These were used for internal work environments, so co-workers could communicate with each other easily without having to use their universal devices. Although UDs did just about everything under the sun, it was easier and more secure to have the small badge for internal communication.

Taking a fresh badge down, she inserted it into the computer that was used for programming them. She input the proper commands so that the new badge was directly linked to her badge. Then she programmed it with a specific tone. That way if she received a communiqué from the new badge, she would know immediately who it was. She intended to give it to the man next time she saw him, so he could alert her when he came through the door. It wouldn't work in his world, of course, but since he'd said the dragonflies didn't let him stay long, she thought it best that he found her the minute he came through.

She had so many questions for him, but the most pressing was Jorge. Where was he and how was he? Had he managed to obtain the sample? She hoped desperately that the man would come back soon. She'd already decided to camp out that night at the spot where she'd originally seen him. It was also the same spot he'd come through with her, and she had the impression he couldn't control the door. That

made sense. He shouldn't be able to use it at all,
so why should he have control of it?

Chapter 35

I really didn't have a plan, but I thought it would calm Clint to think I did. I also knew I needed to talk this whole thing out with someone I could trust. Clint and Kath were street-smart, intelligent, and quick on their feet. If they couldn't help me work through this, no one could.

I sat on the couch, thinking about what Jorge had said. "Use your mind." So what did he mean? Should I concentrate and try and bring the dragonflies to me? Could I also get them to let me stay longer, I wondered?

I decided to try it. I leaned back and took several deep breaths, trying to relax, all the while thinking about them. I heard the buzzing sound and I opened my eyes, and realized the light had dimmed in the apartment as the sun had started to set. I must have dozed off for a while. The dragonflies seemed irritated and were swooping so close to my face it scared me. When they realized I was awake they moved away and congregated, hovering in the center of the room as if waiting for me. Okay, I thought, let's try it. I moved into the swarm and felt the now-familiar feeling of leaving my world.

I landed in the same spot as always and looked around. The light was dim there too, but not exactly the same as what I'd just left. I assumed it was approaching about the same time of the evening, but when I looked up, I could see stars...I mean a lot of stars. It wasn't quite dark enough for stars either, but this place had no light pollution, and these stars weren't quite the same as mine.

I heard a rustle to my left and jumped a little, turning around quickly to find Clarisse standing there. She smiled and said, "I waited for you. I hoped you'd be back tonight." Well, that was good; after all, she was who I'd come to see.

"Clarisse," I said. She looked surprised and I smiled. "Sorry, Jorge told me your name. I'm Frank, by the way."

At the mention of Jorge's name her eyes lit up and she asked again, begged actually, "Where is he? Take me to him, please!"

I didn't move. Instead I lowered my voice to a whisper and said, "Clarisse, Jorge said I could control the dragonflies with my mind. What does that mean?"

She looked surprised at that and took a deep breath and whispered back. "They are connected genetically, mentally, but...." She shook her head in confusion, or frustration, or both. "But they can't be tied to anyone but Jorge and the individuals he programmed them for— it's part of the failsafe."

"What failsafe, Clarisse? Obviously something isn't working right. Jorge is stuck, and I'm moving back and forth between here and there and I don't know why!"

She seemed to think about that for a second then shook herself, and while thrusting her hand out, said, "Here, keep this with you at all times. It's a communication badge. It's tied to mine, and when you come through it will alert me that you are here."

I took the object she was holding out. It was about the size of a quarter and metallic, with what looked like a touch screen in the center. I pressed it and something beeped near her. I looked up and she moved the lapel of her coveralls to reveal an identical device.

"It won't work in your world, but this way when you come through, I can come immediately."

Ah, smart girl, I thought, and so up on her *Star Trek*! The badge reminded me of the "communicators" they wore in the later shows and movies. The thought made me involuntarily laugh, and she looked at me with a questioning expression. "Thanks. Listen, we really need to talk, but we need some time together. I'm going to try and come again, later tonight. I'm not sure, but I think I'm getting the hang of this."

I didn't know why I said that...I wasn't getting the hang of anything. But just maybe I had summoned the dragonflies right as I was dozing off, and maybe that's why they seemed irritated. I looked at my watch. It was only twenty minutes later than when I'd sat on the couch and concentrated on them. I smiled; maybe it was working.

"If we can go back to my world tonight, maybe they'll let us have enough time to talk."

She nodded her head and glanced past me. I didn't need to look. I heard the buzz and then I was gone.

Chapter 36

Clarisse seemed more distracted than usual. Of course, Dyse knew it was probably her concern for Jorge; everyone was aware of their relationship. However, something told him it was more than that. He had watched her go into the supply building and come out about fifteen minutes later. After she came out he went in. She hadn't been carrying anything when she left, so he looked around, trying to figure out why she had been there. It was a large space, and at first he couldn't see that anything was out of place. There was no reason he would know what belonged where, anyway. He was just about to leave when he noticed a light go out...the monitor at the comm badge terminal.

Everything in the compound, and in his world for that matter, functioned with the utmost energy efficiency. If you didn't use it within a five-minute period, it would switch off or go dormant. He assumed she had accessed the terminal. He went over and typed a few commands to ascertain what she had been doing. She'd programmed a new badge to her badge only, and with a special alert tone. Why would she need to do that? All of their badges were programmed to receive communiqués from everyone stationed in the compound. Why would she program one badge that only communicated with her badge? He tried to access the badge so he could track who it was for, but she'd encrypted it, clever girl that she was. Of course, that told him that she was indeed up to something.

Chapter 37

Clint and Kathleen were due any minute, and my excitement level was through the roof. Not only did I think I was beginning to get control of this thing, but Clarisse had given me something, something solid and concrete that I could show them. They'd have to believe me now.

I was turning it over in my hands. I wasn't sure what the metal was, but I guessed some kind of stainless steel or aluminum; it wasn't plastic, that was for sure. The little touch screen was kind of weird too, not like the one on my smart-phone. This was different. It seemed more...more what? Soft? More organic? I wasn't sure, but I'd never seen anything like it, and I knew they wouldn't have, either. As I was pondering this, the door buzzer rang. It had to be them.

Chapter 38

Dyse's concern, aside from finding Jorge, was the attitude of his superiors. They were obviously upset with him, and that would not do, not if he was to achieve his goal. Their goal, of course, was power, unequivocal power. If you controlled the world's food source, then you controlled the world.

He'd studied the governments of the past and the influence the famous and wealthy had on them. In his time, society had evolved, and although there were still wealthy and famous people, they held no power. They were just more easily recognized, and they certainly weren't treated like royalty; they were just people.

He marveled at how much influence those people had had in the 21st century; how the rich and famous and politically connected had lectured the masses about the need to help the less fortunate, all the while doing just the opposite. He was glad that his time was different, but he certainly envied certain aspects of that past world.

In his time, people were treated as equals. It didn't matter if you were a farmer, a doctor, a store clerk, a wealthy socialite, or even a politician. The golden rule in the 22nd century was simple: live healthy, happy, productive lives. But he craved the way people looked up to certain high profile individuals of that former time. He *was* superior to most people. He knew this, and soon the rest of the world would know it, too, and would worship him for it.

By the year 2035 every form of government around the world was under fire. This was inevitable in countries where dictatorships and theocracies ruled; the extreme oppression left the people no choice. But the financial meltdown that began in the early part of the 21st century combined with extremism from opposing political parties sent western countries into a tailspin that would take more than six decades to recover from. Greed and corruption from both political and public sources was rampant. With the use of social media and unfettered Internet capabilities, extremists from every corner of the world could voice their views, and blame the plights of society on their arch enemies. The societal rift had begun and continued with a vengeance, eventually toppling many governments and changing others forever.

As the 21st century moved forward, a younger, more vibrant society began to emerge and with it, the need to change everything. That need was spurred by many different things and would continue to evolve over the next several decades. The 21st century was known not only for its societal upheaval, but also a planetary upheaval. It had been named the *dark decades* by many.

The people who had hired him were of this old world, from the wealthiest families and most powerful political empires. Their ancestors had once been world leaders or had influence of one kind or another. But in this new society, they were powerless, and they wanted that power back. They had done everything they could to fight the changes that had made the world a better place. When they realized defeat was inevitable, they banded together, vowing to someday take it all back.

They came from different backgrounds and beliefs, but all came from old money that had been accumulated over the centuries by their ancestors. Ironically, they were now all on the same side. They had bided their time, waiting for the perfect opportunity to regain the fallen empires built by their predecessors.

This group had been nothing more than a rumor for more than seventy years. To most in Dyse's time, it was simply laughable that they existed at all. These people had been taken down so furiously in the uprisings that no one actually believed they would dare try to re-emerge in the new world. But here they were, and they were ready to regain the control they felt they deserved.

They promised Dyse the one thing he could not obtain on his own—to show the world that he was indeed superior to most, if not all. He was brilliant, more so than Jorge, even though Jorge was thought to be one of the most brilliant scientists. But Dyse knew he was better, and if he brought back the virus and provided the cure he would prove to all that he was indeed the best.

Chapter 39

Clarisse was restless, and so, like many times before, she climbed the steep stairs to the walkway that ran around the perimeter of the main compound. The sun had almost completely set now and the light that drifted across the abyss of snow-covered plains was beautiful. It sparkled like a million diamonds as it bounced off the ice crystals formed by the snow.

She was hoping Frank would be able to come back tonight. There was so much she needed to know and so little she could tell him. But she was relieved about one very important thing, and that was that he knew where Jorge was, which meant she could hopefully get him back soon.

The device she'd given Frank was also a tracking device. Once a person touched the soft center, their DNA was encoded and the device would link with the main system to allow others access to the individual's whereabouts. Often, people turned this feature off. It was a privacy issue and she'd disengaged it many times herself, especially when she was resting in her quarters or when she was deeply involved in a complicated project. For two reasons, this feature benefited her now. First, her device would not be working when she went back to Frank's time, and that could arouse suspicion. Second, she had to turn it off for Frank's device as well. If an unauthorized person turned up on the main system, it would be disastrous.

She had heard some of the other scientists talking. The concern regarding Jorge's prolonged absence, and the fact that time was simply running out, was beginning to build tension. People were getting very worried that they would not be able to accomplish the needed task.

Chapter 40

I buzzed them up. The building didn't have an elevator; it was only three stories, and most of my tenants were young enough to make the climb without any problems. But it did take a few minutes unless you were like Clint and Kathleen and your legs were almost as long as I was tall. So it seemed like a mere second had passed when they came through the front door.

I was still excited and pacing when they walked in. Clint went straight to the kitchen and grabbed three beers, looked at them, shook his head in disgust, and said, "You ever buy anything but this stuff?" as he handed one to Kath and one to me. Clint wasn't a lite beer fan. I was, and it was usually the only kind of beer I bought. Kath didn't really care either way; if it was cold and wet, that worked for her.

I laughed. "Sorry, I should have stopped for something before you got here."

They sat on the couch, shoulders touching. They were both wearing blue jeans and tennis shoes. Clint had on a white t-shirt that emphasized his dark skin and Kath was wearing a black button-down blouse that emphasized her pale skin. Again, I was pleasantly amused at how they always matched each other in some way. It was never intentional and I never pointed it out to them. If I did, they'd be conscious of it and I'd lose out on the pure enjoyment of their mysterious synchronicity.

Kath said, "So, what's going on Frankie? Why are we here?" Her expression was serious, concerned, and curious all at once.

Clint just arched his eyebrows, confirming that his question was the same. I stopped pacing and took a seat on the edge of the armchair opposite the couch. I reached into my pocket and pulled out the device that Clarisse had given me, holding it in the palm of my hand so they could both see it.

Kath leaned forward, touched it gently, then touched the center pad and said, "Okay, what is it?"

I smiled, "It's a communication badge. Clarisse gave it to me when I went back earlier. I controlled the dragonflies this time. I thought hard about it and I went there. It was amazing."

Now they both looked completely perplexed. I was excited and getting ahead of myself. I hadn't told them about Clarisse or about Jorge telling me to use my mind to travel between here and the other place. I took a deep breath and started from the beginning.

I told them how Clarisse had followed me through, how I had placed the rock in the path, and how the dragonflies seemed to be waiting for me to get back to that spot. I explained that Jorge's outburst the day before was because of Clarisse coming through the door. I also told them what Jorge had said about using my mind and how I had tried it and it had worked. And of course I told them what the little quarter-sized device was and where it came from. When I was done they were silent, Clint's brow was furrowed in deep concern. Kath's brow was also wrinkled, but it wasn't concern I was seeing in her face, it was anger.

She leaned forward. "Damn it, Frank! Are you trying to tell us…that you're travelling back and forth between…what…dimensions? Time? What? And this woman, she's from *there*?" she almost hissed.

I didn't understand why she was so mad. This was good news…I was figuring out what was happening to me. I thought she'd be happy about that. I held my hands up, palms facing out in defense, and asked, "Why are you mad, Kath? This is good. I mean, it's not everything, but it's a start. I found someone who can tell me what's happening to me."

"No, Frank, it isn't good! Do you hear what you're saying? It's insane. You need help…you're delusional, and you're dragging this poor kid Jorge into it all with you!"

Ah, that was it. This was beyond her ability to grasp, of course, and why wouldn't it be? Hell, it would be beyond mine if it wasn't happening to me, too. I sighed and looked at her beautiful, kind face. Then I looked at Clint. The painful expression was more prominent now; she'd said what he was thinking.

In a low and humble tone I said, "I know this is hard for you both. I can prove it about Clarisse. Both Joel and the old man that hangs out at the bar saw her, and I'm sure the clerk at the store saw her, too. And this thing," I bounced the comm badge in my palm. "I realize I could have had it made, but I didn't…she gave it to me. Most importantly, you guys know me. I'm a grounded guy with very little imagination. Do you think I just went crazy all of a sudden? This is happening to me. For the last few days I have been traveling back and forth between two worlds. I don't know why or how yet, but I do know that Jorge is the main component…and another thing I know is that Jorge is not from here." My voice had risen with a little anger of its own as I said the last part. I took a deep breath and a long pull on my beer and sat back in my chair.

Now it was Clint's turn, but he wasn't angry like Kath. I knew she wasn't really angry at me, either. It was just her way of dealing with this. He said, "All right; where is Jorge from, then? Did this Clarisse person tell you that? Did she tell you what's wrong with him?"

I shook my head. "I think they're from the future. She said they were here to get something to save their world. I think Jorge came back for it and got stuck somehow."

Of course I was just guessing, but Jorge had previously mentioned that the other place was his time or something like that. It seemed to make the most sense. I didn't know why Jorge's mind was so messed up, but I was hoping Clarisse could help with that, too.

"Why you? Why is this affecting you, of all people?" Clint asked.

I shrugged. "Both Clarisse and Jorge said it was connected to me, tuned to me, but I have no idea how."

Kath looked at me and said, "Can you take us there?"

Ah, there it was. She needed something tangible, something she could hold, feel, see with her own eyes. I smiled. I wished I could, but unless they planned on following me around like a lost puppy all day, I didn't have enough control to try it with them.

I shook my head. "I don't know. I mean, I think I controlled the last trip over, but the dragonflies are very much a part of this. They seem to decide when I come and go, and they definitely decided they wanted Clarisse back…at least it seemed that way."

"They're not real dragonflies, are they? They're machines or something?" she asked.

I nodded and looked down at my half-drank beer. I brought it to my lips and drained it, then said, "Yeah, I think Jorge made them. I think it's part of the device that makes the travel part possible. Clarisse told me he is a scientist." I shrugged again, because again I was just really guessing.

Clint looked thoughtful, and suddenly moved his huge frame forward. It was an elegant and gentle motion that someone his size shouldn't be able to do. "Uh, not to sound as crazy as you, Frankie. But if these folks are from the future, don't we have a bigger problem, like them changing stuff in our time and vice-versa?"

Right. The old time-travel conundrum; could just the existence of a person from the future coming into the past cause an adverse effect that would change or alter their time? Could a person from the past, having gained future knowledge by travelling to the future, change his time, and therefore change the future time? I smiled. All the movies Clint and I'd seen together over the years that involved time-travel said that those were distinct possibilities, and why shouldn't they be? I'd have to bring it up with Clarisse.

"I guess so. She said there was a lot she couldn't tell me. Maybe that's what she meant."

"So when do you think you'll see her again?" Kath asked. She'd calmed down quite a bit, and I was glad.

"I'm hoping to try again tonight. It seems like the daytime hours are the same in both places. You know, if it's three p.m. here it's three p.m. or close to it there. So I think maybe she'd be missed the least if we met at night."

Her brows furrowed again. "What do you mean 'close to it'?" she asked.

Now it was my turn to frown. "Well, the sky is different there. It makes the light different. It's...I don't know, cleaner, I guess. It makes it a little harder to tell if the time of day is the same, but I think it is. I think it's just different…," I shrugged, "because it's a different place."

She stood up and said, "Well then, you better get to it. Call us when you get back, or done, or whatever, no matter how late it is."

She said this in a tone I imagined she used with her students, a tone that distinctly said there was to be no argument, just do as I say. Clint got up too and took her bottle and his to the kitchen. When he returned, he stopped in the middle of the room and looked at me. "Frankie, you said to watch out for Jorge. Is there more to this? Is he in danger or something?"

I realized what he was saying. Clarisse hadn't said anything about danger, but she was definitely concerned about me being seen in her world. She was also definitely concerned about Jorge's safety, but it was Jorge who said he was in danger.

I stood, too. "I don't know, Clint. I'll ask Clarisse, but it was Jorge who said he was in danger, and she's definitely scared about something. Jorge might be checked out most of the time, but we've both seen him break through, so I think we have to consider that he might be in real trouble and not just ranting." I shrugged; I just didn't know.

He nodded his agreement and they left.

I hadn't wanted to try calling the dragonflies while Clint and Kath were there. If it hadn't worked I would have looked nuttier than a fruitcake, and they already thought I was losing it. However, now that I was alone, I decided to give it a try. I put the little badge in the watch pocket of my jeans and then sat on the couch and concentrated. This time I didn't fall asleep, but I did enter a fugue state. Then the buzzing started and I moved to the center of the room. There were only a few and I held my hand out to them. One of them landed on my open palm and then I was gone.

Chapter 41

Selena had thought about the strange man who had visited her and the strange metal case for more than a week, and she was tired of it consuming her thoughts. He said his name was Jorge, and if what he said was true—and she thought it probably was—then he'd be back or send someone like he'd said he would. So she decided to leave it alone, remove it from her mind, and move on.

She decided to refocus on the grant from the Mann Foundation. She'd found out about the foundation from a variety of sources. It was based in San Francisco, making it convenient to work with, and it had very strict guidelines, which told her they were serious about what they funded. But they were also very private and discreet, and that was the most important piece of the plan.

For years she'd been putting together an outline for a program for which she someday hoped to get funding, a program that would help kids from all walks of life obtain an education by working toward a defined goal, which the students themselves would help set. Her idea was a good one, but she knew that if it worked on a small scale, there would be people who would want to control it—politicians, special interest groups, etc.; the same people who had destroyed the education system in the country. Letting them in would be counter-productive.

She had begun some years ago to research major corporations. Most of them had charitable funds for educational purposes, but those funds were generally used for their own benefit. They would recruit from high schools and assist in college funding, and in return the student would come to work for them. Well, what was wrong with that? If children were tested and interviewed to determine their interests and aptitude for something, why shouldn't they get funding for education and then return the favor by working a few years for the company that funded them? The military did it all the time. They paid for college and the recipient served two to four years in return.

To begin with, she wanted corporations to focus on low-income areas. If those children could be educated and given hope for a better future, the possibilities would be endless. Less crime and drug abuse, more self-esteem and personal responsibility. She'd then moved throughout the country, taking on every demographic, in the hopes of turning future generations into productive, healthy members of society. She knew it was a lofty goal, but it was much better than what was happening now.

She didn't agree with everything the corporate world did, but she believed that they could be used to better society if they focused on what was not only important to them, but to the people who worked for them and bought their products. So in her mind, why not create a mutually beneficial system, one in which everyone would win with the proper balance.

Her first meeting with the foundation's attorney had gone well. The attorney worked out of his home office, and his wife, who performed secretarial duties for him, was there also. When she'd finished her proposal, the wife walked her out and continued the conversation in front of the house for another fifteen minutes. The attorney had called last night, which took her by surprise so soon after their meeting. He said that he was very intrigued and wanted a more detailed format of her plan and implementation. She had put that together some time ago, so she spent the evening tweaking it to be sure it was perfect. She told the attorney that she would drop it at his house the following evening. He said he knew that she lived out by Ocean Beach and said that he volunteered at the VA Hospital several days a week and would be there the following day. Why not drop it off at the center? It was much closer to her than a drive to the Marina District. In the morning, she would head to the VA, taking the short bus ride to 42nd Avenue and walking the rest of the way.

Chapter 42

It was time to find out what Clarisse was up to. Why would she need the extra comm badge, and why would she encrypt it to connect only to her badge? Dyse went to her quarters first, but she wasn't there and the door was locked. He checked with her neighbors to see if they'd seen her, but no one had since dinner in the community dining room. She'd also disabled the tracker on her own badge. This wasn't out of the ordinary for her; she often did that when she was deeply involved in a project or wanted some private time—they all did.

He proceeded to her lab areas. Like most people at the compound, she had two areas…one in the large main lab and one small one on the compound floor. Since space was needed above ground for the agriculture, the main lab was located below ground. Access was gained by entering a door in the upper compound, then down to a platform that overlooked the entire lab area and provided a view of virtually all work stations for the scientists and technicians. He scanned both sides; most areas were dark, and the few that were lit and occupied were not Clarisse's. He walked down the stairs to the first occupied station and asked the technician if he'd seen her. The technician was deeply involved in whatever he was doing and didn't immediately respond. When he did, he said he hadn't seen her, but also said he'd barely looked up from his work all day and wouldn't be able to tell him who had come and gone.

Dyse left the lab and started down the path toward Clarisse's on-site station. When he arrived there it was dark and there was no sign she'd been there recently. He began to make his way back toward the personnel quarters when he heard a sound. It was distant, but distinct and clear in the silent night air. He walked faster, knowing what the buzzing could mean. Although the dragonfly wasn't supposed to buzz, his had begun to do so—he didn't know why, and as long as it still functioned, he didn't care. Could Jorge be coming through the door?

He had begun to jog now. If it was Jorge, he needed to intercept him before anyone knew he was back. As he moved faster down the path he realized the sound was fading. He broke into a full-blown sprint, but all that he found was a single dragonfly, lazily bouncing from one plant to the next…a real dragonfly.

Chapter 43

Even though Hugo knew the scientist's full name, he preferred the nickname many used instead…Dyse. He thought of the scientist as the "dice" that his superiors had thrown, hoping to get a winning roll. He had been watching the scientist from afar. He really was an idiot. Hugo smiled; that would be Dyse's new moniker, the Idiot. In the last day or so, the Idiot seemed more focused on the computer scientist, Clarisse, than on the task of finding the missing young scientist and the virus. Hugo knew the Idiot had lost track of Dr. Mendoza in the other time, but he could do nothing but watch and wait. That had been made very clear—do not make contact or interfere with the Idiot's mission. Follow him, and once the sample was obtained, ensure that the Idiot, the young scientist, and the sample were brought to them.

Now there was a new wrinkle. The Idiot had gone to the woman scientist's on-site station. While he was looking around, he had heard something and had run toward the sound. Hugo recognized the sound as well. It was a buzzing, the same buzzing the dragonfly door device had recently begun to make, only this time it was loud, much louder than normal. Since he'd been ahead of Dyse on the path he also saw the woman, Clarisse. There was something else too. A man appeared in the midst of a swarm of dragonflies. She stepped to the man and they both disappeared. Now that was very interesting indeed.

Chapter 44

Clarisse's badge chimed and she jumped a little. She'd been walking from her work station, where she'd first seen Frank, to the spot on the path where they'd come through the door. She'd been listening for the dragonflies' buzzing, but had yet to hear them, when her badge chimed. She knew Frank had come through. She touched her badge and spoke in a whisper, "I'll be right there."

Walking quickly and quietly, she soon saw him. Frank was five feet away down the path, and was accompanied by a group of dragonflies. They were buzzing around his head, but they quickly began to go silent, as if they knew they should be. She heard what she thought were footfalls in the near distance, and Frank heard it too. He reached his hand toward her and she came to him, and then they were gone. Not a word was said until they were standing in his apartment.

Chapter 45

She stepped away from me and looked around, that same odd look on her face from her previous visit to my apartment. I guessed they didn't live like this in her time and it must have been curious to her.

"Clarisse, I don't know how much time we have, so let's get down to business," I said.

She turned, focused her attention on me, and said in that lilting, almost-British accent, "You controlled it this time, did you not?"

I nodded and said, "Yeah, I think I did. But listen, I thought I heard someone running toward us, did you?"

She nodded too, then said, "But they seemed to know. They quieted down. Did you tell them to do that?"

Them? She meant the dragonflies, and now that I thought of it, they did get quiet fast. I shook my head, "No, I think they just knew."

The comm badge had been in my pocket when the door opened, and although the sound was muted, it had still startled me when I heard her voice through it. I hadn't realized you could talk through it. "Do you think whoever it was heard you talk to me?"

She shook her head; she had whispered, but the other place was so eerily quiet at night, you could have heard a pin drop.

"Clarisse, Jorge is really sick, and I think he's in danger, too. He said that he thought 'they' did this to him, that 'they' altered his door somehow and he was stuck. Do you know what he meant?" Her eyes got bigger as they filled with fear and concern, and I thought the realization of something. "Clarisse, tell me, it's important."

She sat down and looked up at me. "There are rumors of a group of people who want to control it. If they do, they would control us all—"

"Control what, Clarisse? What do they want? The door?" I asked a little harshly.

She shook her head. "No…well, they would like that, too, but they want to control the food supply." She sighed. "You see, our agriculture was sabotaged, our food supplies are dying at exponential rates, and we will die with them if we do not find the virus that started this."

Okay, great, I thought; where and why do I come into this? "I'm sorry, but what does it have to do with me?" I asked.

She shook her head and said, "No, not you specifically. The virus was developed in 2007 by a biochemist who worked for your military. He was trying to create a bio-warfare agent that would destroy specific crops, targeted crops. This could be used to destroy illegal drug crops and food supplies. The possibilities were endless from a security and warfare aspect. But after all his work, the government decided not to use it and locked it up…." She sighed again. "They should have destroyed it."

I sat down now, too, and nodded for her to continue. "The scientist who created it stole a sample, and later, much later, he released it. Several variations were created specifically to target certain types of crops. We believe he altered a particular one to target several types of vegetation at once, vegetation that produced the world's food supplies. We began to notice certain crops dying off from an unknown virus approximately fifteen years ago, which was more than twenty years after he said he released it. As it spread, more and more crops began to die, and then other vegetation. No matter what we did, we could not save them. We believe it may have degraded, and we also believe it is mutating, which is why it has been able to affect so many varieties of vegetation."

I got up and got her some water and asked her to continue. "Scientists from all over the world worked together day and night to find an antivirus or virucide, but with every effort the virus would adapt and its strength would increase. The only solution was to obtain an original strain of the virus and create a virucide from that."

She took a sip of water and seemed more composed. "A man came forward with a journal, which had been his great-grandfather's. The great-grandfather had been a scientist in the early 21st century, and had worked at an army base in Kansas that had a research facility. In his journal he describes how he developed the virus and then it was taken away from him, but he'd stolen some of it. He goes on later to describe how he manufactured more, enough to spread around the world. He deployed the sample throughout the world while travelling during his retirement.

"The journal is mostly the ravings of a very disturbed man, someone who was bitter and who had decided to inflict revenge upon the world that he believed had slighted him and his work. The great-grandson said that his great-grandfather suffered from mental illness, illness that began to take hold when the scientist was a fairly young man. So when this journal was found originally, no one really believed it. They simply thought it was the ramblings of a sad but insane man. When information about the blight came to light, the great-grandson remembered the journal and brought it to the authorities. It was a rather simple thing to verify that this disturbed man had been a scientist, that he did work the base in Kansas, and that later in life he did travel to all the places where we believe the virus was initiated."

She looked at me and I said quietly, "Go on."

"We needed the original sample, it was that simple. It was the only way we could fight this blight. Jorge had long ago created the door, in secret, with the help of his parents and his brother Felipe. They, too, are brilliant scientists." She sighed sadly. "Felipe is dead now, a horrible accident involving the early tests on the door."

Then her eyes filled with pride and she said, "Jorge and Felipe came forward with two ideas. First and most urgently, we needed to find a place to grow food that wouldn't be affected by the virus. We tried to do it on our space colonies." With that, my eyes widened and she seemed to realize she'd said too much, but it was too late.

She smiled with embarrassment that she'd divulged the future. "It did not work, though, because we were using our seeds, our soil, all of which were contaminated. They introduced the door technology and said we needed to go back before the virus was released, to a time when the soil and seeds were not contaminated. But of course we could not occupy a time when humans roamed the earth…well, not as they do in your time, or even in the centuries before your time. And so they proposed that we use this door to go back to the Ice-Age and build the bio-compounds. Since our technology is quite advanced, several hundred bio-domes were quickly put in place around the world. We used the soil and water from that time and seeds that had been stored in the early 21st century. From there, we were able to grow food."

I knew what she was talking about. I remembered reading about the seed vaults that were cropping up all over the world in case of a catastrophic event.

"Clarisse, the growth I saw in the other place, it's not new. I mean, it looks like it's been there for years, several decades," I said. Jorge wasn't that old, so if the compound was developed in his lifetime, recent lifetime, then how in the hell did it get like that?

She smiled and said, "As I said, Jorge is simply brilliant. He picked a time in the Ice-Age that occurred in what is now the western United States. We went there and created the first dome so that it could sustain humans and plants. Then we came back to our time and reprogrammed the door for fifteen years later than the dome origination. We went back several times, so within months we had a sustainable bio-dome that was producing food. When we knew that was working, we created several others. We thought they would be enough to supply the basic food needs for most of the planet.

"However, it can't continue forever, and we cannot bring back the soil, as it could change things from a past and future perspective. All we can do is grow what we can and ship it through the door to our time. But most importantly, we need to find the source of the virus so that we can synthesize a counteragent, then remove any traces of ourselves from that time where the compounds are located."

She paused to take a sip of water. "The accident that killed Felipe weighed heavily on Jorge. Even though the door technology was working, he lived in fear that something could go wrong again. He wanted to finish the project and close the doors forever. That's when Jorge volunteered to go back to your time. Using our technology, we created an identity for him and he went back as an enlisted man in your army. It was slow at first, finding the man and trying to gain access to the vault where a sample could be obtained. But in his last communication with us, he said he was close. Then his communications just stopped, and we have not heard from him in weeks. Not only is the sample of dire importance, but Jorge is the lead scientist on this project. Without him we cannot develop the virucide." She sighed, and I realized it was more than that. This woman was in love with Jorge, and her fear for him was practically oozing from her pores.

I smiled at her and said, "You're very close, you and Jorge?" I thought Jorge must have loved her too. How else could he have sensed that she'd come through the door? A flush rushed up her neck and face, and she bowed her head in embarrassment.

"It's okay, Clarisse, I'm pretty sure he feels the same. You know, he cried out the second you came through the door, He knew you were here, somehow."

She looked up and smiled, cocking her head. "How could he have known?" Good question I thought, but not now.

"Clarisse, back to this society that wants to control the food; what's that all about?"

"As I said, there have been rumors about them for years. You see, we've progressed beyond the social divides that your society suffers from. We still have wealthy people in our time, but they do not wield the power politically and socially that they do in your world. But there are some that yearn for the days when their money and lineage entitled them to power and prestige. This group was never considered a real threat, but it was widely known that they would do anything to regain the power of their ancestors." She shrugged. "That would never be allowed to happen again, and Jorge was convinced that they couldn't penetrate the door's security. Therefore they were not considered a threat to the project.

"Jorge mentioned in private to me that he thought he recognized someone from our time, here in your time. He wasn't sure and refused to tell me who he thought it might have been, but he said that possibly they somehow managed to follow him through. At the time I thought that was simply impossible. You see, the doors are coded in two ways. One is the DNA of the user, and the other only allows each door to be used for travel to and from two locations. For everyone but Jorge, our doors are coded from my time in the 22nd century to the compound. And only one person knows how to code it, and that is Jorge. He should be the only person who can use the door from our world to yours." She sighed; obviously that wasn't true anymore.

"Clarisse, I think we can safely say something is very wrong with the door and its failsafe. I'm going through, you're going through, and Jorge thinks someone else is also coming through. What went wrong?"

She shook her head in exasperation. "I do not know…if someone has somehow managed to break the security, maybe it modified the door…." She looked up at me. It wasn't me and we both knew it.

"So you think this someone modified a door to travel to 2013? And Jorge knows who it is? Did this someone's opening of the other door somehow hurt Jorge, damage his brain?"

Now she looked shocked, but a realization of some sort was growing in her eyes. She nodded her head. "Yes, that is possible," she trailed off, a sad expression filling her eyes. I was getting a little annoyed with her; she knew more than she was telling me. Without realizing it, I let that annoyance show.

I stood up and paced for a minute, then said through clenched teeth, "Clarisse, tell me!"

She looked up at me, slightly shocked at my tone. "When Jorge and his brother Felipe were very young, Felipe was very ill, and in order to save him they used some of Jorge's healthy cells and DNA. When Jorge and Felipe perfected the failsafe, they initially programmed Jorge's DNA into it, but then they decided that Felipe would go instead. But something went wrong. Somehow they hadn't removed Jorge's entire DNA, so when Felipe went through, the door detected two sequences, but when he tried to come back, the door only registered one sequence. All that came through was Jorge's DNA. Jorge was devastated, but he didn't give up. He worked day and night to correct the door malfunction.

"He was very careful about the door's security, though, and was adamant that only one person have access to your time, and that was him. When he told me about his suspicions, I created an algorithm that would monitor our timeline as it was on the day he went through the door to your world. If he or someone else somehow did something that caused a rift or change to our time, I would know, but there has been nothing."

"Clarisse, I'm pretty sure this situation is changing things regardless of whether or not someone else is here. Why haven't you picked up on that with your algorithm thing?"

Her eyes widened and again I thought she was holding out on me. Before she could answer, the buzzing began. I looked around and said, "Damn it!" The dragonflies began to gather. Only this time they hovered around her, not me, and then she was gone. I stood there in shock. What just happened? I sat down and concentrated as hard as I could. I wanted them to come back. I needed to know more and I needed it now. After a few minutes of nothing I gave up. They were obviously done letting us talk for the day. I'd try again first thing in the morning.

Chapter 46

After searching for Clarisse and not finding her, Dyse decided to go to the woman in Kansas. He needed to find out what the Army knew about Jorge. His superiors had said that there was no record of Jorge after he disappeared from the base. The plan had always been to erase any evidence of their visit to this past time before they departed for good, but if Jorge had come back to the compound, which he would have had to do in order to leave that world, everyone would have known.

After arriving in 2013, he went straight to the same bar where he'd originally met the young woman. Thankfully, she was there, but her mood soured when she saw him, since he'd left so abruptly last time. He anticipated this. He'd already concocted a sob story that would play well on her sympathies. He told her there had been a death in his family, that he'd left right away to go to them, and simply forgot all else. It worked and she warmed up nicely to him. After a few drinks he told her about his concern for his friend and that no one had heard from him. Had she heard anything? Of course she had not, why would she? He promised to see her tomorrow night and she promised to find out what she could about Jorge. He walked her to her car, which she'd parked in the furthest part of the lot. It was dark and she was frisky and flirtatious with him. He saw no reason why he shouldn't heed her desires. Thirty minutes later he was back on Bio-1, contemplating his next move.

What he really wanted was to go back to his own time. He had a rather elaborate computer system, and was sure that if he could access it, he could find out where Jorge had gone. But he couldn't go tonight because the doors were locked until morning. It was another of Jorge's failsafe conditions; limiting door usage limited the chances of contaminating the timeline.

Even if he went through in the morning, it would cause suspicion because he rarely travelled back to his time. He not only wanted, but needed, everyone to believe he was completely dedicated to the project. Dyse was sure that his superiors were holding something back from him, and his private terminal could help him find out what that was. One of his many and unknown talents was hacking, a term that had survived since the inception of the Internet and computerized age. He was very careful not to let anyone know about this. It served him well to be able to break into most secure systems without anyone suspecting it was him.

In this area, he was self-taught. He had shown an aptitude for bio-sciences, and so he was encouraged to follow that path, just as all children were encouraged to follow the path of their most obvious talents and ambitions. This was all part of an education system developed in the mid-21st century. It was the most innovative and successful education system ever developed, and it had served society, as a whole, well. A teacher from the early 21st century had begun the program in secret, with the help of an anonymous benefactor and other teachers that she had recruited.

Her theory was a relatively simple one— everyone was good at something. All children, and adults for that matter, of all demographics could succeed if they were guided and educated correctly. She began to secretly test children from all over, asking them what they wanted to be when they grew up, what kind of life they would like, what they were interested in. These questions led her to what should have seemed obvious to educators around the world. Every child could be whatever he or she wanted. If the child were properly equipped with the basics, while also learning specific skills, his or her success was inevitable.

With the help of these test results, additional anonymous benefactors, and an unusual pact with private industries, she began specialized training and education for children. It took some time but the success was indisputable, and soon governments and special interest groups were trying to control this new and innovative process of education. Fortunately they were shut out, not only because large companies were funding the education and seeing the direct impact this could have for them, but parents were also seeing the benefits. Politicians and governments had been interfering with education since the beginning of time, and their lack of success was apparent.

It was all so elemental; begin by giving them basic education in all areas, while simultaneously exposing them to ideas in career fields that might interest them. By middle grade level, most children had begun to show interest in certain career paths. It didn't matter if they wanted to be farmers, work in restaurants, retail, auto garages, engineering, education, medicine—nothing was discouraged. If a child began to show interest in a specific area, their education was tailored to it; if they changed their minds later, the program was revised to accommodate that. By helping children understand that they could achieve anything they wanted, they became invaluable to the growth of society.

Private industry understood this, and became the major benefactors of the program. If they could guarantee an unlimited work force that was educated toward their industry, the benefits were exponential.

This new form of education had a ripple effect; by having an educated work force, industries made great strides in medical technology, as well as other technologies that made life healthier.

In the early stages of the program, educators targeted low-income and crime-ridden areas. By showing children and teenagers that their criminal talents could be parlayed into successful careers and happy lives, they eventually wiped out most gang-ridden areas. Naturally, there were holdouts in the crime world, but as people took more control of their daily lives, they no longer tolerated the criminals in their neighborhoods, and fought back instead.

This reform of education was something Dyse had always appreciated about the changes that came about in the 21st century. In his observations of this other time, he knew that he did not want a society like those people had had. His time was certainly better in that regard. Of course, this had its downfalls as well. If everyone was respected equally they couldn't appreciate someone like him, and that was what he really wanted. He wanted the world to know how amazing he was.

Dyse shook off this reverie and accessed the system in his quarters. Since Jorge was a renowned scientist it was easy enough to find out about his immediate family and his educational accomplishments. But beyond that he was a blank page, and that was certainly unusual. Someone had gone to great lengths to erase Jorge's past beyond his parents and brother. This made Dyse very suspicious.

Chapter 47

I called Clint as soon as Clarisse was gone and gave him a brief rundown of what she'd said, leaving out the space colony part. I was actually pretty vague about it all, but I was careful to emphasize the point that there might be someone else from their time lurking around in our time, looking to get at Jorge. But I was distracted, too. Clarisse's departure without my help had to mean something was very, very wrong with the door.

"You listening to what I said, Frankie?" he said a bit gruffly.

"Sorry, Clint, what were you saying?"

He grunted, "I said, why can't you just take Jorge back through this door thing?"

"I think it's broken, Clint. Clarisse said I shouldn't be able to go through, and she also said there was only one dragonfly per person. Tons show up when I go through."

He sighed. "Fine. We need to get some better protection on Jorge then."

"Like what, a guard? Wouldn't that attract just a little too much attention?" I asked.

He sighed again, loudly this time. "Probably. I'm thinking on it. Come by the center tomorrow." Then he hung up on me, which was something I didn't think he'd ever done before, and it really bothered me.

Clarisse and I had spent more than an hour together, which was great, and maybe it meant that the dragonflies would let us have some more time together. I guessed I'd find out when I went back in the morning. I was tired, emotionally and physically.

I stretched out on the couch and flung my arm over my eyes, thinking I'd just sleep right there. Suddenly I heard a voice,—a low sound, almost a whisper—and it said, "Are you there? Please respond. I'm here, I'm alive."

I came fully awake and looked around. The TV was on, but the volume was muted. Something fluttered near it...or was I just imagining that? One thing was for sure...I had heard a voice, and it sounded familiar. My cell phone was on the coffee table next to the badge Clarisse had given me. I picked up the badge and looked at it, then checked my cell phone. I didn't know what I was thinking, and after a few minutes I finally decided that I was either dreaming or maybe it had come from outside.

Chapter 48

The next morning I woke up around six a.m. and immediately tried to open the dragonfly door. It took longer this time, and when I finally got there I had to wait almost twenty minutes for Clarisse. She was disheveled, and it was obvious that my arrival had awakened her. We agreed to meet again that night. I asked if she knew what time it was, as I wanted to confirm that hours and minutes were the same on both sides. They were.

This time I didn't try to summon the dragonflies. They seemed to know that she and I were done for now, and they just appeared as we began to say our goodbyes. I thought that was interesting, and it seemed to confirm what both Jorge and Clarisse had said; they were tuned to me.

Seconds before they took me away, I remembered the voice from last night. "Clarisse, can anyone else talk to me through this badge?"

She looked confused, then shook her head and said, "No, it is only coded for you and me; therefore no one else can access it." She smiled slightly. "No one else here even knows that you exist." Then I was gone, back to my world.

I wandered over to the VA a little before ten a.m. The rec room was mostly empty, but either Clint had made sure Jorge would be there, or that was simply what the staff decided to do with him at that hour of the day.

I saw Clint and Nancy as soon as I entered the double doors. They were halfway in the room, huddled over a chart. They looked up and both nodded to me. I slowly made my way over to Jorge, stopping to say hello to those I knew, to check if they needed anything like specific books or magazines, and made a promise to play a game of Scrabble with one of the guys before I left.

I pulled a chair up to Jorge and touched his arm. "Hey, Jorge, how are you today?" He didn't move or otherwise acknowledge me, so I tried what had worked before.

"So, the dragonfly door...I seem to be getting a handle on it. Clarisse and I were able to have a long talk last night. I know why you came here...well, here as in this time."

He twitched and his head lolled a little in my direction, but that was it. "Jorge, why did you come to San Francisco? Do you have the sample? Is someone else from your time here, too?"

I thought he might be getting worse. He didn't look so good, his skin was sallow, and it seemed as if there was less of him there. Maybe the longer this door situation went on, the more unstable he became, both mentally and physically.

I waited a few moments. I was about to give up when that tell-tale clarity began to emerge in his eyes. He slowly reached for my arm, so I reached out and took his hand in mine and leaned closer.

"She has it...I can't.... It's getting worse...the other door, it must be closed," he said in an almost inaudible voice. I stiffened; this was very bad.

"Jorge, concentrate, please," I begged.

His expression changed; it was slow, but it was good because I could tell he was trying to gain control of his mind. He said in the same low tone, "The door must be closed. I cannot go back if the other door is still open...it would kill me."

Okay, I thought; but was it my door, or the one we thought someone else had opened? "Jorge, which door? Is it the one that I'm using, or is there another one?"

He sighed and I could tell he was losing the internal struggle. "You are my door. There is another...dice...." And then he was gone.

What the hell was "dice," if that's even what he said? I wasn't sure. It seemed as if he slurred the last word. I held his hand until it slipped from mine, and I gently placed his in his lap. I sat there for a moment, still leaning in toward him as if he would speak again, but I knew he wouldn't, not today. He said it was getting worse, and from looking at him there was no doubt that something was getting worse. I knew I needed to talk to Clarisse again, but if there was a spy or whatever, I needed to be very careful going to her. We didn't know who it was or where they were.

I looked around the room for Clint, and saw him near the door talking to Kyle. Clint was six-six and Kyle was around six feet. Clint was hunched down, listening intently to Kyle, and that intensity made me nervous. I walked over to them and Clint immediately straightened up, and said, "Hey, my man, how's it going?"

The greeting put me at ease, a little at least, so I smiled back and said, "Good, how about you?"

He smiled back, not his usual humongous smile but close enough, then he gave me his usual spiel and I felt even better. He may not like what was going on with me, but at least he was trying not to let others see it.

Kyle, on the other hand, wasn't buying any of it, and when I asked how he was, he said, "Fine, we need to talk." He gestured for me to move out to the hallway where we could have more privacy. The three of us left the rec room and huddled out of the way of the general traffic.

Kyle looked from Clint to me and then said, "Look, Frank, I know something is up with you. I won't ask you to tell me if you don't want to." He paused and looked back to Clint, who looked at me questioningly. I thought maybe he wanted me to spill the beans on this door situation, but that wasn't going to happen. I also wondered what made Kyle think something was up. Had Betty suspected something and told him? Had Clint's concerns shown through? I didn't know, and I shook my head slightly and turned back to Kyle.

"Listen, Kyle," I said before he could say anything. "Something is going on, but I just can't share it with you. I may never be able to. I just need you to trust me, okay?"

He looked at me for a minute, then he looked at Clint. He'd known us for more than half our lives, and knew what and who we were. He smiled and said, "I'm not bailing either of your asses out of jail, so whatever *is* going on, you better be keeping your noses clean." With that he turned and walked away toward the building exit.

"How is he?" Clint asked, arching his head toward the rec room.

I shook my head and said, "He's bad, Clint. I think he's getting worse. He said there are two doors open, that mine and his are the same, but the other door had to be closed or he can't go back."

Clint looked at me with the same skepticism as before and said, "Does he still think he's in danger?" I nodded, but I didn't have any more information on that than what I'd already told him.

He was quiet for a moment, then said, "You know Eddie, my friend from the old hood?"

Of course, I knew Eddie. He'd been one of the neighborhood boys that Clint had hung out with when he'd been arrested. Eddie wasn't caught then, but he was later…a misdemeanor only, but caught and convicted just the same. Over time Clint had convinced him to get his act together and he had. With a little help and encouragement from Clint, Eddie finished high school, and went on to train as a nursing assistant and got a job at the VA. I didn't know him well, but I did know that he was liked by the staff and, like Clint, he was a big guy.

Clint didn't wait for acknowledgement. Instead, he said, "I'm gonna ask Eddie to switch to nights, to watch over Jorge." Now that was a damn good idea, and I smiled at Clint.

"Thanks, Clint," I said, as I patted him on the shoulder.

We were still standing in the hallway when, from a short distance, I heard Kyle say, "Hey, Frank." Clint and I turned toward his voice. He was walking in our direction with a woman I didn't know. When they got to us he said, "Frank Mann, Clint Wilson, this is Selena Montenegro."

Clint thrust out his huge hand immediately and said, "Nice to meet you."

I was speechless. She wasn't supermodel gorgeous or anything, but she was extremely pretty. She looked Hispanic, her hair was a silky dark brown that flowed past her shoulders, and she had mocha brown skin and the most amazing grey eyes. As I looked at those eyes it was like I was melting into something familiar and irresistible. I shook my head. What the hell was that all about?

"Hi," I said. It was all I could muster, and Clint nudged me with his shoulder, damn near knocking me down. No doubt he thought I was being rude.

Kyle smiled knowingly. This was the lady he'd recently told me about, the one who'd petitioned the trust. I couldn't stop staring at her, and I knew immediately why he and Trish thought I should meet her. She smiled at me, and a small dimple appeared to the left of her mouth. She seemed a little embarrassed by my reaction so I looked away, but it was hard. I just couldn't stop staring at her.

Kyle began to explain who she was, I guess for Clint's benefit, since I'd already figured it out. She had glanced into the rec room and I was trying not to stare when I realized her expression had changed. I followed her gaze. She was staring at Jorge and her brow furrowed as her eyes grew dark.

She turned slowly back to us and said, "That man, by the window...who is he?"

It hit me hard, why she seemed familiar. I gasped and my mouth dropped open. They all turned to me and I said, "You know him...."

Clint looked from Jorge to Selena, and I knew instantly that he saw it, too. I grabbed her by the arm and started walking her toward the exit. Clint told Kyle to stay and followed us out.

When we got outside I said, "Who are you? You're related to him, I can see it. God, you could be twins!"

She had turned pale and was shaking a little under my grasp, and I let go. Clint was hovering behind her so I didn't worry that she could run from me. She stuttered, "Is he all right? Why is he here? Isn't this a hospital?"

Clint's voice had darkened with suspicion and he said, "He's sick; do you know why? Are you the one that's chasing him?"

She turned quickly. I could see her eyes narrow and she said, "No. I wanted to help him, but he wouldn't let me. How long has he been here?"

This was getting us nowhere fast.

"Selena, how do you know Jorge?" I asked gently, trying to calm what was quickly turning into a confrontational situation.

She looked at us both, struggling with something, and finally said, "How well do you know him?" She said this to me specifically. I wasn't sure why, but she almost seemed to know that I had an unusual connection with Jorge.

Kyle was coming out of the entrance doors at a good clip. He had a worried look on his face that was bordering on anger. When he got to us, I said, "It's all right, Kyle." I looked at Selena, hoping she'd tell him the same.

She just nodded her head and said quietly, "I thought he looked familiar. I was wrong, I'm sorry."

Kyle was no dummy, and he knew that whatever we said was an outright lie, but he didn't say anything. Instead, he waved a letter-size envelope, which I hadn't noticed before, and said to Selena, "I'll review this and get back to you." Then he turned to Clint and me and said sharply, "I meant it, not bailing your asses out." If a man with one leg, using walking sticks, could stomp off, that would be exactly what he did. He was pissed off, and I had no doubt that I was in for it down the road.

I turned back to Selena. "Can we go somewhere to talk?"

She nodded lightly and said, "I think we'd better do that."

Clint wasn't going to be off shift for several hours. I could tell he wanted to be included in the conversation, but I wasn't willing to wait.

"Listen, can I come by tonight?" I asked him. Friday was always date night for Clint and Kath, but I thought this situation trumped that. He nodded and I took Selena's arm, gently this time, and led her around the building toward the back parking lots.

Chapter 49

Clarisse was very tired; not just from the night before, but also because Frank had come early that morning and she had been unable to go back to sleep after that. They had agreed to meet later that night, which shouldn't be a problem as long as she could stay awake that long. She had a lot of work to do. Frank said that whatever was going on had to be changing things, but why hadn't she detected it? She had detected a very small glitch a few days before, but it was so insignificant that she had ignored it; now she thought better of it. As she walked to her quarters, where she intended to work, she thought about the past, about how hard her generation and the ones before had worked for what they now had.

The 21st century had become the new "dark ages" and was eventually termed the "dark decades." Political and religious unrest on a global level had spurred wars and rebellions, expelling governments around the world. The media and information age had only exacerbated the situation. Thought to be a bearer of bipartisan truth, honesty and justice, they instead became platforms for political and social views, and by the mid 21st century it was almost impossible to know who was telling the truth and who was simply promoting his or her own beliefs.

The wealthy and famous were no better. Politicians had long been the recipients and givers of favors for money and power, but it had gone too far; the wealthy ruled the government, and the government leaders had become the wealthy. Simply put, the people were tired, and revolutions of one sort or another were constant.

As if these things were not enough, the earth itself played a role in the widespread changes. Beginning in 2042 and lasting for almost a decade, the countries located on the Ring of Fire in the Pacific were plagued with earthquakes and volcanic activity that destroyed more than half of the infrastructure and killed more than a third of their populations. These seismic disasters lasted for many years, each one larger than the previous. The world simply could not keep up with the humanitarian aid, so a tremendous death toll was inevitable. As the earth calmed in that regard, it lashed out in another.

In the early 21st century, the southern and eastern United States had been walloped by two powerful hurricanes. The east coast was then hit immediately by a powerful winter storm. Although most of the population was prepared and the death toll was minimal, the damage was extensive and it took many years to recover. In 2056 it happened again, this time with even more ferocity, wiping out most of North America. Entire towns were flooded and destroyed, and whole communities across these storm-ridden areas were at a complete standstill.

Powerful storms also blasted much of Europe the same year, and again five years later. The death toll was less than ten thousand, as opposed to the final death toll of the North American storms, which reached over three hundred thousand.

There was more to come. Hurricanes, cyclonic storms, drought, and heat waves that caused firestorms, flash floods, and limnic and volcanic eruptions of an intensity not seen by modern man plagued the planet for another decade.

People stopped relying on government. While it was probably the final nail in the coffins of most governing bodies, it was also the turning point for society in general. They now called on their own resources and rebuilt their communities.

Global populations had been expected to reach almost eleven billion by 2050; however, that number was greatly reduced. The planet's population had been diminished by the events that plagued it during the first and mid-part of the 21st century, and by 2070 the population had reached only nine billion.

The resiliency of humankind took on a process of unification and equalization that was now prominent in Clarisse's time. Her world wasn't perfect, but compared to what was in store for the people of the 21st century, it was practically Utopia.

The people of the 22nd century were proud of what they had overcome, but to be brought to their knees by a mistake from humanity's past like the virus was almost more than they could take. Blame began to circulate and world leaders, both governmental and scientific, were concerned that new threats to peace were on the horizon. The necessity of success of the bio-compounds and development of a virucide had become paramount.

Clarisse knew that anger and frustration toward past mistakes was unproductive and futile. They could not go back and eliminate the virus or its creator. To do so could cause a ripple effect through time and change the future. The only way was to obtain the original pathogen and produce a cure in her time. But her concern and fear for Jorge was mounting, and she was having a great deal of difficulty controlling her emotions.

As she neared her quarters, she stopped abruptly. On the path in front of her was Dr. Blare, and he was staring at her with an odd but slightly amused expression.

"You seemed so deep in thought, Clarisse, that I did not want to disturb you," he said in his usual condescending tone.

She smiled meekly. "Yes, I'm afraid I was allowing my thoughts to wander."

"I see; and where were they going?" he asked.

Before she could stop herself she said, "Dr. Blare, if there were two doors open to 2013, to where Jorge should be, could that cause his inability to contact us or come back to us?"

She'd been unsure of whom to trust and had no intention of asking anyone about it. She was instantly horrified that she had blurted the question out.

Dr. Blare's expression remained blank and he was silent for a moment. Then he asked, "Clarisse, why would you think there is a second door open to that time?"

Was that suspicion she now saw in his eyes? She wasn't sure. To cover herself, she said, after sighing dramatically, "I'm not sure. I was just trying to think of reasons why we have not heard from him."

His expression softened and he said, "Clarisse, we cannot allow this lapse in communication with Jorge to affect the work we are doing now. He developed the door, he alone can use it. I have every confidence that he is doing what he can to get back."

That actually sounded sincere, but it didn't answer her question and she was still uneasy about the look she had seen a moment ago. Blare had always been a vocal opponent of Jorge's control over the door. He'd argued until he was blue in the face that no one man or woman should have singular control. But the bottom line was simple…Jorge did have control, and he had no intention of sharing it. The dangers of timeline contamination were too great.

She smiled at him and nodded her head. "Of course you're right, Dr. Blare. I should think we'll hear from him very soon." That was all she could say. She moved past him and continued on to her quarters.

***

Christian was deeply concerned about Clarisse's question regarding a second door. Because he was the senior scientist on the project, he was privy to many of the discussions concerning the door and its functions. There had been concerns about the integrity and security of the failsafe if it was breached; Jorge simply couldn't supply an answer as to what would happen to him and his door. But Clarisse had not been part of these discussions, and her relationship with Jorge made Christian suspicious that she knew something more about Jorge's prolonged absence.

Chapter 50

I walked Selena around the back side of the VA compound to the path that led up to the Legion of Honor. There was a large circular fountain in front of the museum and we walked to the farthest side and sat on the wall overlooking the golf course.

We'd stayed silent for the whole walk, but now it was time to talk. I said, "Tell me everything you know about Jorge…please."

She sighed heavily and asked, "I'm guessing you know he's not from here?" I nodded and she smiled and nodded in return.

"Jorge told me that he had arrived without being noticed in Kansas, just as they'd planned. After a few weeks, he'd worked his way into the laboratory storage facility and gained the sample he'd come for. He used various instruments developed in his time to bypass the security and go undetected. He said it couldn't have been simpler, but something went wrong. Before he gained access to the lab, he'd begun to notice that he was feeling ill and that his door wouldn't respond when he commanded it. He'd also sensed that he wasn't alone; he couldn't say why, but he was sure he was being followed. On more than one occasion he was sure he'd seen a person that he recognized from his time. He'd returned to Bio-1 to make a report, telling them that one more trip back to our time should do it. He would have the sample and could return to the compound and seal the door to our time forever. He recalled trying to tell someone about this other person, but it seemed as if his memory was worse when he travelled through the door, as if he'd lost something in transit."

I decided this must have been the last visit that Clarisse mentioned, when Jorge had asked her about anything odd going on at her end.

"When he returned to our time he obtained the sample quickly. But before he could go, he had to erase himself from this time. He returned to the library he'd gone to on his first visit and accessed the computers, much as he'd done before. From this point it's vague. He doesn't know if he erased himself, and he's not sure what he did next. But he remembers waking up a few days later. He still had the sample, but he couldn't get his door to open and he was feeling a lot worse." She paused and blew out a breath.

I was watching her while she talked. I couldn't actually take my eyes off her, and it was the weirdest feeling I'd ever experienced. She glanced over at me, but if my staring was making her uncomfortable she didn't show it. Instead she smiled gently, the little dimple appearing by her mouth, and I smiled back.

"He was in Arizona when he woke up the next time, at a bus station in Tucson. He didn't know how he'd gotten there. He said he blacked out again, and when he woke up he was in San Francisco, at the bus terminal downtown.

But this time he thought he knew why he was there, he just couldn't quite grasp it."

"So what did he say, why was he here?" I asked anxiously.

"He said he'd come to see me…that he was in danger and he had to find help. And since I was the only person he knew in this time, in 2013, it seemed obvious to him why he'd brought himself here." She looked anxious now and I could feel my forehead crease in confusion. If he was from the future as he said, how could he know anyone from our time?

She must have sensed the question and answered, "I'm his great-great-grandmother."

I was speechless. What could I say to that? The only thing I could think to ask actually seemed silly. I wanted to know why she believed him; but then again, here I was, and I believed every word. So did that mean she'd been through the door?

"Have you gone through?" I asked quietly. She turned to me and those eyes met mine and I thought I would melt. She smiled again and I saw the dimple, Jorge's dimple.

"No, I…well, I have other reasons to believe him."

She reached into her purse and pulled out a folded piece of tissue, the kind gifts were wrapped in, and I watched her unfold it. Inside was the most beautiful dragonfly pin. The wings were a complicated and delicate design made of silver, so intricate it almost seemed like lace instead of a precious metal. The body of the dragonfly was mother of pearl. The opalescent shimmer reflected the sunlight, causing pastel colors of every hue to bounce off of it. It was amazing.

"I've never shown this to anyone, and the only other person alive that knows about it… well, she wouldn't have told anyone of its existence. But Jorge knew all about it. He described it to me as if he'd been holding it in his hand. He said I'd passed it on to my daughter, who in turn passed it on, until it reached his mother, who he says has it to this day. He said it was the inspiration for the door…well, the door's name and the device design, at least. He said that he'd always admired it when his mother wore it—its complicated design and wondrous beauty. That's what made him create the door in the form of dragonflies."

Chapter 51

So the woman scientist was traveling through the door…but how? Hugo wondered.

Even though he was trained *not* to think, he still did it, and he did it well. However, his egocentric employers didn't think so. In fact they hardly noticed him when he was in the same room as they were, an advantage Hugo relished. It was amazing what people said in front of you when they thought you were either too stupid to comprehend or simply just didn't see you. And they had said a great deal about the door and its functionality, so Hugo knew she should not have access to it.

Hugo had known early on that all they wanted was a drone, someone who did exactly what he was told without question. He was happy to oblige as long as he was instructed to kill occasionally, because killing made him feel powerful, and killing without detection actually *made* him powerful.

The week before his eighteenth birthday, a man had come to the farm where Hugo lived with his adoptive parents. He'd asked many questions of Hugo, primarily about his training, but he'd also asked questions meant to determine Hugo's intelligence. Since he knew what they wanted and expected of him, he only allowed the man to see a boy that was submissive, obedient, and well trained. Before leaving, the man instructed Hugo to take care of his parents, the farm, and any evidence that existed of his upbringing. Then he was to come to them, his current employers and benefactors.

It was Hugo's first kill, and he'd done a fine job of it. Recycling had become a valuable energy source for both urban and rural areas. The farm was no different, and much like the farmers of yesteryear, they used a process of anaerobic digestion to recycle fecal matter, both human and animal, and wastewater produced on the farm. This was far more efficient in his time, but still produced methane gas. Hugo simply rigged the methane to explode. Since the gas was piped into the house and other buildings for various uses, a chain reaction of ignited gas destroyed everything within minutes. Hugo had killed many times since then, enjoying it more and more.

He wasn't allowed to contact his employers for any reason. It was their way of distancing themselves should he be caught. That was fine with him; he really didn't care for them anyway, and he knew he would never be caught. But the woman had to be dealt with; and more importantly, whoever she was communicating with in the other time had to be dealt with. This was a problem. He didn't think killing her in that time would affect his own time, since technically she didn't exist yet, and he could dispose of her in a way that no one would ever find her body. But the person she was interacting with was a different story altogether, because he existed before they did, and his or her untimely death could have a ripple effect.

Chapter 52

Whether I liked it or not, and I certainly liked her, Selena was now part of the mystery, or at least a clue to solving it. I asked her to join me that night at Clint and Kath's. I thought it would help a great deal if they heard what she had to say, and maybe the four of us could figure out what to do. We agreed to meet at my house at six-thirty and drive over together.

Since it was still early and I wasn't due at Clint and Kath's for another few hours, I decided to go to Joel's for a couple of beers. My head was spinning and I needed some mindless chatter for a while. The fog had burned off by mid-afternoon and the western sun was warm and inviting. It was almost a shame to be inside.

I looked around for the dragonflies. It seemed to be an ingrained habit now, but they'd stopped their sudden appearances. I wondered if their original contact was designed to get my attention, which it did; but now that I was beginning to understand them, they no longer needed to just grab me. It was an interesting thought and I smiled, thinking that even with all the insanity surrounding this situation, the thought of control was comforting.

The old man was in his usual spot and he nodded in my direction, which was his usual greeting to me. Joel looked up when I walked in and gave me a peculiar look, but didn't immediately come over.

After I'd gotten comfortable on the stool next to the old man, he asked, "Who was the mystery gal from the other day?" I laughed; no "hello," no "how are you," just right to the point of his curiosity.

"She's a friend visiting from out of town. She was supposed to meet me somewhere else, and caught me off guard…her coming here and all." I thought it was a decent lie, but when I looked over at him I could tell he wasn't really buying it. Joel wandered over and put a beer in front of me, then stood and stared at me.

"What?" I asked, mustering all the innocence I could.

He kept staring. Finally he said, "So what was with the chick? You rushed her outta here pretty quick."

His tone was sarcastic and I decided to fight fire with fire, "Seriously, Joel, if you were me, would you want a girl like that in a place like this?" I was trying to be funny, but it didn't seem to be working, so I just shrugged, hoping that would be the end of it.

Joel let it go, but then said, "That guy was back today."

I didn't know what he meant, so I asked, "What guy?"

"The young kid from the other day," he said.

Oh right, I'd forgotten about that. I asked, "Did he say who he was?"

Joel shook his head. "No, but he left this for you," and he handed me folded piece of paper. I opened it. It was a drawing of a dragonfly, very intricate and delicate.

I stared at it in disbelief. It was almost identical to the pin Selena had showed me. I looked at Joel and said very seriously, "Describe this guy to me."

The tone of my voice caught him off guard, and he said, "You in trouble, Frank?"

I shook my head. "No, it's...well, it's complicated. I really need to know what this guy looked like."

I could tell Joel was concerned. We'd known each other for a long time. Before he could respond, the old man said, "Like Joel said the other day—young guy, Hispanic-looking, longish hair...his eyes were a little sketchy, too. I would've thought drug addict, but his skin was clear and he wasn't grinding his teeth like they tend to do. Besides, he was clean shaven and his clothes were clean, too. Can't be sure, but I'd say he ain't quite right in the head."

I didn't know anyone like that, but the dragonfly drawing had me worried in light of everything else.

Joel finally said, "Guy had a dimple on the left of his mouth, too." I shoved the sketch into my pocket and drained my beer.

"I gotta go, meeting some folks for dinner; maybe I'll swing by afterwards." I threw some money on the bar and waved good bye as I headed for the door.

I was shaking a little as I walked home. Was this young guy the one that Jorge was so afraid of? If so, how in the hell had he found me, and why the bar, of all places?

Chapter 53

Selena arrived at 6:30 on the dot. She'd pulled her hair back into a ponytail and changed her clothes. She had on a grey cashmere sweater the same color as her eyes, skinny jeans, and long boots. She looked casual and comfortable.

We drove to Clint and Kath's place in silence, but it wasn't uncomfortable. It took me a while to find parking. Most people had parked for the night and as usual, empty spaces were few and far between. I finally ended up parking in their driveway, blocking the pedestrian part of the sidewalk, which was usually a no-no. But it was Friday night and the parking patrol would be off work by then.

Kath answered. She wasn't smiling, but she didn't seem to be in the same mood as the night before, so I took that as a good sign. I introduced Selena to her, and since she didn't show any curiosity about her, I figured Clint must have filled her in.

She was wearing jeans again, but this time she had on a cream-colored ribbed sweater that hugged her curves. We followed her into the living room and sat in the armchairs opposite the couch. Kath started toward the kitchen, but stopped to ask Selena if she wanted beer or wine.

Clint was sprawled out on the couch, wearing jeans and a polo shirt. Naturally, it was almost the same color as Kath's shirt. I tried to hold in a giggle, not because they matched again, but because Clint was wearing fuzzy green slippers with dragon heads on the toes. I honestly could not believe they made them in his size, and because his feet were so big, they almost looked like real dragons.

When Kath came back she had two Coronas tucked under her arm and a wine glass in each hand. She passed out the drinks and then sat down next to Clint. As he sat up the dragon heads of his big slippers flopped around, revealing a short red tongue that protruded to the end of his toes. I lost it and almost spilled my beer; Kath saw it too and laughed as well. Selena had an amused expression on her face, but she didn't laugh.

When we finally calmed down I said, "Where in the hell did you get those?"

Kath smiled. "I found them online. Aren't they the greatest?" She started laughing again.

"Well, don't wear them when the kid comes. They're so damn big they'll scare the hell out of the little fella." I fell out laughing again and Clint tried to get seriously defensive, which just didn't play in this situation.

"Hey, they're comfortable, okay?" he said, a smile spreading across his face.

He looked at Selena as if she'd provide sympathy, but she simply smiled back at him. The whole episode relieved most of the tension that had been emanating from all of us, and that was a very good thing.

"Enough making fun of my slippers. What's this about, Frankie? You know Fridays are our night," he said, using his unoccupied hand to wave between himself and Kath.

My initial plan was to try to activate the door and take one of them through, but with Selena now part of the picture, I thought it best to have her tell them what she'd told me earlier.

"I know all of this stuff…this stuff that's been going on with me is really bothering you guys." I paused. "Selena, can you tell them what you told me today?"

She settled back in the chair and recited our earlier conversation. Clint and Kath were riveted and didn't say a word until she was done. I was hoping for a reaction that said they believed now, that they understood, but it didn't come.

"All right; well, I can't see any other way than to prove it to you…I mean really prove it," I said, letting my annoyance show through.

Now I saw at least curiosity in their faces, and Clint said quietly, "How?"

"By taking one of you there. The rest need to stay. I don't know if I can take more than one person; hell, I'm not even sure I can take one…from this time, that is."

Clint's brow furrowed and he said, "What do you mean 'from this time'?"

I shrugged. "I brought Clarisse here a few times, but she's from there…so I don't know; I don't really know how it all works yet."

Kath looked at me and asked, "Is it safe to go there?"

I smiled. "Yeah. We can't stay long, just a minute or two, but it's safe. I've been lots of times and I'm fine." Since she thought I was going insane, she didn't really buy into the part where I said I was fine, but she nodded as if she understood.

"So?" I asked, not needing to finish the question. They knew I wanted to know who would go and who would stay.

Clint put his hand on her leg and said, "You go, babe. I'll stay here with Selena."

We both knew she was going to be the one to go. I just needed Clint to say it for himself. I put my beer on the floor by my chair and said, "Okay, to be honest, I don't know if this will work, but I'm going to try and summon them. There may be just a few of them or it may be a swarm, so don't freak out when you see them. Kath, when I stand up, you do the same and come over and take my hand. Do it slowly."

She nodded and I sat back and began to concentrate. I was hoping this would work quickly, but I was still surprised when it did. Suddenly I realized that I had the comm badge in my pocket. I'd been carrying it around in case the dragonflies decided to just show up. I didn't want Clarisse to know I was there, though, especially since I was bringing someone with me. I pulled it out and threw it on the coffee table. Then I closed my eyes and began to concentrate again. I don't think it had been much more than a minute, but that weird feeling came over me and then I heard them. I also heard a slight gasp from Kath and Selena. I opened my eyes and stood up, and Kath did the same and came toward me. As she did that, several of them moved closer, converging all around us, and then we were gone.

Chapter 54

He'd followed him from the bar to an apartment building. As he waited outside, a woman arrived, and he recognized her immediately. They left together shortly thereafter and he followed them again. He'd "borrowed" a scooter two days back because he thought it would be easier to follow the man, and he felt bad about it. The owner would surely miss it and probably report its absence to the police, but he was hoping to be able to abandon it before they caught up with him.

They'd parked in the driveway of a private residence. The garage was at street level and the living quarters were above it. There was a large picture window facing the street, with sheer curtains that were drawn, but they were thin enough that he could still see inside. After a while the man got up from his chair and a woman, the one who'd answered the door to the house, joined him in the middle of the room. He couldn't tell for sure, but he thought he saw several things flying toward them, and then the couple just disappeared. It was no more than a minute or two later when his badge beeped and it startled him.

Chapter 55

The garden was swathed in moonlight and shadows. The snow-covered plains and mountains beyond the compound's dome were glowing eerily in the reflected moonlight. Kath looked around, turning on the path and occasionally reaching out to touch a leaf or flower. She looked up at the sky. I knew she saw the difference, the purity of the night sky here compared to our time. She turned to look at me and said, "My God, Frank, where are we?"

She kept her voice low, but I shushed her anyway. I had no idea who might come along. "This is the place I told you about, but we have to go now, we can't be caught here," I whispered.

As if on cue, the dragonflies reappeared and began their gentle dance around us, and in a matter of seconds we were back in Kath and Clint's living room. Clint was in shock. We'd only been gone for about two minutes, but I didn't think he'd moved from the edge of the couch where he'd perched himself when the dragonflies first appeared. Out of the corner of my eye I saw a dragonfly on the mantel of the fireplace; it took flight and flew upward, then disappeared, as if the ceiling had absorbed it. I looked over at Selena, expecting the same shock as I'd seen in Clint, but she only had a relieved smile on her face.

Clint's mouth was open as if he wanted to say something. Finally he did. "You just…you just disappeared, shimmered like, and then you were gone."

I smiled and looked at Kath. She smiled back and said, "Clint, it was amazing; this garden, or whatever it was...it was beautiful." She moved over to him and sat down, taking his hand. She seemed to suddenly remember that Selena was there, too.

She looked at her and then back at Clint, and said, "The sky was…different, cleaner, brighter." She appeared to run out of words.

Clint was staring back and forth from me to Selena to Kath. Finally he shook himself and said, "Frank, that thing." He pointed to the comm badge I'd thrown on the table. "It glowed, just as you…disappeared."

I leaned down and picked it up and inspected it. Why would it have glowed, I wondered? Then I heard the voice again, only this time I knew it was from the badge. "Please, are you there?"

It startled me and I dropped the badge. When I picked it up again I ran my finger over the soft pad and said, "Hello."

We were all staring at it, but after a few minutes when nothing else happened, Clint said, "What was that?" I shook my head. I had no idea; maybe Clarisse hadn't programmed it right and someone else was picking up on my signal. I would ask her later. I put it in my pocket and felt the piece of paper Joel had given me. I didn't want to scare Clint and Kath with more stuff, but I needed to tell them about this.

I pulled it out and sat down, drank my beer, then said, "Someone showed up at Joel's looking for me."

Clint's eyes narrowed and Selena turned to look at me, but Kath didn't react, which made me think he hadn't told her about Jorge's concern of someone being after him.

Kath said, "So?"

I looked at Clint and raised my eyebrows questioningly. He told her everything…why not about Jorge being in danger? He cleared his throat and said, "Jorge told Frank that he's in danger, that someone might have opened another one of these doors and come looking for him."

I expected her to be a little pissed that he hadn't told her, but instead she said, "And you didn't believe it." It didn't come out like a question, because like him, she hadn't really believed any of this until tonight either.

Selena said, "He told me he thought he was in danger, too, and he was much more in control of his faculties when I first saw him."

Kath spoke, "So why do you think this person is the one Jorge is worried about?"

"He wouldn't leave a name or anything, but he's been there twice in as many days, and today he asked Joel to give me this."

I reached across the coffee table and handed her the drawing. She sat back and both she and Clint scrutinized it for quite some time, and then handed it to Selena, who gasped audibly.

We all looked at Selena. She finally said, "My God, Frank, how?"

We talked for a while. Now that they actually believed this was real, they had real questions. They wanted to know how it worked, did I just think about the dragonflies? What about before...did they just show up and grab me? What about this guy from the bar...could that be the one Jorge was afraid of? Was I in danger from him? Was Selena in danger? After about an hour we finally left. I'd told Clarisse I would come back later that night, and I wanted to be at home for that.

Although they were certainly still concerned for my safety, I could see relief in their faces. This might be the biggest *Twilight Zone* moment of their lives, but at least I wasn't going nuts, and that mattered to them.

Chapter 56

Selena and I didn't talk on the way back to my house, but as we pulled into the garage she said, "Frank, I…well, I guess I'm afraid to go home…by myself."

I could understand that. I wasn't feeling too comfortable about being alone either. Since I owned the building, I also had the biggest apartment, and although I never actually had any out-of-town guests, I still had a pretty nice guestroom.

"Stay here tonight…I have room."

I got her settled and then told her how I'd promised to see Clarisse again tonight. She asked if it would be okay to meet her, too. If not, she'd stay in the guest room until Clarisse left. I thought it would be fine. I tried the door again. It took longer this time, but finally I went. Clarisse was waiting for me; she looked haggard and more concerned than usual. She came to me as soon as I appeared, and we went back to my time.

"What's wrong, Clarisse?" I asked as soon as we were in my apartment. She looked around and stopped abruptly when she saw Selena.

"Clarisse, this is Selena; she's Jorge's great-great-grandmother." The look on Clarisse's face was priceless, but the resemblance between Jorge and Selena was undeniable.

Clarisse finally said, "It's an honor to meet you, Mrs. Mann." She shook her head and inhaled deeply, then said, "I'm sorry, I meant Miss Montenegro."

My jaw dropped and I looked over at Selena. A slight flush was rising up her cheeks, but she smiled the most amazing smile, as if she'd known all along.

Clarisse dropped heavily into a chair and put her head in her hands. "Oh dear Lord, what have I done...?" Selena moved toward her and crouched in front of her chair, gently removing Clarisse's hands from her face.

"Clarisse, it's all right. Look at Frank...I mean really look at him."

She did and it felt weird being scrutinized so intensely. Clarisse suddenly smiled and said, "Of course; how could I not have seen it? The sharpness of the chin, and the nose...." What in the hell were they talking about?

Selena stood and sat back down on the couch, and looked at me and said, "I knew the minute I saw you and Jorge at the center; he looks like you, too." And there it was...that was the connection. I was Jorge's great-great-grandfather.

Clarisse shook herself and said, "I suppose you would have connected eventually. Hopefully, knowing that you will marry...won't change anything. I'll know when I get back." Then she turned to me and said, "Did you come through earlier?"

How did she know? Then I remembered Clint saying the badge glowed; it must have transmitted when the door opened. I blushed...I was busted. I said, "Yes, I had to.... Well, I had to convince my friends that this was happening, so I took one of them through the door."

She gasped and turned a whiter shade of pale. Her obvious worries about the timeline were now amplified.

"It's okay," I said hurriedly. "They won't tell anyone, it's just that...they're my friends, and they know Jorge. They're helping me take care of him."

She looked up at me, still pale, but more composed, and said, "You don't understand. The more people that know of us from your time...you could destroy us."

I sighed. I knew what she meant, and I said, "Look, I know that whatever you tell me could alter the future—your future, my future, everyone's future—but I can't do this on my own. I promise they won't do anything to jeopardize the timeline." Of course, how could I know that? How could I know that by showing them I hadn't already changed things? On the other hand, how could I know this wasn't what happened anyway?

But there was something else in her face, something that was bothering her. "Is there more, Clarisse, is something else wrong?"

She sighed loudly. Tears welled up in her eyes and she rubbed them away, and said, "I...I may have made a grievous error. Dr. Blare knew something was wrong. I blurted out the question about two doors. I didn't mean to…I don't know if I can trust him."

She was very distraught, so I got her some water. When she'd sipped some and seemed more composed, I said, "Do you think this Dr. Blare is the one who followed Jorge through the door?"

She shook her head "no" but said, "I don't know, Frank. He has always been very jealous of Jorge. He made many arguments that he should be the one to travel back in time. He's also one of the few scientists that could have any understanding of how the door works."

I narrowed my eyes at her. "Clarisse, I thought you said only Jorge knew how it worked."

She nodded this time. "That is true, but Dr. Blare worked closely with him. If anyone could have figured out how to open a second door, it would most likely have to be him."

I looked at Selena, then turned to Clarisse. "Okay, listen, you need to try and find out what you can, see if you can follow him around or something. Maybe he'll go through and you'll see or hear the dragonflies. I mean, I'm guessing they'd swarm for him too, right?"

She nodded, but then shook her head. "I don't know. You see, there is not supposed to be a swarm, just one dragonfly mechanism for each person." Well, that was interesting and scary, too, because I definitely had a swarm.

"All right, I'm going to go see Jorge first thing tomorrow. Selena, can you come too?

Maybe your presence will help him come around. We'll see if he can tell us why there are so many when they come to me."

Clarisse seemed a little relieved and said, "I will try to follow him, but he is very clever. Next to Jorge, he is probably one of our best and brightest scientists."

I didn't like the idea of sending Clarisse on a clandestine mission to find our second door man, but who else was going to do it?

"Clarisse, Jorge said the word 'dice' today. Does that mean anything to you?"

She looked perplexed and seemed to be thinking. Finally she shook her head and said, "No, I don't know what he could have meant."

Selena said, "Frank, what about the voice we heard?"

I'd totally forgotten about the voice. I turned to Clarisse and said, "When we came back through tonight, a voice came through the badge. It happened yesterday, too, after I came back."

Her brow furrowed. "A voice? That's not possible. The badge is only programmed to communicate between you and me. But…," her eyes widened. "Frank, does Jorge have his badge?"

I didn't have a clue and I shrugged. "I don't know, Clarisse, why?"

"Well, the dragonfly technology is malfunctioning, so it stands to reason that the badge technology could be malfunctioning as well. It's possible that when the door opens, it engages Jorge's badge. Could it have been his voice?"

"I don't know; the person was sort of whispering, but I'll see if I can find out," I said.

She smiled tiredly and asked us, "Please tell me about Jorge."

We told her what we knew. After we'd finished, she looked frightened and I knew it was not just for Jorge but for her, as well.

"He's getting much worse. Take me to him. I may be able to help him," she said. I could hear the rising fear in her voice.

I shook my head. "Clarisse, I don't think we should risk that. What if this other person is following you? We'd lead him or her right to Jorge."

She sighed and lowered her head. "Yes, of course, he must be kept safe until we can return him to our time."

She shifted in her seat and said rather anxiously, "I need to go back. I have to check the timeline." Then she became thoughtful, almost as if she was talking to herself. "I think I may know of one way which it has already been changed, but I cannot be sure when it happened."

I looked at Selena and could see the concern in her eyes. She said, "Clarisse, what are you talking about?"

"In our time it is very easy to learn about people, especially people of historic importance. Jorge is considered a great scientist, as are his parents. When I remembered my conversation with him about his great-great-grandmother being here in San Francisco around this time, I attempted to research her."

She smiled admiringly at Selena and then continued. "I remembered him telling me that you had become famous. I found your encyclopedic page, but it was not linked to his as it should have been, and there was very little about you. Just your name and major accomplishment, and where you lived the latter years of your life. That is very odd, especially for someone like you—" She stopped suddenly; obviously this was *future* territory and she couldn't say any more.

I wasn't sure what to make of that, but I've looked on Wikipedia enough to know that if the person you're looking up has famous relatives, they're almost always mentioned.

"So what you're saying is that someone altered both Jorge's and Selena's information, to exclude them from each other?"

She looked up at me, realization in her eyes, and said, "Yes, that is exactly what I think has happened. But when was it done? A year ago? Yesterday?"

I got up and paced, then an idea hit me and I said, "Clarisse, try this scenario on for size. Jorge figures out he's being followed and that someone has messed with his door. So he does the only thing he thinks may work...he goes to Selena, gives her the virus for safekeeping, with the idea that he'll somehow figure it all out and retrieve it from her. But something goes wrong and he ends up at the VA. Anyway, he eventually makes it back, gets everything fixed on your end. Then travels back, to...what? I don't know...some other time, and somehow erases his connection to Selena, therefore protecting her from the future, or the past...." I shook my head. Did that make any sense, I wondered?

She smiled at me and said, "Yes, that is very convoluted, but I think you are onto to something. Now we must figure out how to close the other door, so that he can come back." She was sad again; so was I, because we needed to figure out who opened the other door first.

I said, "Listen, you've been here a while, so you need to go back. But do what you can to find out about this Blare guy, okay? Just be really careful."

As if on cue, the dragonflies started to appear. I looked around the room. There was one perched on the TV, one on the picture ledge, another fluttering near the kitchen door. We hadn't noticed them arrive and that always surprised me. They began to converge on us and we both stood at the same time, and off we went. I was back in under a minute.

Selena was smiling when I returned from taking Clarisse back. It lit up her eyes and her face, and I couldn't help but return it.

"So...." I didn't know what else to say. According to Clarisse, this woman was my future wife, and the dragonfly swarms were nothing compared to the butterflies that were currently invading my stomach.

She laughed lightly. "I'm sorry Frank...I knew it the minute I saw Jorge in the hospital. He's a combination of us both. I just didn't think telling you that, on top of everything else, was a good idea at the time."

I couldn't actually blame her for that. It must have shocked her to realize who I was, too.

"That's okay; I mean, what were you going to say to me? 'Nice to meet you, Frank; by the way, we're gonna get married someday....'" I had to laugh. That sounded as stupid as I thought it would. But she laughed, too, and the sound of her voice made me relax. I was pretty sure I was already madly in love with this woman who I'd only met that afternoon, and that was just weird.

She stood. "I'm tired, and I'm sure you are, as well...goodnight." She disappeared down the hall and I heard the door close to the bathroom. I grabbed a beer, sat on the couch, and blew out a big breath, thinking the day had been more insane than the first day I'd gone through the door.

Chapter 57

The girl in Kansas had come through for him, but the information perplexed him. She had tracked Jorge to a veteran's hospital in San Francisco, but she was unable to find out exactly how he got there, or what his exact malady was. However, she was able to speak with someone there and determined that at best, he had severe mental problems that had incapacitated him. This brought several concerns to the forefront.

Dyse's first concern was that he still needed Jorge to give him the sample, which he was convinced Jorge had obtained. The second concern was that Jorge would be incapable of helping when they returned to his time. Although he knew he was certainly smarter than Jorge, he still needed him to assist with developing the virucide. He wondered how and why Jorge had ended up in San Francisco. There was no reason that he could think of; none of their research into the past or the virus' origins led to San Francisco. He shrugged to himself; it didn't really matter…what mattered was getting to Jorge.

He sent an encoded communiqué to his employers, informing them where Jorge was and that he needed his door reprogrammed for San Francisco. He thought about having them program it for several days earlier, but he didn't know where Jorge had been before he was sent to the hospital, so he had no idea what day or exact place to have the door open. Messages from Bio-1 to his time could be sent only when a door was activated and open. Fortunately, this was happening now, as it was the normal scheduled time to send harvested food through. The door would remain open for an hour, the maximum amount of time allotted. His employers knew this, so hopefully they would be monitoring for incoming messages.

He received a reply within minutes. Again there was a tone to the message that he did not like, a tone that implied they were unhappy with him. Well, that couldn't be helped. They were foolish if they had thought this would be easy. They would have his door reprogrammed by mid-morning, and they were quite clear that he was to travel to 2013 immediately, and return with both Jorge and the sample, no more delays.

Chapter 58

Hugo woke up in the bushes. He'd been hiding there since last night, near the path where the woman, Clarisse, and her friend had first appeared and disappeared. She'd come and gone again last night, so he thought it best to maintain his position in case she came back for another trip through the door. Suddenly Hugo's UD beeped and surprised him. He received very few messages, and this one was from someone in his time.

The message was encoded, and there was no sender shown, but he knew it could only be his employer. They'd been quite clear about communication with each other, so he knew that something had not gone as planned. Did they know about this woman, Clarisse? It didn't matter, the communiqué was simple and it made him very happy. The Idiot would be going to San Francisco 2013 later this morning to retrieve both the sample and Dr. Mendoza. Hugo was to go as well and return with only the sample; the Idiot and the doctor were to be disposed of. He hadn't killed in months. What a wonderful day it would be.

Chapter 59

Clarisse had tried to follow Dr. Blare the next morning, but it was almost impossible to do so without being noticed. She had duties of her own, and could not be absent from them. There was, however, one way. If she was caught, the repercussions would be devastating to her career and possibly land her in legal trouble. But what choice did she have? If Dr. Blare was the one who had created another door, a door she was now convinced was wreaking havoc on Jorge's door, then she had to find out.

She went back to the supply building where the main comm badge computer station was located. Fortunately, no one was there and she was able to quickly access the station and Dr. Blare's badge signature. She reprogrammed his badge and linked it to her UD, which she had with her at all times. This link would allow her to trace his every movement, and it allowed her to turn on its microphone feature and listen to any conversations he was having. It didn't give her any visuals, but if he remained on Bio-1, she could gain that by hacking into the surveillance cameras. If he was the one travelling to 2013, she would know as well, because the badge would become inactive. She also reprogrammed his badge so that if he turned it off, it would appear so to him, but in actuality, she could still track him.

Once she'd completed this task, she quickly left the supply building and headed back to her quarters. She'd started an analysis on her algorithm program to see if there were any changes in her time. It was a complicated request and had been running since she'd returned the night before, but she thought it would be completed now and she was desperate to see the results.

As she was walking there she heard footsteps behind her and turned to see who it was. She smiled as soon as she saw him, but once he caught up to her, she saw that his face was drawn and tired.

"Jonathan, are you all right?" she asked with concern.

He sighed loudly, hung his head a bit, then said, "I suppose. I'm tired, Clarisse. I want to go home for a while."

Although it technically took many, many years to develop and cultivate Bio-1, those years were on the prehistoric side of the timeline (where the compound was actually located). But from their side of the door, it had taken less than a year to develop and fully occupy the domes. Jonathan had been there since the beginning, and as far as Clarisse could remember, she didn't think he'd taken any real time off. That was typical of Jonathan. He was very dedicated and probably felt a personal responsibility to be there always, working toward a solution that would save mankind.

She gently touched his arm and said, "You should. Without Jorge we cannot proceed any further and the compound is running smoothly. It's the perfect time for you to go."

He looked thoughtful and after a minute said, "You know…you're right. I mean, I could monitor my projects while I'm away. If something comes up I could be back soon enough."

He smiled as if a heavy burden had been lifted. "I'm going to see Blare right now, and get him to approve it." She smiled in return and he peeled off on another path toward Dr. Blare's office, his step lighter and his head held high. She was glad for him. He really did need a break. They all did.

She looked around as she made her way to her quarters; the beauty of the compound was really quite astonishing. Because this was the first and main bio-compound, it was the largest. Aside from the main dome, there were several smaller domes that were connected via glass-enclosed corridors. From space, what appeared to be a vast network of glass domes spread across thousands of acres would appear to be floating on a bed of snow, and for the most part that was true. Bio-1 was the only compound that was anchored below ground level. The others sat on the surface and only housed agricultural fields. Bio-1 was sunk two full stories below the ground, primarily because they needed the lab and storage space and did not want to take up surface area for those facilities. It was also the tallest of the domes, which allowed it to have the catwalk that ran the perimeter.

They'd tried everything in their time to revitalize their agriculture, but no matter what they did, the virus still took hold. Eventually they realized that the virus was capable of spreading and adapting to anything and everything. It invaded both the soil and the existing growth, making it impossible to engineer a seed that would be resistant.

Jorge's idea to build the bio-compound was really the only solution they had. Several seed vaults had been instituted in the early 21st century, and more were developed by mid-century. By 2050 every plant known to mankind, both current and extinct, was represented in the vaults.

They'd tried bringing soil back to their time, but it quickly became contaminated. So they began the aggressive growth and worldwide placements of the domes in the Ice Age. Unfortunately, the virus began to take hold of non-agricultural plants as well. So far, the spread was slow, but if all plant life was infected, the earth would be uninhabitable. The hope was that they'd find the original virus, develop the cure, and then bring it all back to their time, where they could cultivate and rejuvenate the world with healthy flora.

The group of scientists that had been tasked with finding a solution to the virus and their ever-growing food needs carefully selected plants for the compounds so that they could provide the most food. But this couldn't go on forever. Jorge was convinced that the longer doors from one time to another were open, the higher the risk to the timeline. They estimated that they could only occupy this prehistoric time for approximately fifty years, and then they'd have to remove it in its entirety or risk irreparable damage. But for now, this was the only thing keeping humanity from starvation.

Chapter 60

I dreamed of Selena. We were walking on Ocean Beach; the sun was just beginning to touch the horizon, a golden glow spreading across the ocean. We were hand in hand, not talking, just walking. Dragonflies were everywhere, flying all around us, but not too close. The sun was bouncing off their colorful bodies, making their wings look like tiny stained glass marvels. I turned to her; the sun was bathing her face and her grey eyes were sparkling.

She said, "It will be all right, Frank." And I knew she was right. I woke up with that feeling, and I knew it would be okay, but I also thought we had a tough road ahead of us.

It was Saturday morning and not quite seven a.m., and a feeling of euphoria from my dream lingered. I got up and showered and then made coffee, a nice strong Kona blend that I bought at a specialty store in the city. Selena appeared in the doorway to the kitchen. Her hair was messily tied up in a bun and she was rubbing the sleep out of her eyes. But she was still beautiful, even in that disheveled state. I prepared a cup for her and we drank in silence.

Finally she said, "I need to go home, shower, and change."

"Sure. Why don't I follow you over, then we can take my car to the VA from there?" She nodded in agreement.

"Selena, the box that Jorge gave you...did you open it?"

She shook her head. "He said not to."

"Okay, good; where is it?"

A small, almost sinister smile spread across her face and she said, "It's behind a secret panel in my apartment."

I cocked my head at her; a *secret panel*?

She laughed. "When I bought the place it needed a lot of work, mostly cosmetic, so I figured I'd do what I could on my own. Anyway, there's wainscoting all along the hallway walls, and one of the panels seemed to be popping away, so I thought I'd just remove it altogether. But when I tried to pull the broken panel off, I discovered it was hinged. When I finally got it open there was a cavity in the wall; a secret hidey-hole, I guess." She shrugged. "So I fixed it so that it would close properly and left it there. You know, it's sort of cool having a secret panel."

Yeah, that would be cool; maybe I'd put one in my own apartment.

"Good, so it should be safe. Let's leave it there for now." She agreed and left the room to get dressed.

Chapter 61

Felipe was so cold. He'd spent the night outside the man's apartment and his light-weight jacket just wasn't enough to keep him warm, especially when the fog rolled in and the cold became a bone-chilling dampness. He'd been sleeping in a doorway across the street, but as the sun began to rise, he knew he couldn't stay there. Fortunately, he didn't have to. The garage door to the man's building opened and the woman walked out and to her car. A minute later the man's car began to pull out. He smiled when he saw the woman; he couldn't help it. She looked so like his mother; well, actually, his mother looked like her. He scrambled to his scooter and started it up. When she pulled away from the curb the man followed, and he followed both of them.

When he had become trapped in 2013 he knew he was in trouble and would need help. But how to obtain that help was a problem. His head wasn't right...he couldn't think straight, couldn't concentrate. He was wandering aimlessly around the streets of Junction City, near the Army fort that housed the virus. He was eventually picked up by the police and subsequently dropped at a homeless shelter, where he stayed for several days. As the days went on, his head began to clear.

Aside from the clothes on his back, he'd had only two other things with him when he came through; his comm badge and his universal device, or UD. Once he was thinking straight again—well, mostly straight…he still wasn't a hundred percent—he modified his UD so that he could access the computer systems of this century. He accessed an identity and a bank account. At least then he could find somewhere to stay and get food.

There was no way to know when or if Jorge was coming for him, and after a month of no contact, he decided to leave Kansas and go to San Francisco. At that point he knew he was stuck for good. He wasn't actually sure what he would do once he arrived in San Francisco, but it was the home of his ancestors and it made him feel connected to this timeline. It wasn't like he could contact either one of them, but for some reason it made him feel better to know he was close to them.

When his badge had started beeping a few days earlier, there was a glimmer of hope. He knew the only way the comm badge could be engaged was if the door was open again, and someone with a badge was in close proximity. They were designed to be used in professional working environments; the range was usually limited to the size of the campus where a person was employed. His badge was originally programmed for the scientific foundation that he and Jorge had been part of, but it was also specifically coded to Jorge's badge as well. That way they could communicate with each other privately. The campus was one of the largest in the world, so its range was approximately two-thousand meters, a little over a mile. After he'd become stranded, he reprogrammed the badge to pick up any signal. The problem, however, was that if Jorge was contacting him, a specific tone was used, and this was not Jorge's tone. But that didn't matter, because it was engaged, and that meant someone from his time was there, in 2013, in San Francisco.

In the past months, he'd had a great deal of time to think about what had gone wrong with the door. The only thing that made sense was that the genetic code had been contaminated somehow. The minute he'd engaged the door to return he had felt a change in himself. He knew something was wrong, he just didn't know what it was. After he'd recovered at the shelter, he started to realize that this feeling he had was familiar...he'd felt it before, a very long time ago. And then he knew, and why they hadn't thought of it infuriated him.

He'd been born with a terminal lung disease; it was a slow-progressing disease that didn't materialize until he was five years old. By then it had metastasized to a point of crisis, but it wasn't incurable. The doctors used the stem cells that were harvested from his umbilical cord at birth and infused them into the affected lung after extracting the damaged tissue. The cells should have regenerated the damaged portion, curing him and allowing him to live a long and healthy life. But the disease had been there in utero; therefore his harvested cells were also contaminated and of no use. So they used his brother's cells, and that had worked. His body had assimilated those cells into its own, but even all these years later traces were still there. He thought that because the door had first been programmed for Jorge, that they must have somehow not cleansed it of those cells, and when the door was opened for his return, it only registered Jorge's DNA, causing Felipe, minus a thing or two, to remain in the past.

Now he felt a pressure in his lungs. Sometimes it was difficult to gain his breath, to fill his lungs with air. And that meant he would begin to become very ill again, just as when he was a child. He had to get back to his own time, to his own medical technology. He just didn't know enough about this time to figure out how to find the person who was accessing the door. He needed help.

His great-great-grandfather had kept a diary starting in late 2013 until his death in the late 2070s, and Felipe had read it front to back. The diary never said where Frank had lived, but it did mention his friend Joel, who owned a bar in what was known as the Richmond District of San Francisco. He didn't know the bar's name, but he knew the owner's first name. He spent endless hours at the main library downtown scouring public records to find ownership.

There were only four bars in the city with an owner who had that first name. Two were nowhere near the Richmond District, the third was near Golden Gate Park, and the fourth was on Cabrillo and 38th Avenue. He started with that one—it just seemed reasonable. After a few days it paid off. He wasn't sure how he was going to convince Frank of who he was and what he needed; in fact, he had no reasonable expectation that Frank could help him, but he had to try.

Chapter 62

The last thing I expected to see on Saturday at the VA was Betty. She worked ten hours a day during the week, and unless there was an emergency, she always took the weekends off. The other thing I didn't expect was the police. There were two federal cruisers, a city cruiser, and an unmarked police car at the entrance to the building. When we entered, we saw more federal and local cops walking away from the elevators. The VA was under federal jurisdiction, so their presence wasn't unusual, but if the local police were involved, that usually meant something very bad had gone down.

Selena took my hand and said, "What's going on? Why are the police here?"

"I don't know." I nodded toward Betty. "But she will."

Betty was standing in the middle of the corridor with a man. The guy was extremely well-dressed in a tailored suit, white dress shirt, and silk tie, and he had "lawyer" written all over him. He also looked vaguely familiar. They were engaged in a heated conversation, and Betty looked pissed off like I'd never seen her before. I guided Selena as close to them as I could, but didn't want to interrupt her.

The corridor was loud and busy with staff and the police. Something had happened and it wasn't good. We were close enough to Betty to catch snatches of what she was saying. "You're not going to see him and I don't care who you are or what paperwork you have. He's very sick, and after last night, he's also injured."

The man replied in a condescending tone, "I don't think you quite comprehend my authority, Ms. Garner. I am his lawyer, and I am authorized by his family to ensure he is receiving the best care."

Betty narrowed her eyes, but didn't respond immediately. Something flashed across her face and I knew that look...it was pure anger and suspicion.

Clint was coming down the hall; he saw us, and Betty saw him. She waved him over and said, "Clint, take Mr. Fields to the waiting area." Then she turned to the lawyer and said in a poisonous tone, "You can wait there. It's going to be a while. Don't bother my people and keep out of their way."

She nodded to Clint and he grabbed the guy by the arm and led him away. Betty turned and saw us; she walked over, looking haggard and pissed.

"What's going on?" I asked without saying hello first.

Selena and I were still holding hands and she looked at this, then turned to me and said, "Who's this?"

I smiled, couldn't help it, "This is Selena, she's...let's just say she's a very good friend."

Betty smiled a tiny little knowing smile, and then turned back toward the end of the hall where Clint had gone. He was coming back around the corner and she waved him over. I hadn't noticed it before, but he looked terrible, sad and tired and worn out and I didn't know what else, but none of it was good.

When Clint reached us, Betty said, "Follow me." We made our way through the maze of corridors until we were in her office. She shut the door and went around to her desk and sat down. She took a deep breath and let it out loudly.

"Betty, what happened? Why are the police here?" I asked.

She held a finger up angrily and looked at Clint, then back at me. Through clenched teeth she said, "You two...Clint, it's my understanding that you asked Eddie to switch shifts, to watch over Jorge. Why?" She glared at him.

He shifted on his feet and pulled a chair over, sat heavily, and looked at me.

"Jorge said someone was following him, that he was in danger. We thought it would ease his mind if he thought he had a...you know, someone familiar watching over him," I said.

"And you didn't think to talk to me or anyone else about this?" She slammed her fist onto her desk, causing everything and everyone to jump. We didn't have an answer, at least not one we could share with her. When we didn't respond, she said, "Well, I guess he was right, wasn't he?" She glared at Clint.

"What do you mean?" I asked.

She sighed. "Someone broke in last night and made their way to Jorge's room, and beat the hell out of his roommate Alex. Eddie was at the nurses' desk down the hall and came running when he heard the commotion. The intruder killed him. According to Alex, the guy was small, but strong and quick. He stabbed Eddie in the chest multiple times. Eddie bled out. Jorge had started screaming by then and woke the whole ward, and the intruder ran and got away. But Eddie's still dead, and he might not be if I had known what you two were up to!"

"Oh my God, is Jorge all right?" Selena asked.

Betty turned to Selena and her eyes were like daggers, but softened almost immediately.

"Honey, I don't know you," her eyes narrowed. "You seem familiar, but that doesn't matter right now." She waved her hand at Selena and then turned to Clint and me and said, "I have a bigger problem. That man you escorted to the rec room, he says he's Jorge's lawyer and was hired by his family."

I stiffened. "Betty, you said he didn't have any family."

"Precisely. So who is this jerk, and why is he showing up now, coincidentally on the morning after someone tried to get at Jorge?" she demanded.

"Do we know for sure that this intruder was after Jorge?" I asked.

Betty nodded her head. "Alex said the guy came into their room around four-thirty. He knows the time because Jorge had been talking in his sleep again and it had been keeping him awake. The guy came in the room, and after looking around for a second went right to Jorge and started to pull him out of bed. Alex jumped up to try to stop him and the guy clocked him something fierce. Jorge had started to scream and so had Alex. That's when Eddie arrived—"

"I heard you tell the lawyer that Jorge was injured. How is he hurt?" I asked, looking from Clint to Betty.

"He's mostly just scared and shaken up. I just said that to try and keep the lawyer away. Jorge doesn't need some jerk in a thousand-dollar suit bothering him right now. Plus, I have no reason to believe this jerk is who he says he is."

"So what now?" I asked.

Now the daggers were directed at me. "Well, the right thing to do would be for me to hand your white butt over to the police for questioning, because I am damn sure you know a lot more about this than you're telling me. But I'm not going to do that, and because I know you two boys real well, I'm going to assume that neither of you are going to tell me what's up, or you would have done it already. Is that correct?"

I nodded my head. "Betty, I can't. You have to trust me. And we need your help, but we just can't tell you what's going on."

She leaned back in her chair, clasped her hands on her ample stomach, and stared silently at us. When she finally spoke, she said, "What do you need?"

I couldn't believe she was throwing in the towel this easily and it made me uneasy, but I needed her, so I went with it. "Can you tell that lawyer that Jorge is being transferred to another hospital for treatment? Then can you help us get Jorge out of here?"

"Excuse me?" she said sharply. "I don't think so, not with the police all over the place. My God, a man has been murdered, Francis!" The use of my given name was never a good thing and I cringed.

"I'm going to call Kyle Mason, get him to come down and throw some lawyer crap back at the guy, see if we can't get him out of here for at least a day or so. That should give us some time to figure out what to do." Kyle didn't have any real authority, but hopefully the thousand-dollar suit in the waiting area didn't know that.

She picked up her phone, made the call, and after a brief explanation she hung up. "He'll be here soon. Now, I'm going to make sure they transfer Jorge to the secured hospital wing, where you," she looked at Clint, "will be pulling an extra shift until further notice."

In a calm and soothing tone, Selena turned to Betty and asked, "May we see Jorge?"

Betty sighed and said, "I shouldn't allow it, but I'll try. Clint, escort them to Jorge. If the police let them see him, fine, but only for a few minutes. If not, you two get the hell out of here."

I got up, walked over to her, leaned down, and gave her a kiss. "Thanks, Betty."

She waved her hand in dismissal and we all left. As we made our way through the maze of corridors and offices to the elevator bank, Clint sighed heavily.

I said, "I'm so sorry, Clint; I had no idea."

"I know, but he was a good man." Suddenly his expression grew dark. "If that asshole comes back tonight to finish the job, I'm gonna kill him myself."

I knew he could, too. Clint wasn't just big, he was extremely strong. I'd seen him restrain men even bigger than himself. But he wasn't impenetrable, and if this guy had a knife or gun, I didn't see how Clint could fight that.

At the moment I thought Jorge was pretty safe. The hallway surrounding his room was filled with cops and crime scene people. A nurse was in his room with him, sitting in a chair reading a magazine. Jorge was curled in a ball on his bed, his breathing calm and even. I thought maybe he'd been sedated.

Clint exchanged a few words with the nurse and she left the room. He said, "They gave him a sedative, but that was a few hours ago; should be wearing off now."

Selena and I moved to the bed and sat down. She gently rolled him over and shook him until he opened his eyes, but it was clear he wasn't seeing her. She said, "Jorge, it's me; can you hear me?"

He didn't move, and I said, "Jorge, come on, come back; we have to talk about the door."

That did it, more or less. He wasn't quite all there, but enough. "Jorge, when the door opens for me, there's a swarm of dragonflies, lots of them. Clarisse says that's not right. Can you tell me why that's happening?"

He was struggling but finally said, "The link, it has to be the link."

Selena laid her hand down on his and said, "Jorge, Frank is your great-great-grandfather. Is that why they came to him?"

Jorge's expression changed and he said, "Yes...of course. I must carry much more of your gene structure, that's how they found you, but...."

He was fading. "But what, Jorge? Please, this is important!" I pleaded, but he was gone. I stood up and said, "Damn it!" as I ran my hands through my hair.

Clint put his hand on my shoulder and said, "Calm down, Frankie, I'll be with him for the next several hours. Maybe I can get him to talk."

Clint stayed with Jorge while Selena and I made our way out of the facility. On the way we passed the waiting area. Kyle was there, and he was talking to the lawyer. Betty was there, too, a satisfied look on her face. I stopped for a minute; the lawyer really looked familiar, but I couldn't place him.

We exited the building into bright sunshine. The fog had burned off quickly, but I couldn't enjoy it. My car was parked around back, so we began to walk that way. As we made our way around the building a man stepped into our path.

Chapter 63

Hugo went immediately to Dr. Idiot's quarters and waited. He emerged a half-hour later and Hugo followed him. Dr. Idiot summoned his dragonfly and so did Hugo. His employers had reprogrammed his door to open at the same location as the doctor's, and within a few seconds they were gone from the compound. Now all he had to do was follow the Idiot to Dr. Mendoza's location.

It wasn't far. They'd materialized in a quiet residential neighborhood, and the Idiot walked a few blocks to a sprawling campus full of buildings, parking lots, and some green areas. It was only three in the morning, so the Idiot couldn't possibly be planning on going in now, but nothing he did surprised Hugo. Hugo knew from his communiqué that this was where Dr. Mendoza was, and he intended to deal with the young doctor right there and then. He'd let the Idiot go; he knew he'd be back, and then he'd kill him, too.

Hugo gained entrance to the building through a service door at the back, then found an open office and accessed a computer terminal, which told him what room he could find the young doctor in. As quietly as possible, Hugo made his way to the second floor, passing a sleeping nurse on the way. When he entered the appropriate room, he saw two bodies lying in narrow beds opposite each other. He didn't dare turn on the lights, so he crept close until he could be sure Jorge Mendoza was one of them.

He was simply going to suffocate him, a nice quiet death…not his favorite kind, but good enough. Just as he was about to slip the pillow out, he was jumped from behind. He turned under the man's weight and managed to push him back, then delivered a punch to the man's throat. It wouldn't kill him, but it would certainly knock him down for a while.

When the man went down, he hit the bedside table, knocking over a lamp. Dr. Mendoza woke and began to scream. Within seconds, another man was coming through the door, a very big man at that. Hugo pulled out the knife he kept sheathed in his boot and stabbed the big man in the chest several times.

By now, there was too much chaos. Dr. Mendoza was screaming and so was the roommate; well, as best he could with a semi-crushed throat. Hugo rushed out of the room and down the hall to a door labeled "emergency exit," which took him down a staircase to an outer door. He was out of the building within a minute, but he'd also tripped the emergency alarm in the process.

Lights inside and out began to come on and alarm bells were screaming, along with the occupants of the building. The moon was high and bright and lit up the parking area, so Hugo used the shadows of the other buildings to cover his escape, and soon he was back on the quiet residential street.

He walked a ways and discovered a park. No, it wasn't a park, it was a golf course, but it would do. He found a thick grove of trees and sat down in their black shadows, away from the moonlight that lit the fairways.

It had gone incredibly badly, but he would rectify the situation. When morning came he would return to the facility and wait for Dr. Idiot, then he'd figure out his next step. He realized now that his desire to satiate his murderous appetite had clouded his judgment. Dr. Idiot couldn't possibly have the sample yet, and killing either of them before he'd obtained it would have been disastrous. So maybe this was a   good   thing   after   all.

Chapter 64

Clarisse had run her analysis, but couldn't make sense of its results. Technically, nothing had changed, and that was a relief. But there were blips that she didn't understand; she studied these intensely. They had occurred several times over the last few days. There wasn't really a pattern to them, and even more mysterious was that there were two separate types. The first blips had appeared several days ago. After scrutinizing these carefully, she realized that some of them coincided with when she'd first seen Frank, and also when she and Frank had subsequently met. So she assumed these were results of his door opening.

The second blips were different. There were only two, and they were so slight that she'd never have seen them if she hadn't refined the algorithm and run the analysis. One of these two had occurred yesterday evening. Hadn't Frank said that his comm badge activated and that someone had spoken through it? Could that be it? The other was the night before last. She would have to ask Frank about that. For now, there was no indication that the timeline was affected, at least on her end. She thought about performing another analysis to determine anomalies in 2013, but realized any change there would almost definitely be reflected in her time.

Chapter 65

Selena grabbed my hand and was squeezing it painfully. The guy standing in front of us had a thin veneer of sweat covering his forehead and upper lip, like he was feverish or something. His hair was clean but long and unkempt, the same for his clothes. His eyes were green, the same shade as my own. It all came together for me at once, like an avalanche.

I smiled and said, "Hello, Felipe." Selena's grip tightened and then relaxed.

Felipe also visibly relaxed and said, "How did you know?"

"Come on, let's get out of here." I gently took Felipe's arm with my free hand and guided them both to my car. We drove in silence, and when I had them both comfortably seated in my living room, each with a glass of water, I told them what I thought.

"I'm glad to see you Felipe. Jorge's going to be pretty damn happy, too." I smiled at him; this was my other great-great-grandson. "Now I'm not a science guy and obviously this is all way beyond what our science is capable of anyway. So you're going to have to fill in the blanks, but give me a minute to tell you my theory." I paused to catch my breath and then continued. "So, here's what I think. Jorge came through, but you were already here, and whatever happened with your door was still lingering. The longer Jorge stayed, the more that affected his door. Someone else—we don't know who—has also opened a door to this time, but it was unauthorized, so I gotta guess that might be screwing with Jorge's door, too. When Jorge came to San Francisco, the dragonflies, which were already broken, caught a whiff of my DNA, which I think must be pretty close to yours and Jorge's. That caused this swarm that keeps popping me back and forth, but I think it's also causing some serious damage to your brother. Clarisse—do you know her?" I didn't wait for an answer, but he nodded anyway.

"She said there's only supposed to be one dragonfly per door, and I've got a lot more than that. What really tipped me off was the badge. That was you talking through it, right?" He nodded again; his relief was apparent.

"Right. Well, when you left that drawing at the bar, that did it for me. Selena said she'd never shown the pin to anyone, and Jorge told her your mother wears that pin all the time. I knew about you, and I knew Jorge didn't leave it at the bar."

Selena reached over and took Felipe's hand. "How did you survive?"

He didn't look too good and that worried me, but maybe now that we had a scientist that understood the door and its workings, we could figure this out together and get them both back home where they belonged.

Felipe told us his story, and confirmed that he was indeed ill, but he was adamant he could help us, and if he could get home within the next few days his doctors could repair his damaged lung. He wanted to see Jorge, too, more so than Clarisse had expressed; but that wasn't going to happen just yet, and I explained why.

"Sir, ah, Frank…." He shook his head.

I laughed. "Frank's fine."

Felipe smiled. "Frank…do you think whoever broke into the hospital last night was the person from our time?"

"Yeah, I do, and they killed someone, Felipe, so they're very dangerous. Do you have any idea who that could be?" He didn't; I hadn't expected that he would.

"Look, I think we need to get all of our big brains together, including Clint and Clarisse, but both of them are probably out of reach right now. I'm going to go through and tell Clarisse we need her tonight. Hopefully, Clint will be free by then." I looked at Felipe and said, "You look like you need to lie down for a while. Why don't you go into the other room?" He nodded, and Selena stood and led him to the room she'd slept in the night before.

I concentrated on the door and the dragonflies came quickly. I thought maybe that was a good sign…that they understood the urgency and were trying to cooperate. As soon as I was on the other side I brought the badge to my mouth and whispered Clarisse's name.

She responded immediately. "Frank, where are you?"

"It doesn't matter. Listen, I need you tonight…can you be available at, say, seven?"

She whispered "yes." I said, "Clarisse, I'm going to need you for a while, probably a few hours, okay?" She responded with an almost silent "yes."

I summoned them again and was back in my apartment in less than ninety seconds. Selena was sitting on the couch smiling at me, as if a person disappearing and reappearing was a daily occurrence for her.

"How come you're not shaken up by all of this? You're really calm," I asked as I sat next to her.

She laughed lightly and said, "Remember, I've had a little longer to assimilate all of this. I guess I just accepted it all weeks ago. Now everything else just seems…I don't know, par for the course of…extreme weirdness."

That was as good an explanation as any. My cell rang and I got up to answer it.

Chapter 66

From his hiding place in the trees, Hugo watched and heard the emergency vehicles speed up the street toward the campus. The noise and flashing lights disturbed everyone in the quiet neighborhood, and lights began to pop on in the houses that ran along the street opposite the golf course.

When daylight came he walked back to the VA campus. It was still a mess. Most of the larger emergency vehicles were gone, but there were still a few vehicles that had seals on their doors. He assumed they were law enforcement. People were lingering all over the place, some still in their sleepwear. Eventually those that looked like patients were led back into the building, but there was quite a crowd of pedestrians lingering, and he moved through them without notice.

He kept an eye out for Dr. Idiot. Hugo wasn't sure where he'd gone, but he knew he'd be back soon. It was another two hours before he reappeared. The Idiot had changed his clothes. He was wearing a tailored suit of this time and carrying a case of some kind. He strode with purpose to the entrance and surprisingly, the law enforcement personnel guarding the door let him in. Another hour passed and Hugo was growing impatient.

Finally, just when Hugo was deciding he may need to gain access to the building again, the Idiot emerged. He looked irritated and that made Hugo smile. He couldn't wait to kill him, but he told himself to be patient. Dr. Idiot looked around and his gaze settled on three people standing at the corner of the building. He couldn't see their faces, but the Idiot could and he looked unsettled by them. The Idiot started toward them, but for some reason he stopped suddenly and turned in the other direction.

Hugo followed Dr. Idiot out to the street and a few blocks away to a busier street, where they boarded a public transport vehicle. It was huge and had an accordion-like section connecting what appeared to be two cars; it stunk horribly, and provided a rather long and bumpy ride. The vehicle filled with many people, and at one point Hugo lost sight of the doctor. They came to a stop at another busy intersection, and as Hugo was looking out the window, he saw the Idiot exit from another door. Hugo lunged for the doors, barely getting out before the vehicle began to pull away.

He looked around, noticing that he was on a street called Van Ness Avenue. He hadn't had time to study this city before coming, but that was okay; he would just keep following Dr. Idiot. The doctor walked north for a bit and then crossed the street and entered a building with a bright green sign that said Holiday Inn. When Hugo entered he realized it was a hotel of some sort. Aside from the unfamiliar decor, it wasn't that different from the hotels of his time. Dr. Idiot went straight to an elevator, but Hugo didn't think it was a good idea to follow, so he lingered in the lobby and waited.

Chapter 67

My cell was ringing. It was Kyle and I wasn't sure I wanted to answer. I knew he would have talked to Betty and that wouldn't have gone in my favor. I sighed and hit the button. "Hey Kyle, how are you?"

"Don't give me that shit, Frank. What the hell is going on? What are you and Clint into?"

I hadn't expected *that* response and it took me off guard. I took a deep breath and said, "Kyle, I can't tell you, and I'm sure if you talked to Clint he told you the same thing. You have to trust us, please!"

"Yeah, fine. Listen, that guy isn't a lawyer. I don't know who he is, but he's got what looks like a valid court order to see Jorge, and he was pretty adamant about it."

"How do you know he isn't a lawyer?" I asked.

"Because as soon as I saw him I snapped his pic and sent it to Trish, along with the name he gave and the firm he said he worked for. She ran him; there is a lawyer by that name at that firm, but according to the photograph on the firm's website, it's not this guy."

That wasn't good at all. "Does he know you know that?" I asked.

"No, I'm not an idiot, but one of the detectives investigating Eddie's murder is an old friend of mine. I got him to hustle him out of the building, for now at least. He'll be back, though."

"Kyle, I'm sure Betty told you that Jorge doesn't have any family, so whoever this guy is, he could be related to the person that killed Eddie and tried to attack Jorge." I sighed. "Kyle, he could be the guy that killed Eddie, for all we know."

"I know all of that and I told Rice, the detective. He said that didn't mean much—maybe Jorge lied on his papers, who knows?—but he'd check it out."

I really wanted to tell Kyle everything. I wanted to tell Betty, too, but I couldn't risk it. Finally I said, "Thanks, Kyle, for getting rid of the guy, even if it's only temporary."

Kyle sighed into the phone and said, "Yeah, okay." Then he disconnected.

Selena was staring at me with concern and I went back to the couch and sat down again. I explained the call and she took my hand and just held it for a while. Then we talked for a few hours about everything under the sun. The conversation was easy and smooth, as if we'd known each other forever. The next thing I knew, the sun was lower in the sky and my cell phone was ringing again. I grabbed it and heard Clint's voice on the other end. He said that Jorge was safely tucked away in the secure ward, which was guarded. I thanked him and asked if he could come over before seven. Things were breaking and we needed to brainstorm. I didn't bother telling him about Felipe, he'd find out soon enough.

Felipe emerged from the guest room looking groggy, but better than he had before. I suggested he clean up a bit, and since we were the same size, I gave him some fresh clothes to wear and sent him to the shower. Selena had gone into the kitchen, scrounged through my meager pantry, and had somehow found enough stuff to make us some dinner.

I smiled and said, "Sorry, not much of a cook...."

"Apparently not, but I'll make do," she said with a wink.

While she emptied three cans of albacore into a bowl and mixed it with mayo and relish, I set the table. By the time Felipe had finished showering and dressing, she'd put together tuna melts with Ruffles chips on the side. We sat and ate in almost complete silence. Felipe ate with a vengeance, and I wondered where he'd been staying, and how he'd managed all these months without money.

"Felipe, how did you survive here?" I asked before I stuffed the last of my sandwich in my mouth.

He finished chewing and sat back. "My UD...it's a universal device much like your smart-phones, only...smarter," he said with a smile. "I reprogrammed it to access your vital records databases and one of your banks. I accessed an identity, a bank account, and had all the paperwork sent to a post office under general delivery." He looked from me to Selena. His expression was an odd mixture of pride and guilt. "That was how we'd planned it. You see, we knew that Jorge had to have an identity, a background, so we created a program and loaded it onto a device, similar to your flash drives. Once he arrived he would go to one of your libraries and use the device on a computer there. Since the libraries of this time are Internet-enabled, the device was able to access the necessary databases and create his background, without any trace of having been infiltrated. I didn't have the complete program on my UD, but was able to alter it enough to at least access your systems. I…eventually it will look like identity theft, but I had no choice."

That's what the guilty look was all about. Basically he'd stolen from the bank, and also hijacked someone's social security number and identity.

I smiled. "Okay, well, I guess that couldn't be helped. But answer this; I'm not sure I understand this door thing. Why can Clarisse come through with me if the doors are only programmed for one DNA strand?"

He shook his head. "I'm not sure; it shouldn't be that way. But you said that there was someone else accessing another door. I don't know how they could be doing that. Jorge and I were very careful about the programming; the encryption process alone takes a complicated series of algorithms for each door. I think you were correct, at least regarding Jorge's door. I think that our mistake, the one that stranded me here, is probably what corrupted his door initially. I must still have been in Kansas when he came through. I think that a portion of his DNA must have remained in me and confused the door further, and each time he used it, it corrupted the programming a little more. But when I left Kansas, and his dragonfly couldn't find me anymore, it began to degrade or change somehow. It's also possible that this second door caused additional damage. When Jorge arrived here in San Francisco, his dragonfly was now picking up not only his strand but yours and mine. I also think the mental link that we programmed between traveler and door became very unstable, and somehow it's affecting him."

"But that doesn't explain why I can take people through, and why it isn't affecting you and me," I said in an exasperated tone. I didn't think I would ever understand any of this and it was frustrating, I was a pretty smart guy, but this was way beyond me.

He shook his head. "I don't know, but I think part of it has to do with this other door being open. We took security precautions at every turn; each door is explicitly linked to one person. If someone tried to access another person's door the device would self-destruct. Each door was programmed to only allow access from our time to Bio-1. If someone tried to reprogram the destinations, again, it would self-destruct. The programming device itself looks like a UD, so no one would think twice about it, and if they did suspect its correct function, they wouldn't know how to use it.

"Jorge was the only one whose device could access this time…well, aside from the original device that stranded me. The final precaution we took was quite simple. You see, we both have an eidetic memory. His is more developed than mine, but we can pretty much recall anything. Only certain aspects of the functionality of the door are recorded, the rest is in here." He tapped his temple and smiled. "So essentially, you'd have to be in our heads to have the complete schematics of the door."

He inhaled deeply and flinched, I thought because it hurt him to do it. He took a few shallow breaths, and once he was composed again he said, "I can't be sure, but I think whoever is opening the other door had to already have his own door, which means he has to be a staff member from one of the bio compounds."

Selena had been quiet up until now, but she asked, "Why, what do you mean?"

He smiled affectionately at her and said, "You…my mother looks so much like you." She smiled in return and waited for him to answer the question.

"You see, that was the final security precaution. If for any reason Jorge's door was compromised, all of the doors would activate and return everyone from the compound to my time, and then the doors would deactivate. But that didn't happen. Someone has broken the encryption to the point of being able to reprogram their door to access this time, but they also somehow removed that last failsafe."

"Why couldn't it have been someone in your time, not someone from the compound?" I asked.

"Because the doors only have two destinations and one is always the compound, so in order to get from my time to this time, you have to travel to the compound first."

"All right; is it possible someone gained unauthorized access from your time to the compound and then to this time?" I asked.

He shook his head. "No, we decided to program the other doors so that they were linked with each other, so they knew there should only be so many...no more, no less. If an additional door was added it automatically triggered the final failsafe and everyone would have been returned to my time. But if someone who is already in that link somehow reprogrammed his door from Bio-1 to this time, and the dragonflies are corrupted as we suspect...well, it might not have triggered the return."

"Does anyone else know about the various security precautions?" Selena asked.

He nodded his head. "There is one other person that knows. If the last failsafe is activated, he would receive a one-minute warning so he could sound the emergency alarm that indicated immediate evacuation of all compounds." He smiled as if that was funny and said, "You know, in case someone was in the shower or toilet, they had a few seconds to make themselves travel-ready." I snickered at the mental images.

"Is that person Clarisse?" I asked. He looked at me and then shook his head.

Chapter 68

Clarisse had decided to run a new and more in-depth analysis. She was concerned that these small blips had gone virtually undetected and that maybe there were others. After an hour or so, the computer alerted her that indeed there was another blip, only this wasn't a blip per se, it was an actual change to the timeline.

A man had disappeared from the past, and he should have existed for another few months. She scanned her saved data of what she called the "pre-door timeline." He should have died in the fall of 2013, an accidental drowning. But the new analysis showed that he'd been murdered on yesterday's date in 2013. Clarisse began to panic; this wasn't supposed to happen. She began a comparable analysis of what this man might have affected had he lived, and what was now changed. There were ripples, but they were slight. This man had apparently been a loner; no living relatives, unmarried, and no children.

It was sad to see that he was so alone, but her data showed he'd been a good man, and he was missed by the few who knew him. Not only that, but now there was a criminal investigation in the new data, one that went on for months. In the end his killer had eluded the authorities, but the event had caused another ripple. She began to program a new analysis; she needed to be sure his death wouldn't have an adverse effect on her time.

While she did that, her previous analysis, which was still running, alerted her again that another ripple had been detected. This one concerned her even more because it wasn't an identifiable ripple or blip. It was like a shimmer…there, but not there, and she had no idea what that meant.

Her comm badge beeped and it startled her. She'd lost track of time and Frank was there to take her to his time. She locked her computers and her quarters and made her way to the spot on the pathway she now thought of as Frank's passage. When she arrived she couldn't see him anywhere and she began to panic. Suddenly an arm shot out of the bushes and pulled her in, and then she wasn't in the bushes any more.

Chapter 69

Clarisse had been acting very strange of late and Christian was suspicious that she knew a great deal more about the door and its functionality than either she or Jorge had led him to believe. Her comment about two doors was of even more concern, because he'd begun to think that something was indeed very wrong, days before she said anything to him.

He decided he would have a little chat with her. As he approached her quarters he saw her locking the door and hurrying away toward the center of the compound. He followed her as best he could. He didn't want her to see him, but he wanted to know what she was up to. He lost sight of her as she worked her way around a bend in the path, and when he arrived there she was nowhere in sight. He continued on for a bit, but still he didn't see her.

He activated his comm badge and signaled her. No response, which meant one of two things—she'd deactivated her badge or she was out of range. Since you could only be out of range by leaving the compound and their timeline, he assumed she'd deactivated it. Part of their security was to limit travel between this place and their time to once a day, at eight a.m., and of course, it was now a little after seven in the evening.

Chapter 70

When Dyse had been talking to the obnoxious black woman at the VA Center, he'd noticed a man and woman about his age, lingering off to the side. They were both eerily familiar, but he was having trouble placing them. A while later, while he was arguing with the one-legged attorney, they passed the room he was in. The young man lingered for a moment, a faint look of recognition on his face.

There was no way anyone could possibly recognize him in San Francisco. He'd never been there in this time, and he didn't plan on staying long, either. A moment later a plain-clothes police officer arrived and shuffled him out the door. He was very irritated and almost didn't see the man and woman on the sidewalk.

They were just about to turn the corner of the building when they were stopped by another, younger man. Dyse almost fell over in shock and took a deep breath to regain his composure. Was this possible...could he really be alive? Obviously he was, and more importantly, he knew why the couple had seemed familiar. They could be his older siblings, which was impossible. He started toward them and then stopped himself. He didn't want Felipe to see him. Felipe would recognize him right away. He turned and left the center; he needed to think about this.

Chapter 71

Because Clarisse wasn't there when I arrived in the other place, I had to wait almost ten minutes for her. In the meantime, Clint and Kathleen had arrived at my apartment, and when Clarisse and I returned, I had a sudden feeling of claustrophobia. My apartment wasn't small by any means, but I didn't entertain much and when I did, it was only Clint and Kath. Now the living room was full of people, and Clint's enormous size alone seemed to take up most of the space. They all turned and looked at us. Kath had an expression of awe on her face, but she was smiling, too.

Clarisse looked around and suddenly inhaled sharply, and her jaw almost hit the floor. She began to stammer a bit, and I realized she was seeing Felipe, who she thought was dead. He came over to her, smiling, and embraced her.

"How?" she mumbled, her eyes moist with emotion.

Selena took charge of the situation and said, "Sit, Clarisse; everyone please sit."

They did as they were told. Clarisse sat in one of the armchairs and Felipe perched on the arm of the chair she was sitting in. She was clutching his hand tightly and it looked painful. Clint and Kath sat on the couch and I took the other armchair.

"Okay, let's just get some things out of the way first. Clint, Kath, this is Clarisse, the lady from the other place, the one I told you about. And of course, Felipe; he's Jorge's brother and we all thought he was dead, but he's not," I said, smiling.

Everyone but Selena and Felipe seemed a bit dazed with the rush of introductions. Selena said, "Frank, I think you're forgetting something." She was smirking at me, and I knew she wanted me to cop to being a great-great-grandfather, which I thought might send Clint and Kath over the deep end.

"Ah, well, yeah, there is one other thing," I said hesitantly. "Felipe and Jorge are my great-great-grandsons."

Their jaws dropped in unison, then Kath started to get this look of understanding in her eyes. She smiled and said, "I see it, of course." She nudged Clint and said, "Look at him, he looks like them both. The eyes and jaw line are Frank's; the nose, forehead, the dimple, those are Selena's."

Clint looked from Felipe, to Selena, to me, and finally said, "Well all right," and turned to Kath. "Jorge too; he looks like her mostly, but man, oh man," he said, turning to Felipe. "You two boys could be twins."

And that was it. The introductions were made and now we needed to get down to business.

I asked Felipe to fill everyone in on his situation, how he'd come to be here, why he came, and that he was sick and needed to get back to his time ASAP. We also went over our theory regarding Jorge's door and the second door, and why I had become involved.

Then Clarisse said, "Something came up on my timeline. A man—he's dead and he shouldn't be." She looked distressed and I glanced over at Clint. His face took on a pained expression. He was mourning his friend and Kath gently took his hand.

I told Clarisse what had happened and her immediate response was to ask about Jorge. Was he all right? She began to panic and Felipe tried to calm her. Finally she relaxed. Clint assured her that Jorge was safe for now, but also that he was working on getting him out of there.

Finally I said, "So I guess the big question is this; can I take Jorge and Felipe back through my door?" I looked at Felipe and Clarisse. This was their area, not ours; we were just lowly 21st century pawns in the game of 22nd century time travel.

Felipe seemed to be concentrating hard, so we all just waited him out. It was Clarisse who spoke finally. "We may have a larger problem. We know someone else is accessing this time." She looked around as if she needed confirmation. "I've detected a ripple...well, more like a shimmer in the timeline. I don't know what it is, but it is there, and I believe it is because of this other person. Thus far, everything he has done hasn't had a detrimental effect on the future, but it will if we don't stop him and get him back to where he belongs."

That was something even we laymen could agree on, and we all nodded our heads in confirmation. Clint said, "So how do we find this dude? I mean, we don't know what he looks like, who he is, right?" He was looking around as if he'd hoped that one of us would contradict him. I sat back. Selena was sitting on the arm of my chair and her hand slid to my shoulder, resting there in an intimate way. Kath was watching us and she smiled; she knew what this was. So did I, and I smiled back.

"Jorge said something about dice. Remember I asked you about that, Clarisse? Felipe, does that mean anything to you?" I asked.

Felipe's brow furrowed and he said, "Not really…." He turned to Clarisse. "Aside from the obvious game implications, the only other dice I know is Jonathan, Jonathan Dyson, or Dyse. It's a nickname from his college days. I don't think he cared for it, but Jorge called him that often."

Clarisse shook her head. "No, it can't be Jonathan; he's too grounded, too dedicated." She seemed unable to believe it could be this person.

I said, "Well, what does he look like? I mean, I'm sure your friend isn't our bad guy, but describe him. That way Clint and I can rule him out as anyone we've seen hanging around the center." That seemed to placate her and she began to describe him. Then I remembered my first trip to the compound.

"Clarisse, the first time I went over, I saw you with a man. He was kind of distraught, and he had on black-rimmed glasses. Is that him?"

She smiled affectionately and said, "Yes, that's Jonathan. He's a bit old-fashioned…he doesn't much care about how he looks."

It was there, at the tip of my brain, wanting to come out, but I just couldn't grasp it. Clint said, "Sorry, I don't remember seeing anyone like that. The only person that sends up red flags for me is that lawyer from this morning."

Oh crap; I snapped my fingers. "That's it, that's him! Clarisse, it's him. I mean, he removed the glasses and he slicked back his hair. But I'm positive that the lawyer from this morning is the same guy I saw you with that first time!"

Everyone was looking at me, but Clarisse seemed to be in shock. Then she began to shake her head in denial. Felipe placed his hand on her shoulder and said, "Why are you so sure it isn't him, Clarisse? What do you actually know about him?"

She let out a long breath and said, "He's just a biochemist. We've worked together for years. He…he…oh I don't know, we've just always been friends. I never thought…."

"It's okay, we'll need to learn more about him, confirm that it's him. Can you do that when you get back?" Felipe asked in a gentle tone.

She nodded, but then asked, "How, Felipe? Everyone was thoroughly vetted. If

Jonathan had the scientific knowledge that is needed to alter a door, wouldn't we know?"

Felipe thought for a minute, finally saying, "Well, he and I never really got along, and I always got the impression that he wasn't very fond of Jorge, either. I just don't know him that well, but I do know he's more than just a biochemist. He has very serious computer skills, hacking skills."

Clarisse almost seemed to get angry. She turned to Felipe and said, "What are you talking about? He can barely program his UD!"

Felipe tried to calm her with a smile, that little dimple becoming more defined the wider his grin became. "He roomed with a friend of mine from college. My friend told me that Jonathan used to hack into all sorts of things, just for fun, to see if he could do it. He asked Jonathan why, if he was so good at it, he didn't make that his primary field of study. Jonathan became defensive and told Peter that he wasn't that good at it, and to mind his own business."

Clarisse didn't seem to be buying Felipe's theory that Jonathan was hiding a seasoned talent for computer hacking. To be honest, I wasn't sure that was enough either, but I was sure that it was him I saw, and that made him our primary suspect.

I tried to use a sympathetic tone with her. "Clarisse, I'm sorry, but I know that was him. Regardless of what you think you know about him, he was definitely here."

Kath took charge, moving the conversation away from Jonathan. "What about those little badge things? Was that you that talked through it the other night?" she asked Felipe. He nodded and she said, "Okay, well, doesn't Jorge have one of those too? How come you couldn't communicate with him directly?"

Clint answered, "I checked through all of his belongings when I transferred him today. The only things he had on him when the police brought him to us were the clothes on his back and his ID and dog tags, nothing else." Well, that answered that. If Jorge had come through with his badge, then he'd lost it along the way.

"So how come it didn't work right away? I mean, Frank had his for a while before Felipe made contact," Kath asked.

Clarisse answered, "They're from our time, powered by our technology, so they could only work when the door was activated and a link to our system was made."

I shook my head. "But in both cases I heard his voice *after* I'd come back."

She smiled a sympathetic smile, the kind you'd give a child that didn't understand something. "You see, the dragonfly is designed to open a tunnel, so to speak, and we travel through that tunnel. Once we've reached the other side, they retract and the tunnel slowly collapses upon itself until it's sealed. But that can take a few minutes, and I believe those were the minutes that Felipe activated his badge and communicated with you."

I was sure there was a much more complicated answer to that, but what she said was good enough except for one thing. "Clarisse, you said my badge was only linked to yours, that no one else could detect it." Her brows drew together and her forehead creased. I'd stumped her.

Felipe smiled and raised his hand. "That would have been my fault. You see, when I realized I'd been stranded here, I modified my badge to pick up any signal from my time, just in case someone came through that wasn't in my comm group."

She smiled at him and said, "Bravo, Felipe; you amaze me."

Felipe blushed slightly and said, "I'm more than just a brilliant physicist, you know. I do have many other talents."

She laughed and said, "Oh bloody hell, your modesty is astounding!" This was some personal joke between them, but it lightened everyone's mood and we all laughed and relaxed a bit.

"So, back to taking you guys back; can we do it?" I asked Felipe, since he was the physicist in the room.

He shook his head. "I think we have to close the other door first. Something about that door is causing a serious problem for my brother. And there's another concern. If we return, if we get everyone back where they belong, the dragonflies, the ones that are linked to Frank and Jorge and this other door, will most likely shut down and self-destruct. I'm not sure why they've managed to stay active this long. Once the corruption was detected they should have shut down immediately. We need to find this other person." He looked at Clarisse. "We need to find Jonathan before we attempt to go through. If he becomes stranded here, it would irreparably change our timeline."

Chapter 72

Christian had scoured the compound for Clarisse. He hadn't found her, and now he was more than concerned, he was angry, too. He and Jorge had gone to great lengths to ensure that people perceived them as rivals; this was imperative. After what happened to Felipe, Jorge was even more convinced he needed someone who could assist with any malfunctions of the door on this side.

When Jorge and Felipe were fourteen and thirteen, respectively, they began their first year at MIT. Because of their ages, the campus counselor and the dean thought it a good idea to provide them with a mentor, someone who knew what it was like to be so young, and so brilliant.

Christian was twenty-five at the time and had returned to MIT to study for one of what would be many doctorates. He didn't start at the same age as the Mendoza brothers, but still he was only sixteen when he became a freshman his first time, giving him ample exposure to the perils of youth and naiveté in a big college environment.

He liked them both immediately. They were personable, and although Jorge was a bit shy, it hadn't taken long for him to warm up to Christian. He liked them better than most of his peers and spent a great deal of time with them. By the next year, the three of them had become almost inseparable when they weren't in classes.

One fine spring evening, Christian wanted to attend a last-minute concert, and popped over to their dorm room to see if they wanted to go. When he got there they were engaged in a complicated project. Before they could switch the screen on the tablet they'd been hovering over, Christian saw something that concerned him greatly. He questioned them relentlessly until they admitted to what they'd been up to. It was the door. They'd almost perfected it, and what Christian saw was enough of the formula to suspect what they'd been working on. They argued. Christian knew enough about these boy-scientists to know they could do this; they could create a link to another time. And he also knew they simply were not mature enough to understand the disastrous implications and ramifications.

Eventually he secured a promise from both of them to stop working on it, to destroy the technology they'd developed. He spent hours going over all the various cons of such a project, and emphasizing that there simply were no pros. To ensure that they would do as he asked, he called their parents that evening. He never knew what was said between parents and children, but the relationship he'd enjoyed over the last eighteen months no longer existed. He'd always kept close tabs on them, not because he was concerned they'd break their promise, but because he'd loved them like brothers and he wanted nothing but success for them both.

Many years later he'd joined the Global Scientific Consortium, a think-tank that had been founded by the world's leading energy companies in the mid-21st century. Its original goal was to gather all the energy producers, be it petroleum, natural gas, solar, wind, hydro, nuclear, etc. and work together to develop clean, alternative sources of energy. Government restrictions and subsequent failures by those governments had made this a necessity and it was highly successful. They eventually expanded to cover every scientific field of study known to man, and the staff consisted of the greatest scientific minds available.

When the agricultural disaster stuck, the world governments turned to GSC without hesitation. By then, Christian had achieved a great deal of seniority and was a highly respected scientist in the institution. He was involved in all the discussions regarding the possible solutions, and when everything failed, he felt he had no choice but to contact the Mendoza brothers. They, unbeknownst to him, had already decided to reveal the device. They met in secret. Christian had thought long and hard, and he felt it was best to keep knowledge of the door to a minimum. The meeting was tense, and to Christian's great disappointment, the doctors Mendoza informed him that they'd broken their promise and perfected the door; "the dragonfly door," they called it. They'd made a prototype, but they hadn't physically tested it. However, they knew it would work, and Christian did not doubt them.

Since the Mendozas were respected scientists themselves, they were well aware of the plight facing mankind. They'd actually discussed approaching the GSC with the door technology, but with an unlimited list of conditions. Having matured a great deal since he'd last seen them, they now realized he was right all along regarding its dangers. They also agreed that a third person, a back-up so to speak, was a good idea. So they maintained the appearance of estrangement, and when it was decided that Christian would head all the bio compounds, the Mendoza brothers feigned displeasure at having to work with him. They went so far as telling people that when he'd been their mentor, he'd been jealous of them, and Christian's jealously was what had caused the parting of ways.

Chapter 73

Dyse rested comfortably in his hotel room. It wasn't quite as nice as the hotels he frequented in his time, but it was relatively quiet and very clean. So many questions plagued him. Had Jorge known that Felipe was alive? Was that why Jorge came to San Francisco? Who were the couple he'd seen at the VA Center? They were definitely related to Jorge and Felipe—that was indisputable.

He wished he could go back to Bio-1 and then back to his time, where his computer was, so he could search this time for Jorge's relatives. Then he remembered his previous searches, and how they'd come up empty. Had Jorge and Felipe somehow managed to jump ahead, and erase these two people from the databanks? That could only mean that Jorge and Felipe survived this and returned to their own time. This would also mean that they provided the sample and saved humanity. And if all that happened in the future, what would become of him? His employers would not let him live if he failed, that he was sure of. They couldn't risk exposure.

After much thought, he decided he needed to find these people, and he thought the only way to do that was to stake out the center where Jorge was being held. He was sure they would be returning, and he thought, based on what had happened there earlier, they'd want to move Jorge to a safer location.

Chapter 74

It was almost nine and I was getting nervous for Clarisse since I wasn't sure how long she could be absent before someone noticed. I decided that we needed to address two more things with her before I took her back.

"Clarisse…." I looked at Selena. "We know where the sample is. Can you take it back with you?" She brightened a little and looked at Felipe questioningly.

He said, "She should be able to return with it, but…for the time being, won't it be safer if we leave it here? At least until we know we can get everyone back?" He had a good point and I nodded in agreement with him.

"Okay, well, one more question. Felipe, you said there was someone else at the compound that knew about the door and how it functioned. I think we should bring them in on this; we may need their help."

Felipe shot a look at Clarisse, then turned to all of us and said, "Yes, I think you're right." He turned back to Clarisse and said, "It's Christian…Dr. Blare."

Her eyes narrowed into deadly slits as she turned to Felipe. She began to shake her head, as if denying what she'd just been told. "No, that can't be…he hates you both. Everyone knows that!"

"He doesn't…it's an act. The three of us planned it before we even told anyone of the door's existence. We felt it was important to have a back-up, in case something happened to

Jorge and me, and we wanted to be sure someone could destroy the technology if that became necessary."

She didn't respond, but she looked hurt, like he'd offended her somehow. Maybe she thought her relationship with Jorge warranted being brought into the loop on this. But we didn't have time for hurt feelings; she could deal with that later.

"Clarisse, find him as soon as you get back. Tell him what's going on and ask him if there's something else we need to be doing," I said firmly.

I stood up and reached for her, and she hesitantly joined me. The dragonflies came almost immediately.

Chapter 75

Less than a minute later I was back. Everyone was staring at me when I returned.

Clint said, "So what now?"

I went into the kitchen and grabbed a beer for everyone. Selena took a sip of hers and then said, "I think we should get Jorge out as soon as possible." She turned to Clint. "Do you think we can do that tomorrow?"

He began to shake his head and then said, "I don't know. We'll need Betty's help with that." He looked at me. "And I'm not sure she's in a helping mood...."

Kath and Betty volunteered together on other projects and they'd become good friends over the years. She said, "I can talk to her; I haven't pissed her off." She smirked and winked at me and then rubbed Clint's leg affectionately. "I think I can convince her that you two yahoos are only trying to do what's best for him."

I could only smile back at her; she was probably right. Betty had been privy to most of mine and Clint's shenanigans over the years, and she was definitely not on our side right now. Kath, on the other hand, was golden with her.

Clint nodded his head and said, "Where do we take him? I don't think your place is a good idea, Frank."

I agreed with him, and Selena said, "He can stay at my house, with Felipe."

We all agreed that was probably the best place. Kath turned to Clint and gently placed her hand on his. "Clint, they need protection. Maybe…maybe we could ask Darrel."

Darrel was Clint's older brother by two years. He was as tall as Clint, but bigger, broader, and he could be outright mean. Darrel hadn't emerged quite as lucky as Clint; he'd been arrested many times as a minor and an adult. But he'd finally realized there was a better way, and now he helped run a youth center in Hunter's Point. He was a good guy…street-wise, and knew how to defend himself. However, I knew what Clint was thinking. Eddie had been killed quickly and right under our noses by an unknown assailant. How could he put his only brother in danger like that? This made me realize something, and it scared the crap out of me.

"You guys, we missed something. Oh man…," I said, running my hands through my hair.

Clint's eyes narrowed. "What?"

"Alex, Jorge's roommate. Betty said he'd described the guy who attacked them. He said the guy was small, with dark hair. Jonathan's at least my height and has blond hair."

Everyone's eyes widened at once. None of us had even considered that. It meant one of two things; either this was a random attack and had nothing to do with Jorge, or…there was someone else coming through the door.

Chapter 76

Dyse wished he had a gun. He'd actually considered bringing one from his time, but that would have backfired horribly. It wasn't illegal to own one, but in his time all weapons were tracked. The violence during the dark decades had exploded to the point that most businesses and governments were under constant attack. It had become impossible for them to conduct day-to-day operations, causing a standstill of productivity and the growth the world so desperately needed.

By then, the GSC had expanded to cover a larger base of the scientific community. Because it was never the intention to turn a profit, the companies that started the GSC used a rather brilliant business plan to fund their research, attract the brightest minds, and continue to have the most up-to-date facilities and technology. The scientists who worked for the GSC were encouraged to create and discover outside of their daily duties. If they invented or discovered something that had a great deal of monetary potential, the GSC asked only that they donate some of their profits back to the facility, and the scientist would retain the rest. This also encouraged companies outside the consortium to use the GSC as a back-up to their own research and development departments. If a company's R&D needed assistance perfecting or developing something, they could go to the GSC; in turn, they would only have to donate a portion of their profits to continue support of the consortium.

A young scientist, who'd been concerned about the violence that constantly plagued the GSC's benefactors, created a device that would automatically detect any weapon that used explosives or projectiles. It was integrated into the security systems and scanned not only the facilities themselves but anyone or anything approaching them for miles around. The device ran and adapted constantly; if your intention was to assemble your weapon once you were inside a facility, the device would detect the combination of components and alert the proper authority. Because of this technology, there would have been no way of transporting a weapon through the door.

The open-minded concepts at the GSC had been one of the deciding factors for Jonathan to join them. But soon he realized that he did not stand out, that no one thought he was more brilliant than the next scientist…and he was. This he knew definitively. As such, when he was approached by his new *secret* employers to obtain the sample of the virus before Jorge could, and was told that the rewards would be ample, he jumped at it.

He was sure that his employers had a spy at the GSC, otherwise they wouldn't know so much about the blight and the door. He was also sure that this spy had to have access to Jorge and Felipe's research, but how was another question. The Drs. Mendoza had made it clear from the onset that they would not share it with anyone, and once the situation was resolved, they intended to destroy the technology and all research pertaining to it.

Chapter 77

Dr. Idiot finally emerged in the lobby. It had been several hours and Hugo had actually considered finding out which room he was in and just killing him right then and there. But again, he reined himself in and remembered that he needed the Idiot to lead him to both Dr. Mendoza and the virus sample.

Hugo followed him out of the hotel and south on Van Ness Avenue until the neighborhood began to change. As he turned onto a street called Turk, it was clear that they'd reached a less than desirable area. The buildings were run-down and covered in graffiti, the streets were littered with debris and trash, the curbs were lined with dilapidated cars, and the people who inhabited the doorways and street corners looked worn out, dirty, and a bit dangerous.

Hugo couldn't figure out why these people didn't have more self-respect. Why would you want to live like that? In his time, people of lower income kept themselves and their environments clean, and even though they were not wealthy, they were happy.

After a few blocks, Dr. Idiot stopped and talked to a shifty-looking man wearing a long duster of indeterminate color. The coat seemed a bit large on him and bulged in certain areas. They talked for a few minutes and the doctor pulled something out of his pocket and handed it the other man, then turned and started to walk back toward Hugo. When he was close, Hugo simply stepped toward the curb and the doctor walked right past him, never noticing him.

Hugo followed him back in the direction of the hotel, but the doctor turned into a place called Mel's Drive-In instead of continuing on to the Holiday Inn, several blocks north. Hugo looked around. He couldn't figure out what "drive-in" meant, as it appeared to be just a restaurant and he couldn't even see any type of dedicated parking area. He shrugged. This society was so odd, but he was hungry so he went in, too. The doctor asked for a table by a window that faced a side street. Hugo moved to the counter, picking a seat that would allow him to keep an eye on the Idiot.

They were both finishing up their meals when the man in the duster entered the restaurant. He looked around until he sighted the doctor, and then he casually walked over and sat down in the vacant seat across from him. The man pulled something wrapped in newspaper out of his coat. He slid it across the table and the doctor opened the paper just enough to look at its contents; he then slid the package into his own pocket.

Hugo watched this with interest and wondered what the doctor had received. When the doctor pulled out a wad of money, Hugo assumed that he'd purchased something illegal from this man. He'd seen quite a few old films from this time; he found them amusing and more interesting than the films of his time. Based on that cinematic knowledge, Hugo figured the doctor had purchased either illegal drugs or a weapon of some sort.

Chapter 78

After he'd given up looking for Clarisse, Christian returned to his own quarters. He'd find her first thing in the morning, but for now, he was tired and just wanted to rest.

A communiqué was waiting for him. It had come through while he was looking for her, and that was indeed a serious problem. Since the doors to his world were strictly monitored and only opened once a day, the fact that his boss at the GSC had opened the emergency communication door this evening to send the message meant something had to be wrong.

He read it over and over again. He just couldn't believe that the one thing they feared the most had happened. He and the Drs. Mendoza had gone to such great lengths to protect the door technology. But unlike the brothers, he just had a great memory. He'd needed to record the information in case he had to access it later, so he'd put it on a microchip that was smaller than the tip of child's pinky finger. He'd hidden the chip in his comm badge, something he was never without, but somehow someone had found it and obviously copied the information off it; but when?

According to the communiqué, a communication stream that had been sent through the emergency communication door had been detected a few days before. It had taken them time to track down the source because the woman who'd sent it, a renowned and well-respected programming technologist, had covered her tracks brilliantly. In fact, they might not have detected it at all, but she'd been seen by an intern going into the office of the only person with access to the emergency door. Once they'd figured out what she'd done, they were able to trace back several earlier communiqués, all of which were sent to two unknown recipients at Bio-1.

The messages were highly encrypted and it took time to decipher them, but in the end, the result was the same. Someone had gained access to the technology that programmed the doors, and was sending directives to these recipients. One recipient was assigned to follow Jorge and obtain the sample from him. The other was assigned to follow the first person, and once the sample was obtained, that first person was to be eliminated.

He immediately thought of Clarisse; she'd asked about two doors. But the bigger question was, who had wanted to interfere with the mission, and why? He leaned back in his chair; he could think of only one group. Although most people thought they were just a rumor, Christian knew that they did indeed exist, and were similar to the secret societies that had always existed throughout time. They'd been closely monitored for years, but for the most part they were considered harmless. They were the ancestors of spoiled political and monetary families that thought the old ways were better.

Interpol, an organization created in the early 20th century, now encompassed all countries and the moon colonies. They, too, had taken heavy fire for corruption during the dark decades, but were now considered one of the most wholesome and effective world agencies. They issued monthly reports regarding this secret group, and had deemed them an annoyance at best.

Now Christian wondered if this group had infiltrated the Interpol ranks, too. It wasn't impossible. The GSC had a very good system that vetted its employees every six months, and they'd been penetrated. If they could manage to infiltrate the GSC's security, it wasn't unfathomable to think they'd made their way into Interpol as well.

However, knowing who was behind this was one thing; knowing who they'd employed was the more important thing. He knew he'd never sleep now, so he began a scan of the bio compounds' personnel to assure himself that everyone was accounted for, and more importantly, had not left without authorization. What he found surprised him. Clarisse had left on several occasions in the last few days, and she hadn't gone to her own time; her biorhythms simply stopped transmitting.

He and Felipe had developed the biorhythm monitoring system for two reasons. One was simply for added security; the other was to be sure no one decided to go beyond the confines of the compounds. Although the terrain outside was impossible most days, confinement and curiosity could lead to misconduct, and it was imperative that their presence here did not touch the world beyond.

The only other person whose rhythm was undetected was Jonathan Dyson. He'd requested leave, and Christian had granted it. He would check in the morning to be sure Jonathan had gone home as requested. But he didn't think it was him. Jonathan was a competent biochemist, an amicable but meek man. It would take a great deal of personal risk, combined with courage and to a degree, arrogance, to pull this off, and Jonathan just wasn't that sort of person.

Chapter 79

Selena and Felipe spent the night at my house, and we were all up early the next morning. I drove them over to Selena's. As we approached her building entrance, I spotted Darrel sitting on the edge of a planter fiddling with his phone. I was very relieved to see him because I wasn't excited about leaving Felipe and Selena alone.

I was used to Darrel's size, but if you didn't know him, he looked outright threatening. As we neared, he stood up. A long pink scar ran down the left side of his face, starting at his hairline and intersecting a corner of his eye, ending mid-cheek. It made him look even meaner than his three-hundred-pound, six-foot-six body did. Darrel had shaved his head since I saw him last; there were more scars on his shiny bare scalp, some keloid-like, some indented. It was a reminder of a dangerous time in his life, and hopefully it scared the hell out of the kids at his youth center.

Like Clint, he had a big broad smile, and when he flashed it, I could all but feel the tension ease out of my companions. I put my hand out to shake his and he pulled me into a bear hug that damn near flattened me. Introductions were made and we headed into Selena's apartment.

I pulled Selena aside. "Listen, we didn't mention the hiding spot for the sample to the others. Why don't we keep that to ourselves until we know we can send it back?"

She nodded and turned to Darrel and Felipe. "Can I offer you gentlemen some coffee?" They heartily accepted, and while she was making it, Darrel pulled me aside.

"Hey man, good to see you. Clint didn't...well, wouldn't...give me any details. You wanna tell me what's up?" Yeah, I did, but I couldn't.

"Sorry, Darrel, you gotta trust us on this; we just need to keep these two safe. Chances are we're overreacting, but—"

"All right, but I don't break the law anymore, so you two better not be up to no good," he said, semi-scowling down at me. I nodded that I understood, then we exchanged cell phone numbers and I left for the VA.

Chapter 80

It was pretty early for visiting hours, but I was well known at the center and no one gave me a second look. I made my way to Betty's office, and when I got there, heard a familiar voice. It was Kyle. I poked my head in and smiled at them, but any hope that they'd calmed down since the day before vanished when I saw the narrowed eyes and thin-lipped scowl on Betty's face. I slumped into a chair next to Kyle and prepared to be verbally mauled.

"Did you *really* think having that sweet Kathleen call me would work? That girl must really love that dumb oaf she's married to, to agree to get involved in whatever you two are up to." I glanced over at Kyle. There was a slight, amused smirk on his face, and I knew that whatever Kath had said had worked.

I leaned forward in my chair and said, "I know you're pissed, that both of you are pissed, and you both deserve an answer, but we can't give you one right now. Right now the most important thing is—and this *is* imperative, you have to believe that—to get Jorge out of here and somewhere safe, where no one knows where he is."

She sighed heavily and relaxed a little. "I gathered that from what Kathleen said." I started to say something and Betty wagged her index finger at me, "Ah, ah, ah, don't get your knickers in a bundle; she didn't tell me what was going on, just that she was privy to it all and she supported you both." I leaned back and relaxed. I should have known better than to question Kathleen's tactics.

"So," Kyle said, "we have some logistical problems. First, we can't move him today, but Betty and I think it can be done tomorrow morning."

"What are the logistical problems? I think it would be better to do it today," I said, hearing the desperation in my voice.

Kyle held up his hand. "Detective Rice and the feds will be back today to interview Jorge; they couldn't do it yesterday. If Jorge isn't here it's going to cause major problems."

"Can't we move him after the detectives see him?" I knew I was sounding desperate, but I couldn't help it; there were two people trying to get at Jorge, and I didn't really know what one of them looked like.

Kyle looked at Betty and she shrugged her shoulders. "Maybe," was all she said.

I blew out a breath in frustration and said, "Can I see Jorge?"

She picked up her phone and made a call. When she hung up she said, "Meet Clint in the rec room, he'll take you up." She pointed at me and said, "And don't upset him, do you understand?"

I saluted, which usually made her smile, but not this time. I smiled weakly and said, "Thanks, to both of you. I'll stop by on my way out."

Chapter 81

Clint was waiting for me at the entrance to the rec room. When I looked inside I saw a few people that I knew, but most were still either in their rooms or possibly at the cafeteria having breakfast. Alex was there, though, sitting by the window, staring out. I asked Clint to hold on a minute and went over to talk to him.

"Hey, Alex, how're you holding up?" He looked over at me; his throat was the color of a rotten pomegranate and looked painful. I flinched a little at the sight of it. It must have hurt like hell, and I thought he was lucky not to have been more seriously injured.

"I'm okay," he said a little hoarsely and without interest.

"Listen, I'm really sorry about what happened. We're all just glad you're okay. You're kind of a hero you know, trying to fight off that guy."

He didn't seem to care much about that, but finally he said, "So why is someone after Jorge?" It bothered me that he thought I would know that answer, which of course I did.

I said, "Don't know; we don't really know what happened to Jorge when he left Kansas. Maybe he crossed this guy somewhere along the way." I thought that was a reasonable explanation, and apparently so did Alex, as he nodded his head in agreement.

"Alex, can you tell me what this guy looked like?"

Alex turned back to the window and said, "Well, it was dark, and…," he pointed to his throat, "I got clocked pretty good, but I can tell you the guy was around five-eight to five-ten. He had dark hair, and I'm pretty sure he was a white guy." He shrugged. "Sorry, that's all I saw."

That described half of the men on the planet, so it was really of no use to us. I thanked him and went back to Clint, and we headed up to see Jorge.

Chapter 82

Clarisse woke early and made her way to Dr. Blare's quarters. She wanted to get this over with; and of course, if he could help Jorge, she would endure whatever was necessary. He answered his door immediately. He didn't look like he'd slept. His clothes were wrinkled and his hair was sticking up as if he'd been running his hand through it repeatedly.

"Ah, Clarisse, I was just going to go look for you. Would you care to come in?"

She hated his smarmy smile and arrogance, but she had to suck it up and get this done. "Dr. Blare, we need to talk," she said forcefully. His eyebrows rose in amused curiosity, and he waved his arm toward a chair and shut the door behind her.

She began immediately. She was afraid if she didn't, she'd lose her nerve. She told him everything from the very beginning, and when she got to the part about Felipe his eyes lit up.

"He's alive?" he said in a shocked but excited tone.

This was an expression she'd never seen on Dr. Blare. His eyes watered and he smiled broadly. She realized then that everything really had been an act with him. He'd wanted people to believe he was a jerk and that he disliked the Mendoza brothers a great deal, but now she knew that simply wasn't true. Her tone softened at this realization and she told him the rest.

When she'd finished, he was thoughtful for a moment, and then said, "That explains a great deal." He told her about the communiqué.

"You were all so clever and careful…but someone is cleverer. Dr. Blare, what are we going to do?" she asked.

"I don't know, but at this point I think we should seal the other doors. I believe I can do that, but I may need Felipe's help. I can put my plan on a UD and you can take it to him, and have him approve or revise it as needed."

"But Felipe thinks these other doors might be part of the problem affecting Jorge. If we close them and they're somehow tied to him…."

He nodded. "Yes, of course…." He went back to being thoughtful and finally said, "These 'shimmers' you mentioned. Is there any way to refine them, to try and find the source? If we could, maybe we could figure out who the second person is."

"I can try." She stood to leave and he walked her to the door.

He gently placed his arm on hers and said, "Clarisse, I can't tell you how relieved I am that you are not the source of this problem. Jorge loves you a great deal; it would have devastated him."

She smiled up at him. She realized that she had a new affection for him, one she'd have never considered.

Chapter 83

Clint and I made our way up to the secure ward. Jorge was lying in his bed when we arrived, propped up with pillows, and his eyes were vacant.

I sat down next to him, took his hand, and said, "Jorge, can you hear me? It's Frank."

He was unresponsive and I shook his shoulder gently. "Jorge, Felipe is alive. He's fine and he's going to help me get you home." Jorge's pupils began to focus, but he was still staring forward.

I waited a minute and then said, "He's with Selena. Jorge, we know Jonathan is trying to hurt you, do you know why?" He moved his head toward me and his lips moved as well, but no sound came out. I waited another minute and then turned to look at Clint. He shook his head sadly and I turned back to Jorge.

"Jorge, Clint and I are going to get you out of here, to a safer place. Hang in there, okay?" I didn't know if he heard or understood me, but it was all I could think to say.

We made our way back to Betty's office. She wasn't there, but one of the other admins said she'd be right back, so we sat and waited. She returned a few minutes later. She was reading a file when she entered the room and stopped short when she saw us.

"Huh," she mumbled sarcastically, and then moved to sit at her desk. I loved Betty, and it pained me a lot to know she was disappointed in me, but it was even worse to know that I'd hurt her by lying to her. She took off her glasses, rubbed the bridge of her nose, and said, "The detectives will be over around two this afternoon. I suggest you two tell me what your plans are to get Jorge out of here." We hadn't really discussed an actual plan, but apparently Clint had given it quite a bit of thought.

"We get deliveries all day long. I just happen to know one of the delivery guys. I called him and asked what his schedule was today; he said he had a delivery coming here this afternoon. If we can give him a specific time, he'll work his route to show up when we ask him to. I'll take Jorge down through the loading bay, put him on that truck, and Frank will meet us at the next stop." I was impressed…it sounded like a great plan.

"I see; and you will be accompanying Jorge, and making sure he's all right? How do you plan to do that and perform your duties here?" Betty said, glaring at Clint.

Clint shifted in his chair and said, "Uh, well I already told my supervisor that my mama was sick and I'd probably need to take a few days off. He said it was okay."

She grunted. "Well, then, glad to see all the practice you had lying to me is paying off." I saw Clint flinch out of the corner of my eye.

Chapter 84

Dr. Idiot left his hotel early the next morning, and of course Hugo followed him. Now they were both sitting in the VA parking lot. The doctor didn't try to go into the facility this time. Instead he found a bench with a view of the entrance and sat, pretending to read a newspaper. Hugo positioned himself so that he could see both the entrance and the doctor, and he waited.

A short while later Dr. Dyson came to full attention. He was watching a man approach the entrance from the parking lot. Hugo realized he'd seen the man the day before. It was one of the men that Dyson had been staring at yesterday, only he was alone this time. A little over an hour went by before the man came out of the building. As soon as he came out, the doctor dropped his paper and rushed toward the edge of the parking lot, where several yellow taxi cabs were idling. Hugo had been standing not far from these, so he casually went over and got into the back seat of the last one in line. He told the driver to follow the doctor's cab.

When the man's car passed the cab stand, Dyson's cab pulled out and so did Hugo's. The driver was either used to this kind of request or just not interested. He didn't ask any questions and he didn't follow too closely. They crossed the big street where both Hugo and Dyson had caught the bus the day before, and continued south for a bit. They entered a residential neighborhood, and after a few turns, the man pulled into the garage of what seemed to be a residential building. Hugo told the driver to go past the building and the doctor's cab and turn the corner. Then he paid the driver and walked back.

Dyson was now lingering across the street from where the man had gone in. He had no idea what the idiot intended to do, but he knew what he was going to do. Dyson had recognized this man, which meant, he guessed, that there was some connection to him and Dr. Mendoza. Hugo was getting tired of following Dyson around using this time's public transportation. It was loud, crowded, and smelled horrible.

He walked to the end of the block and stopped. Sitting at the curb was what was known in the late 20th century as a standard or naked motorcycle, known for its simplicity, which made it easy to access. His adoptive father had been quite fond of these vehicles and had had several that he'd restored. Hugo learned to ride them, and since most of the bikes his father had obtained did not come with ignition keys, he also knew how to start them by what his father called "hotwiring."

He looked around, and then looked over the bike, found the ignition wiring, and in a few minutes had it started. He went around the block and stopped where he could see the man's building. Hugo hoped the man would come out soon, though, before the owner of the bike showed up. He didn't need that type of attention.

All of this took place right in front of Dyson. He truly was an *idiot,* and totally oblivious to everything around him...unless of course it had to do with him. What had the guy on the bus said yesterday? A man had bumped another one and the response was "Asshole!" Based on the inflection and the other man's reaction, the term had to be derogatory. Yes, he thought, Dyson was an *asshole*. He smiled; he liked that term better than *Dr. Idiot*.

Chapter 85

Clarisse had gone back to her quarters and spent over an hour trying to identify the "shimmers," but there wasn't anything definable…they were just there. She was relieved that whatever they were, they were not affecting the timeline, at least not yet.

She also decided to break into Jonathan's quarters to see if she could find anything. She had no fear of being caught because Dr. Blare had confirmed that Jonathan was not in any of the compounds. It wasn't difficult to penetrate the locking mechanism, and she was in within seconds. She looked around the room. Like hers, it was sparsely furnished…a bed, a desk, two chairs, a built-in dresser, and shelving. She didn't think Jonathan was stupid enough to have any evidence of what he'd been doing in the room, but it was worth a try. She went through all of his drawers, checked under the mattress, and began to go through the items on his shelves.

Finally she sat down at his desk and attempted to access his personal computer tablet. The encryption pass codes were good, but she was better, and after a few tries, she was in. Most of the data was related to his work at the compound and all very normal. But hidden under many layers was a document entitled "acceptance." She opened it and began to read. When she finished, she leaned back, rubbed her eyes, and said out loud, "My God, he's absolutely mad!"

She copied the file, made sure everything was as it had been before she entered, and then went to find Blare.

Chapter 86

I'd noticed the cabs pull out behind me when I left the VA. I decided since Selena and Felipe were safely tucked away with Darrel, I'd let them follow me home. Before I closed the garage door, I noticed the first cab stop just past my house. The second had continued on, but I didn't see where it went. I ran up to the second-floor landing and looked out the window. A man—I thought probably Jonathan—was standing in the shadows of the recessed doorway across the street. I went up to my place and looked out again. I didn't see a second man, and since I wasn't sure if they were working together or not, I couldn't be sure the other cab had been following me or if its route had just been coincidental. I called Darrel's cell phone, and he answered on the second ring.

"Hey, Darrel, how's it going?"

"Oh man, this woman of yours, she is some cook!" He was chewing and groaning, so it was hard to understand him, but I laughed anyway.

"Yeah, she's pretty amazing," I said. I'd only experienced her tuna melt, but for reasons I couldn't explain, I didn't have any doubts she had other culinary talents as well. "So, is everything good there? You haven't seen anyone lingering around, have you?"

He swallowed audibly and said, "No. I been taking quick little perimeter walks every fifteen; all is good so far. But your friend Felipe, he don't seem so good. Seems to be having some trouble breathing. Think maybe we should get a doctor for him?"

I didn't like that one bit. "Can I talk to him?" There were some fumbling noises and then I heard Felipe say "yes" in a breathless tone.

"You doing all right, Felipe?"

"I'll be fine, but we need to hurry…not just for me, either."

"I know. We should have Jorge out by this afternoon. I'm going to try to get in touch with Clarisse, find out what she's been able to determine. I'll call you guys in a while, once we have a plan in place."

I called Clint, told him that I thought Jonathan was following me, and that I thought maybe he'd need to handle Jorge on his own. He agreed and said he'd get Kath to meet him at the pick-up spot, and would call me later to confirm it all. I also told him about Felipe's labored breathing. After all, he was a nurse. He said he'd get a portable oxygen tank and bring it with him; it was really all we could do for now.

Chapter 87

Christian had contacted his superiors at the GSC the minute the door was opened at eight a.m. He told them everything he knew and was assured they would act quickly. They had already contacted Interpol. The people they suspected as being behind the theft of the door technology and project interference were very wealthy, but that didn't matter in his time. Wealth no longer bought protection. Interpol would respond without haste. This was more than just a matter of breaking the law; this was a matter of life or death for all people on earth and on the moon colonies.

He was getting ready to make his rounds when someone knocked on his door. Clarisse entered, looking quite disturbed. "What is it? Did you find out what this 'shimmer' is?" She shook her head, moved into the room, and sat heavily in his guest chair.

"Dr. Blare, I...well, I broke into Jonathan's quarters." She looked at him expectantly and he just smiled at her.

"And?" he asked, slightly amused at her hesitation.

She sighed. "I found a document on his tablet. He'd hidden it well, but...well, I was able to access it. Dr. Blare, he's gone completely mad!"

He moved to the other chair. "Clarisse, tell me?"

"It's something like a manifesto, but in the form of an acceptance speech or something.

He…says that he has seen the world we were born from, a world of hate and ignorance, but a world that at least had the intelligence to acknowledge those who were preeminent, who were entitled to acknowledgment because of their distinctive intelligence and the superiority of their lineage."

She had loaded the document on her tablet, and now she brought it up and handed it to Christian to read. She added, "He also says that proof of his greatness is evidenced by the fact that *he*, not Jorge, obtained the sample that will save humanity. And that humanity will be grateful by acknowledging not only his supreme intelligence, but by following his leadership and the leadership of his superiors."

Dyson had written a great deal more than that. If what he outlined were true, Jonathan and the people he worked for intended to hold the virucide hostage, therefore controlling the world's food sources. Jonathan had also documented a family tree of sorts, to show why he was so entitled. He said he was the great-great-grandson of one of the world's most notorious criminals (though he didn't use that term).

This man had been a financier in the 20th and 21st centuries. He'd created a persona that drew in a surprising variety of followers, from the most ignorant and gullible to the intelligent and productive. He was also intimately tied to most of the world's wealthiest people, government leaders, and politicians, and the latter had hitched their wagons to him because of his influence. Some thought they had paid with their souls.

This man was known as a great philanthropist, whose mantra was reform through social programs, organized labor, and dismantling of large successful corporations that did not heed and conform to his idea of how a company should run. He'd formed and/or funded activist groups designed to spread his political and social views. But he'd also secretly funded groups for the opposition; the intention was to undermine support on all sides, to create dissent and hate for the existing political structures and governments. This would allow him to promote his ideas of a new government, and they would be a refreshing and welcome change for everyone. In actuality the hate, lies, and violence that erupted destroyed the very concept of peaceful protests and free thinking. On the outside, he appeared to be a great man, with great concerns for society. His actual agenda wasn't revealed until it was almost too late.

By the time the dark decades had begun, he was still wealthy, while many of the people who followed him were living in extreme poverty. Many influential people were tied to him, and people saw this as a betrayal, so his empire, along with most others, went down in flames.

When his true agenda was known, the world gasped, more because he'd come so close to accomplishing it than because of their disappointment in his false pretenses. He wanted one world government, a single-party system that disallowed free thought. He also wanted to cleanse society from the burdens of the terminally ill, the disabled, criminals that couldn't be rehabilitated, and the elderly populations that were unable to work. His plan was to bring humanity to its knees, and when they were at their weakest point, he would step in and show them a better way, one he controlled in its entirety.

He was compared to the greatest villains of all times. His family, out of fear or shame, disappeared quickly and changed their names. Not much had been heard of them, and eventually people simply didn't bother to try and find them. There were simply too many other problems that needed to be addressed.

Christian could see how Jonathan would have believed he was one of those "favored" ones. Maybe that was true; any record of that family had been mysteriously deleted early on. Jonathan seemed meek, but Christian would never have thought he was this weak and gullible. This could also mean something else; that this family was alive and well, and most likely part of the secret society that Christian feared was behind the current situation.

After he'd finished reading, he turned to Clarisse and said, "I'll report this, but aside from outlining the reasons for Jonathan's betrayal, it doesn't tell us who he's working for."

She sighed. "Isn't it obvious Dr. Blare? He thinks he's part of the entitled, the elite of the past. It must be the group for Social Supremacy."

Christian frowned. This was what he suspected, but it hurt to hear it put into words. The SS was established long ago. No one really knew how the name came about, but it was often thought of as a reminder of the 20th century paramilitary group under one of history's most nefarious political leaders. In many cases, the correlation wasn't inaccurate, but no one had ever thought of them as a real threat until now.

"Interpol will investigate them, but I have another concern that you may be able to help me with." The compound had a surveillance system—everything in their time did. He could go to the security station and ask them, but he didn't want to alert or involve any more people in this situation. He knew Clarisse was a brilliant computer scientist and that she should be able to access them.

"We know the door has been compromised. I don't know how much you know about the security protocols that we put in place…." She looked hurt…he thought because Jorge hadn't taken her into his confidence, but that couldn't be helped.

"We had to have a back-up in case something went wrong. Jorge and Felipe were the only two who knew the entire workings of the door and the devices that programmed and activated them. We put all of that knowledge onto a chip, and I am the only one, aside from them, that knows it exists…at least I thought I was. Two of the directors at the GSC knew of the connection between me and the Mendozas. So it wouldn't be a far leap for them to think that Jorge and Felipe had read me in on everything. I think one of the directors must be working with our adversaries, and that is how they knew to look for the information with me. I attached the chip to the one thing I have never been without, my comm badge. However, I now believe that someone gained access to it. The only time I ever remove it is when I bathe."

She was nodding now; she was a very intelligent girl, and he thought she had made a leap of her own. "Yes, I see. Whoever gained access had to enter your quarters while you were in the bathroom. Is that what you believe?"

He nodded and she moved to his stationary computer and began to work quickly. In a matter of seconds she'd accessed the security center's databases. "When do you think this happened? I would think early on, when we first arrived." She looked to him for confirmation and he nodded again.

She began a search, focusing on the hallway that led to his quarters. On the second day the compound had been fully staffed, a man, keeping his head turned from the cameras, approached Dr. Blare's quarters, accessed his locking mechanism, much as Clarisse had done with Jonathan's, and went inside. There were no cameras inside the private quarters, so she couldn't tell what he was doing, but he was only there for a short time.

After they viewed it, she said, "How will we know which director is working for them?"

Christian sighed heavily. He'd always reported simultaneously to both directors, so they both knew what was transpiring now. And without knowing which one was the spy, he couldn't go to either of them. There was only one person he could think of to go to, his own father. They'd always had an amicable relationship, but his position had kept him away from home most of Christian's life, and after his mother passed away they'd drifted apart. But his father was an honest man of impeccable standards and morals, and more importantly, he was one of the highest-ranking officials at Interpol.

"I know who to contact. Please go about your daily routine. We need to act as if things are fine and moving along."

She rose from the desk and started for the door. As she was opening it, her badge beeped; it was the tone for Frank. She looked to Blare and smiled. "I gave Frank a badge so I would know when he came through. He's here now. I need to go."

He smiled. She was indeed a clever girl. "Go," he said.

Chapter 88

I'd summoned the dragonflies so that I could talk with Clarisse. They came quickly and furiously, and there were more this time than I'd ever seen before. They seemed to be frantic, buzzing loudly and running into each other. It worried me, but I travelled through just like before, and they dispersed as soon as I was on the other side.

It took Clarisse a good ten minutes to get to me, and she was out of breath when she arrived. "Sorry…I was with Blare."

"What does he think?" I asked.

"We haven't identified the second man yet, but we know how he gained access. We also believe we know who is behind this. Dr. Blare is going to put his plan on a UD, and I'll need to give it to Felipe so he can tell us if it will work. What about Jorge?"

I put my hand on her shoulder and squeezed gently. "We're getting him out today. I think he's worse, but it's the only thing we can do. Felipe is getting worse, too. We need to move fast, Clarisse. We have to get them back to your time."

She nodded and said, "Come back in a few hours. I'll let Blare know."

"Before I go, tell Blare this; the dragonflies, I think something is wrong with them." I told her how they'd acted this time.

She frowned. "I'll tell him. I don't know what it means."

As if on cue, the dragonflies reappeared...not as frantic, but there were certainly too many of them.

Chapter 89

Once I was home I looked out the front window again. I could see the shadow of someone in the doorway across the street, and I was still pretty sure it was Jonathan. I wanted to flush him out, but what was I supposed to do with him once I did? Could I somehow subdue him and then take him back to the bio-compound? I paced for a while, trying to think it through. I wasn't a fighter...physically, anyway. I wouldn't know how to go about subduing Jonathan. He'd probably be able to kick my butt. So what should I do? After a while I called Selena and told her what was going on. Just hearing her voice made me feel better.

"That's a tough one, Frank. I mean, yes, I think getting him back there is a great idea, but how?"

"I was thinking I might try something. I've got a buddy who runs a bar down the street. He knows me pretty well and I think if I could get Jonathan to follow me there, I could get Joel to help me...capture him, I guess."

She laughed lightly and said, "Sweetheart," which made my heart pound a thousand miles a minute. "What would you tell Joel? What reason would you give him?" she asked. She had a very good point...what would I tell him? I was silent for a moment and she finally said, "You still there?"

"Yeah, I'm here; just thinking about what I'd tell Joel." I laughed. It was a ludicrous idea...we already had way too many people involved in this. "So what do you think then? Do you think I should try and lure him into my apartment? That would be a more controlled environment."

Now it was her turn for silence. "Yes, if you could. If you could alert Clarisse as to what you were doing, make sure she had security in place, maybe you could get him through and she could handle him on that end."

"Okay, I like that, and Jonathan knows who I am. Well, maybe not exactly who I am, but he knows I'm involved with Jorge. I think I should just walk right up to him, tell him we should talk. What do you think?"

"To be honest, I don't really like the idea of you doing this on your own. Can Clint be there? You know, in case he gets violent?"

"No, he's got to stay with Jorge. I think I'm on my own on this, Selena."

She blew out a breath. "Can you bring someone from the other place over, a security guard, or this Dr. Blare?"

That was a good idea, but since the dragonflies were acting strangely and we already knew that the multiple doors were causing serious problems for Jorge, I wasn't sure bringing someone else through was a good idea. What if it messed with Jorge even more? I said all this to her, and then I heard her talking to someone else in the room.

Felipe suddenly came on the line. "Hi." He sounded breathless again. "Selena told me your idea. I…I just can't be sure that will work, and I agree that at this point we need to limit the usage to those who have already come through. Besides, Jonathan has his own door; it isn't like Clarisse, where she's somehow riding on your door. If he goes through your door, I have no idea what will happen. His door could completely destabilize, and if it's somehow tied to what's happening to Jorge, it could kill him."

Kill Jorge or kill Jonathan? Well, to be honest, I didn't care if it killed Jonathan, but I cared very much about Jorge. I didn't bother asking, though; there was no point.

"So what do you think I should do, Felipe?"

"What is Blare doing? He must have ideas as to what we can do." I told him what Clarisse had said. "Yes, that's very good, but can we get that sooner rather than later? I'll need time to analyze everything; ask him to download every bit of data he can, regardless of how inconsequential it appears. I need to figure out how it all ties into Jorge, so I can figure out how and why it's affecting my brother."

We hung up and I immediately summoned the dragonflies again. It was the same as before, but this time I didn't bother trying to travel through. Instead I touched the badge. Clarisse responded immediately and asked why I'd come back so soon.

"Clarisse, I'm not there, I just opened the door so I could tell you something. Listen closely." I repeated my conversation with Felipe and she said she and Blare would drop everything and get moving. She asked that I come back in an hour.

In retrospect, that was the moment when it seemed that time began to speed up. All of a sudden, things started moving very quickly and very dangerously.

Chapter 90

Hugo was tired of waiting. Dyson was still lingering in the doorway across the street from the man's building, and it was obvious to Hugo that he had no idea how to proceed. Did the asshole plan on just waiting until the man emerged from the building? Then what? He had no transportation—how did he intend to follow him? He shook his head in annoyance and mild frustration. He knew what would make all of this better, and it would make him feel immensely better. He smiled at the thought. He pushed the motorcycle into an alley and hid it behind a large metal trash receptacle. Then he casually walked back up the street to where Dyson was lingering.

Hugo stopped on the sidewalk in front of Dyson, startling him. In a shocked tone, Dyson asked, "You! What are you doing here?"

Ah, so Dyson *did* know who he was…or at least he'd noticed him at one point or another. "I was sent to make sure you did your job, but you've failed; I always knew you would."

Dyson stared at him in confusion. Hugo moved forward quickly, simultaneously pulling out the Blackhawk Hornet II knife he'd acquired in Kansas. The tip and first inch or so of the knife was smooth and razor-sharp; the second half of the blade was serrated. He liked the feel and size of the knife, and it had done a nice job on the man at the VA center.

He plunged the knife into Dyson's abdomen and forcefully yanked it upward. The knife blade wasn't very long, but the serrated edge and Hugo's personal strength made quick and easy work of Dyson's torso, ripping it up to his collar bone. Hugo pulled the knife out and watched Dyson slowly sink to the ground.

As Dyson took his last breath, a dragonfly suddenly appeared. It hovered for a moment, and then dropped to the ground in the pool of blood that had begun to flow out of Dyson. Hugo brought his booted foot down on the dragonfly, crushing it and splattering blood all over the sidewalk and outer walls of the building. Then he bent over, wiped the blade on Dyson's jacket, and checked his pockets, finding the gun that Hugo had suspected was there. He then walked casually back the way he'd come.

He smiled as he retrieved the motorcycle. That had felt so good, so wonderful, so satisfying. Nothing could compare to watching a person take his last breath.

Chapter 91

I checked the street again. Jonathan had moved further into the shadows of the building entrance so I couldn't see him. A man in jeans and a light-weight jacket was coming up the street. I couldn't see his face, but he seemed so casual that I figured he lived in the neighborhood. Would he see Jonathan and wonder why he was lingering in that doorway? No, this was the city; people were oblivious, and Jonathan didn't look like a thief trying to break in.

But the man stopped at the doorway where Jonathan was and Jonathan stepped forward. I could see the surprised look on his face. I couldn't believe my eyes as I watched the next few minutes. After the man stabbed Jonathan, he simply turned and casually strolled back the way he'd come, leaving bloody footprints in his wake.

I stumbled backwards and started to hyperventilate, then fell into an armchair and put my head between my legs. It took a minute or two for me to regain my composure. I ran my hands through my hair so forcefully I actually pulled some out. The pain was sharp, but it snapped me out of it. I went back to the window. Jonathan was lying there in a pool of blood. Even though people tended to mind their own business, this wouldn't go unnoticed or unreported for long. I grabbed my jacket, car keys, and cell phone, and headed down to the garage. I didn't know where I was going, but I had to get out of there before the police came and the street became impassable.

I drove a few blocks and pulled over. I was still shaky and needed to calm down and think. I had to assume that the guy who'd killed Jonathan was our other man, the one who'd killed Eddie and tried to attack Jorge. He matched the description that Alex had given me.

I tried to call Clint but my hands were shaking so badly that it took me three tries to access his number. Before Clint's phone picked up, my call waiting beeped. I saw it was him, so I switched over and said, "Holy shit Clint." I was still a little breathless.

"Frank, something's happening. Jorge, he just…I don't know, he cried out, but it was more like a scream. Then he grabbed his head, like it was gonna explode—"

Clint was rambling and I said, "Slow down Clint; tell me what happened again?"

He took a deep breath and said, "I was going to check on him. The detectives are here and Betty wanted to be sure he was awake. I heard this scream, like someone was killing him, and I ran to his room. When I got in there he was holding his head and rocking back and forth. He won't say anything, but he's white as a ghost and I think he's in serious pain. The doctor is talking about taking him down for an MRI; they think something burst in his head."

"How long ago did this happen?" I asked.

"Ah, about ten, fifteen minutes ago. Why? Wait, you said 'holy shit' when you answered; why?"

"Clint, someone walked right up to where Jonathan was hiding across the street from my place. He killed Jonathan, stabbed him…my God, Clint, it looked like he gutted him."

"Hold on a sec," Clint said. I could hear a lot of background noise. As it began to fade I realized that Clint must have been standing near Jorge's room, where there was probably a ton of medical personnel around.

While I waited I realized something. Whatever had fluttered down into Jonathan's blood had refracted the light, like the dragonflies did. I was pretty sure that's what it was….it was Jonathan's device, and when his heart stopped it materialized from wherever they went when they weren't in use. If the other doors were interfering with Jorge, maybe the fact that this one had been destroyed so suddenly was the reason Jorge had cried out, and maybe its destruction was causing the pain.

When Clint came back on I told him what I thought. He said, "Call Felipe, ask him what I should do. Be quick about it…they're talking about taking Jorge down to radiology for the MRI. I might not be able to get him out of here once they do that."

I hung up without saying goodbye and dialed Selena's cell phone.

Chapter 92

Once he'd turned the corner he moved quickly to retrieve the bike and get back to where he could watch the man's house. Just as he came around the corner, the man pulled out of his garage and headed south. Hugo followed at a distance and the man pulled over to the curb a few blocks later. Hugo pulled in between two parked cars and watched. The man was talking on a communication device. Hugo could only see the side of his face and he couldn't hear what was being said, but the man looked quite distraught. Hugo wondered if he'd been watching while he took care of the Idiot, and he smiled at the memory.

While he watched, he thought about the timeline. Killing Dyson in this time could have an effect on their time; after all, there would be an investigation. The police here would have an unexplained murder of an unidentifiable man. Hugo didn't think it would be a big deal. Eventually they would have to give up. He didn't know what people in this time did in these situations, and he honestly didn't care. But he should have checked Dyson's pockets more thoroughly, just in case Dyson was carrying any of his devices from their time. He chided himself for that...it was sloppy. Maybe he should go back and hope that the police weren't there yet. No, that was too risky. What was done was done.

***

What Hugo didn't know was that Dyson also had the keycard for his hotel room on him, and the police would be going there. They would find Dyson's comm badge and UD, and they wouldn't know what it was; nor would they ever figure it out, but it would leave a ripple. He'd also left a crushed dragonfly in Dyson's pooling blood, and that, too, would baffle the authorities.

Chapter 93

I quickly told Selena what had happened, and her first reaction was to ask if I was okay. That calmed me immediately. I'd only known her for a short time, but the connection was so strong I felt like I'd known her all my life. Once I assured her that I was fine she put Felipe on and I repeated everything. He was so quiet for so long I was sure the call had disconnected.

"I think we can safely assume that our theories about the other doors are correct," he finally said.

"What do you mean?" I asked.

"Well, we thought that they were somehow connected or tied to Jorge's door. When Jonathan's door was destroyed, the link to Jorge went with it. I can't say for sure if that's good or bad, but from what your friend Clint is saying, it's certainly causing him a great deal of pain and anguish."

"So what do we do, Felipe?"

"Get him out of there and find that other man. I don't know what else to do."

Both of those things were way easier said than done. I disconnected and called Clint, who sounded panicky. "Clint, calm down okay? I can't come there; I can't take the chance I'm being followed." This, of course, made me look around, because I hadn't even thought of that when I left my place. I didn't see anyone, so I figured I was okay. "Clint, you have to get him out of there; can you do that?"

"Yeah, yeah, I'll figure it out. The delivery guy will be here at three." He paused. "Its two-thirty now. I need Betty's help with this…I gotta go talk to her. I'll call you back." He hung up without waiting for my response. I thought maybe I should call Betty too, but decided to wait.

I pulled away from the curb and headed toward the beach. I made a bunch of unnecessary turns and stayed at stop signs too long. A man on a bright yellow motorcycle was in my rearview most of the way. I wouldn't have put much thought into it, but he was without a helmet, and although I didn't get a good look at his face, I was pretty sure this was the guy who'd gutted Jonathan. I figured it was a safe assumption that this guy wasn't familiar with the city, and especially not the maze of roads and paths in Golden Gate Park. I headed that way, hoping I could lose him there.

I came into the park at 30th Avenue, and when I hit JFK Drive I went west. It was a weekday and the road was relatively clear of cars, bicycles, and pedestrian traffic. That was good because I could drive at a good pace; but bad, too, because the man on the motorcycle could easily follow me. As I passed Spreckels Lake and the bison paddock, I knew I wasn't going to lose him this way. I was coming up on the golf course; I quickly pulled over and parked illegally, then ran into the trees that surrounded the course.

He was quick and on my tail in a matter of seconds. I ran out into a fairway; there were three guys and a young woman at various points, and three more people lined up at the tee. They all started screaming at me to get out of the way. I veered off into more trees. I didn't want to do it, but couldn't think of any other way. I summoned the dragonflies.

They came fast and again there were way too many of them, but they also took me quickly, faster than they'd ever done before. As I went over, I heard more yelling from behind me. The man must have interrupted the golfers as I'd done. I had just enough time to glance back, and I saw him coming quickly. All I could do was hope they'd close the door before he could come through with me.

Chapter 94

I found myself in the same spot on the path where I always seemed to arrive. I jumped into the nearest bush and waited to see if my pursuer had followed me through. After a few minutes I decided it was safe, and I buzzed Clarisse on my comm badge. She must have been close because she arrived in less than two minutes.

"Good, you're here; come, we must go see Blare." She turned and walked quickly down the path, and I had to jog to catch up.

"Clarisse, wait!" I said. When she stopped and I caught up, I told her about the man following me and killing Jonathan. Her eyes bulged and began to tear up.

I touched her arm gently. "I'm sorry about Jonathan, but I think he would have done the same to Jorge and Felipe if he was able to."

I'm not sure if that made her feel better or not, but she straightened her shoulders and said, "That may explain something. Come, we must go see Blare."

Chapter 95

Hugo dropped the motorcycle without even shutting off the ignition and ran after the man. They ran through trees, a green area full of people, and finally into another grove of trees. Hugo saw the swarm immediately. It was massive, fifty or more of them, and he knew that was not right. Then the man disappeared.

Hugo summoned his own dragonfly. It took well over a minute for it to appear, and when it did, it moved lethargically. It should have come directly to him and opened the door, but instead it slowly fluttered to the ground, much like Dr. Idiot's had done after he was dead. Hugo stared in shock. What did this mean? He picked it up and turned it this way and that. It was twitching and making little electrical sparking noises, then it just disintegrated. Hugo let the dust fall to the earth and wondered what had happened. His superiors had said they would tie his door to Jonathan's; that way Hugo would always go where Dyson went. He realized that by killing Dyson, he'd inadvertently destroyed his own door.

His fists tightened in anger; his nails dug so deep into his palms that he could feel the blood begin to ooze between his fingers. How could he have made such a grievous error? He was furious with himself. He began to take long, deep breaths; he must calm himself, formulate a plan.

He walked through the golf course to where he had left the bike. Fortunately, it was still there, but the engine had sputtered out. He started it again and slowly made his way from the park. He wasn't familiar with where he was, but once out of the park he quickly realized the streets were in a grid pattern, more or less, and from there he backtracked until he reached what he thought was his point of origin, the man's building.

It was easy enough to find the man's street; there were police and emergency vehicles everywhere. He guessed someone had reported Jonathan Dyson's body on the walkway. He went around the block and back to the center where Dr. Mendoza was being held. If he could monitor Dr. Mendoza, he was sure the other man would show soon. He could then use the other man's door much like the woman scientist had been doing. But he also had to find the sample. Maybe he could take Dr. Mendoza hostage and demand both the sample and his return to the bio-compound. Yes, he thought, that was really his only choice.

He approached the center from the front entrance and circled around the parking lot area, finally deciding to go around back where he could ditch the bike. He would then monitor the main entrance for the man associated with Dr. Mendoza.

Chapter 96

Clarisse remained quiet on our walk through the compound. Since I hadn't seen much of it before, I was in complete awe of the size and lushness of the place. We came to a series of metallic buildings, one story tall with tons of windows. People were coming in and out of them, most wearing the same jumpsuits I'd first seen Clarisse in.

Before we entered what appeared to be the main building, I caught a glimpse of what I guessed was the world beyond the compound's dome. There was nothing but whiteness as far as the eye could see. There were hills and mountains, but all covered in snow and barely discernible. The wind must have been blowing out there because I could see drifts moving along like ghosts across the plains, some running into the curves of the dome itself before they disappeared into the boundless land beyond the compound.

Clarisse cleared her throat, and when I turned to her, she was smiling wanly and waving for me to follow her into the building. A quick glance past her revealed more of the dome wall and what looked like many more domes beyond it. The place was amazing and I wished I had time to see more of it. She led the way through a labyrinth of hallways until we reached Dr. Blare's quarters, knocked lightly, then entered. It was a sparsely furnished room; not big, but enough for the three of us. He stood when we entered.

"Dr. Blare, this is Frank Mann," Clarisse said with a shy smile.

Dr. Blare smiled broadly and thrust his hand out. "It is a pleasure to meet you, Mr. Mann. Tell me, how are the doctors?" I guessed he meant Jorge and Felipe.

"Call me Frank, please. They're okay for now, but that's not going to last." Then I told him the same things that I'd told Clarisse. She didn't cry for her friend this time; the reality had set in.

Blare sat down in his desk chair and waved toward the two guest chairs for us to do the same. He rubbed his forehead absently and said, "I suppose that explains a great deal." I wasn't sure what he meant and looked to Clarisse for clarification.

"We were putting the data together for you to take to Felipe. Dr. Blare was running an algorithm on the existing doors to be sure he didn't miss any information. He found two doors that were created, but not by Jorge. These had been created after the facility was staffed and Jorge had gone through. They don't have the exact configuration as Jorge's doors, and they are interfering terribly. We believe Jorge's door was already malfunctioning because it detected Felipe. Once the altered doors opened and Jonathan went to your time, Jorge's door detected them and tried to integrate them, thus becoming corrupted. We believe the contamination continued when Jorge went to

San Francisco and his door detected multiple, but similar, DNA strands."

Okay, I thought I understood and nodded my head. This time Dr. Blare spoke.

"But that is not the only problem. You see, the doors must complete certain cycles before they can be shut down. The final cycle is always the return to its origination *with* its traveler. The two doors, the copies, shut down on their own. I am now sure that one of them was Jonathan's door; it would deactivate the minute his heart stopped. The other must be the man who killed him."

"Why do you think the other one belongs to that guy? He was alive and well twenty minutes ago."

Dr. Blare frowned slightly. "Whoever created the door for Jonathan also created the second door, and tied them together. I think they did it so that they would both always travel to and from the same places."

I had to think about that, and when I realized what he was saying, I said, "You think this guy is now stuck in our time?"

Dr. Blare and Clarisse nodded in unison. She said, "But there is more. He's done damage to the timeline. So far, it doesn't look too bad, but the blips and ripples are now identified. An investigation will be conducted on Jonathan's death. They will find his comm badge and UD in a hotel room, and they won't know what they are. They will remain in an evidence locker for twenty more years, his death will never be solved, and the items will eventually be destroyed. So far that is all, and we can live with that. But if we cannot find this other man and get him back, it could get much, much worse for us all."

I didn't know what to do, but I knew I needed to talk to Felipe. I needed to know if Jorge was safe, and I desperately wanted to see Selena, because I knew just looking at her would help calm me down. "I need to go back. Is that thing for Felipe ready? Can I take it to him?" I hoped I didn't sound as desperate as I felt. I was beginning to get a tightening in my chest that could only be fear and panic.

"Yes, he may need more information though. Come back if he does," Dr. Blare said, handing me a device that looked similar to an iPhone.

"Wait, do you think you could open the door when you are with Felipe, and he could use your comm badge to talk to us?" Clarisse asked.

Dr. Blare looked at her admiringly and smiled, and then he turned to me with a questioning eyebrow.

I shrugged. "I can sure try." I started to get up and then realized something. I had no idea where I was going to end up when I returned if I left from Dr. Blare's quarters, and I sure didn't want to end up back at the park. Then an idea hit me.

"Can you two figure out how to configure this place with San Francisco? What I mean is, if I leave from here I don't know where

I'll end up. If I go back to the path where I arrived, I could run into that guy again. If we use the spot on the path and overlay a map of the city onto a map of your compound, then we could find a spot that I could leave from that should be harmless for me to return to on my side." I had no idea if what I said made any sense.

But Clarisse must have thought I did. She smiled broadly and went to Dr. Blare's desk and began to type quickly on his computer. Within a minute she had what looked like a map of the city, but an underlying map was beneath it. I pointed to Ocean Beach, a spot that would put me on the sand (though hopefully not in the water), and a quick walk from Selena's apartment.

Chapter 97

"What do you mean you want to get him out of here now?" She almost screamed at him and Clint flinched. Betty was a good-sized lady; she was mean and fierce, and Clint knew better than to cross her.

"Please, Betty! Frank said that he thinks the man who attacked Jorge also killed that lawyer dude. It isn't safe for him here," Clint pleaded.

Betty's eyes widened in disbelief, then narrowed. "What the hell are you talking about? Murder? Who got murdered now and by whom?" she demanded.

Clint was exasperated. All he wanted to do was tell her the truth, but hell, he barely believed it himself; and not only that, she'd lock him up and throw away the key if he did tell her.

"Betty, that lawyer guy followed Frank home today. Before he knew what to do about it, another guy that fits the description Alex gave of the attacker came up and stabbed the dude. Frank split, but he's not sure if that other dude, the attacker, is following him. So will ya help me get this done, please?"

Betty angled her head at Clint. His tone, the words he used—they all screamed desperation. She'd known this giant man since he was a giant youth and she did trust him, that much she knew. She sighed heavily and said, "Yeah, let's go. I'll handle the doctors and nurses up there; you just get him loaded into a wheelchair and headed down to the loading bay."

As Betty headed toward the door, Clint pulled out his cell to call Kath. They decided to eliminate the middle man and just have her show up with their SUV at the loading bay.

Betty turned and pointed her index finger at him, "You boys *will* tell me what the hell is going on here when you get that man to wherever you're taking him!" Clint nodded. He'd leave that part to Frank. He couldn't think what they were going to tell her that would make any sense at all and not screw up this timeline thing.

Chapter 98

I landed in the sand, and since it was uneven, I also fell down. As I stood and dusted the sand off my hands and knees, I saw a woman with a small terrier standing about three yards away with a perplexed look on her face. I guessed she'd been looking in my direction when I suddenly appeared. I just shrugged and trudged up the sand to the highway. I glanced back once, but she was on her way and didn't seem to think much of it. It took me ten minutes to get to Selena's apartment, and when she answered the intercom, she sounded a little frazzled. When I got upstairs to her apartment I could see why. Felipe was very pale, and his breathing was really labored. Darrel was pacing back and forth anxiously.

He said, "Frankie, man, your friend here needs a doctor something fierce. I can't get ahold of Clint either. What the hell is going on?" I could hear his frustration and panic, and looking at Felipe I could understand.

"Darrel, Clint should be here soon, okay? I need to talk to Selena for a minute. Can you just stay here with him?" Darrel nodded but didn't seem too happy about it.

I pulled her to the hallway and toward what I guessed were bedrooms, and said, "Listen, I just saw Clarisse and Dr. Blare. Jonathan's death is causing some problems with the timeline, but even worse is that the other guy, the one who murdered him, may be stuck here." I told her about the chase through the park and the visit to the compound.

"Does that mean you'll have to find this man and take him back, like with Clarisse?" She looked worried, and rightly so. This guy had just killed another man a little more than an hour ago, his second murder since coming to our time.

"I think so, but first we gotta do something about Felipe." I pulled out my cell and tried Clint's phone. It went to voicemail, so I tried Kath's.

She answered, "Frank, can't talk right now. I'll call you in ten or fifteen minutes."

I stared at the phone. What was going on? I had a sinking feeling in my gut and I didn't like it. We went back to the living room and all of us began to pace, with the exception of Felipe, who was busy scanning the device Blare had given me. But his breathing seemed better and that was a relief.

Chapter 99

He was just about to ditch the bike when he saw a woman in a large car pull around and head toward some large doors at the back of the building. For some reason it made him suspicious, so he watched her. She parked parallel to the loading bay, and then went around and opened the cargo door at the back of the vehicle. After a minute or two a very large black man came out with another man in a wheelchair. Hugo immediately recognized him as Dr. Jorge Mendoza, and he smiled. It was a good thing he'd held onto the bike, since he would need it to follow them.

The man and woman loaded the doctor into the back seat, and then the man loaded the chair into the cargo section. The woman got in back with Dr. Mendoza, and the man got in the driver's seat and started to drive away. This vehicle was much larger and easier to see from several cars away than the one he'd followed earlier, and he didn't think these people were looking out for him. But he was cautious and did his best to stay as far away as he could and still keep track of them.

Chapter 100

My cell phone rang…it was Kath. I took a deep breath and answered it. "Hey, what's going on? Have you talked to Clint?"

"I'm with him and Jorge; we're on the way to you now," she said. Then she asked for directions and we hung up. It was another agonizing fifteen minutes before Selena's intercom buzzed.

Clint had Jorge in a wheelchair that had an oxygen tank attached to the back of it. Jorge wasn't using the oxygen, but he didn't look good either. Felipe jumped up as soon as he saw his brother. I could tell it took some effort, but I could also see the rush of adrenalin he was getting from the reunion. He knelt down in front of Jorge, took his hand, and said, "Jorge, can you hear me?" His breath was ragged, and as I started to say something, Clint leaned forward and put his giant hand on Felipe's shoulder.

"Felipe, let me take a look at you; you don't sound good." He turned to a pocket at the back of the chair and pulled out a bunch of clear tubing wrapped in plastic. He unwound it and attached a nasal cannula to it, then attached the tube to the oxygen tank. Clint still had his stethoscope in the pocket of his uniform and he pulled it out. Felipe let him do a quick examination, then let him affix the cannula around his ears and into his nostrils. He remained on the floor in front of Jorge the whole time. I didn't think we'd be able to pry him away, either. I pulled an ottoman over from the corner so he could sit more comfortably.

After a few minutes he removed the cannula and looked up at Clint. "Thank you." Gesturing with the hand still holding the tubes, he said, "It is helping." Then he turned back to Jorge and said, "Can you hear me? We're in a bit of trouble, brother, and I need your help."

Jorge didn't stir at first, but after what seemed like forever he began to move. The hand Felipe was holding began to twitch and his eyes seemed to focus; not much, but some, at least. Felipe was patient, quietly talking to him, almost whispering. By now Clint had moved Darrel to the opposite side of the room. He didn't want Darrel to overhear anything, and I thought he was trying to send Darrel home. It didn't seem to be working, though.

I knelt down next to Jorge and took his other hand. I said, "Jorge, we need to get you both home, but we need your help; can you understand us?" I wasn't sure if my voice and touch did anything to revive him, and I didn't care, but he seemed to be coming out of it, more and more each second.

When he spoke, his voice was weak and low, and Felipe and I had to lean in to hear him, our heads almost touching. "Good to see you, brother." A small, faint smile spread across his face, the first one I'd seen from him. "We...the door, I think the door closed...."

"No, not your door, Jorge; but mine is closed and Jonathan's is closed. He is dead,

Jorge. Another man—we do not know who, but he is from our time—he killed Jonathan." Felipe let that sink in, and Jorge seemed to understand.

"Yes, that must be what I felt…Jonathan's door closing. But another door closed too…I felt it as well; it hurt." As if in response to that memory, a painful expression flashed across his face. "How will you get back?" he asked Felipe. All along I thought Felipe would just go with me, or Jorge, but the expression on Jorge's face led me to believe that might not be possible.

Felipe looked at me and then turned back to Jorge. "Christian has provided data on what we believe was done. Your door is corrupted. It isn't closed, but I don't think it's wise for you to use it, and I don't believe I can use it. I think we need to go back through Frank's door. I believe it is a hybrid of some sort, created by our combined DNA, so it should accept us."

Jorge turned to me and smiled. "Of course, I couldn't grasp it until yesterday. I knew that there was a connection, but it was as if it was stuck in my head. I couldn't quite reach the knowledge." He squeezed my hand and I suddenly realized that all this time, he never actually knew who I was. His damaged mind wouldn't let that little bit of family history through to him. I squeezed back and smiled in return. I also realized that he seemed more coherent than I'd ever seen him before.

"Jorge, you seem better...you know, mentally," I said, and looked over at Felipe. Neither of them said anything for a minute, and I was beginning to think they didn't understand what I'd said. Finally Felipe spoke.

"It's you," he said, smiling. "Jorge's door became corrupted because of me, and then it became worse, much worse, when the other two doors were opened. But when they encountered you, they were able to reconnect. Now they have three close strands and they are feeding on them. It's helping him," he said, nodding toward Jorge. I had no idea what that meant, and it must have been apparent in my expression. "The door that opened...your door. Somehow that is a combination of all of us. I think that is why it's so...self-aware, why it directed you. It wants us back where we belong...it is part of us," he said in an almost wistful tone.

Chapter 101

Christian was furious. He slammed his fist into the wall and turned to his desk, shoving his chair so violently that it tumbled across the room and slammed into the visitor chairs.

His father had called from the GSC headquarters twenty minutes ago. Interpol had known all along that the SS was gearing up for something big, and they suspected that they might have sent someone to the compound. He could not believe that he had not been told of this, especially since his father was Interpol's chief inspector. If they'd done so, he could have found out who the infiltrator was and possibly prevented what was happening now. His father had tried to calm him, explaining that they couldn't just make accusations without evidence. Evidence! Christian thought, sparking a new bout of fury in his already fuming mind. For God's sake! The compound, Jorge's success…these things were absolutely vital to the survival of mankind. How could Interpol have thought it wasn't urgent, that *action* wasn't urgent?

He took a deep breath and calmed himself as best he could. He needed to be calm, and he needed to think. His father said that Interpol would be sending men over to help him find the perpetrator. Christian had laughed at him, rather maniacally at that. What good would that do them now? The man was already in the 21st century, had killed two people, had affected the timeline, and they had no idea who he was.

Suddenly his computer let out an alarm that a secured communiqué had just come in. Christian picked up his desk chair and replaced the visitor chairs. He then sat and opened the message. It was from his father again; they'd broken down the scientist who had helped with the devices for Jonathan and the unknown assailant. Her name was Dr. Joan Bectle. She said she'd received the information on the door technology shortly after the compound had been staffed. She wasn't sure who sent it to her, but she did have the DNA for the two people for whom she was supposed to program the doors. The first was Jonathan and the second was an unknown, which was deeply concerning. The majority of the population was DNA-printed at birth; it was like a fingerprint, only better. But more importantly, anyone who came to the compound was printed; they had to be in order to make the journey. If this unknown had never been printed, then there was no way to know who he was or how he got there, for that matter.

Dr. Bectle also said that she'd been approached by one of the directors, a man whom Christian had always admired and respected; now he felt only loathing for him. His father had said the director was also in custody, but would not talk about who he was working for. The only thing the director would say was that it was too late, that they had the sample and would soon be in control of everything. Christian didn't think that was true. He could account for everyone who'd gone through the door from the compound to his time; no unknown had used a door. But what if the unknown had sent the sample through alone, disguised as something else...food or other scientific data?

Christian replied to his father's message, telling him that he thought the director's statements were false, a bluff to buy the SS time to get the sample. The SS may not be aware of Jonathan's demise, or of the unknown's inability to obtain the sample from Jorge. He was just about to call Clarisse when there was a knock on his door.

Chapter 102

Hugo parked the bike at the curb and walked around the building. He saw the man and woman with Dr. Mendoza enter a parking area, but he didn't want to pull into it in case they caught sight of him. By the time he made it to the entrance, the black man and white woman were just entering the building with Dr. Mendoza in the wheelchair. He waited until they were out of sight and then tried the double glass doors; they were locked. He looked around; there was a panel on the wall with many buttons next to what he assumed were the occupants' names. He had no idea who they had come to see, and even if he did, he wouldn't have contacted them directly.

He walked away from the entrance and sat on a retaining wall that allowed him a view of anyone coming and going through the glass doors. He sat quietly, assessing the situation and what he knew. First, he now knew where Dr. Mendoza was, and he thought he could reasonably assume that the sample was probably in this building as well. The black man was huge and probably a formidable opponent. Hugo was confident he could kill the man, especially since he now had Dyson's gun, but if there were others there—and there most certainly were—he may not be able to get them all before they got him. The next concern was the man who was travelling back and forth; he needed him so Hugo could get back. He was sure if Dr. Mendoza's door was working properly that he'd have gone back to the compound already, so it was a safe assumption that his only way back was the other man.

He wasn't sure how long he'd been sitting there, lost in his own thoughts, when the doors opened and the large black man emerged. But no, this wasn't the same man; this one was a bit larger, his head was bald, but the resemblance was indisputable and Hugo knew this man had something to do with the one who had brought Dr. Mendoza. Hugo followed him to his vehicle…a shockingly small one, considering this man's size. Before the man could get into the car, Hugo pulled the gun out and placed the barrel in the center of the man's back.

"Do not move. I have no concern about using this, and it will surely blow your heart out through your chest." Hugo grinned; he'd like to see that actually, but first things first. "Where is Dr. Mendoza?"

Darrell's shoulders sagged slightly, but otherwise he didn't move. "I don't know anyone named Mendoza, you got the wrong dude." His voice was deep and Hugo detected a threatening tone; he would need to be very careful.

"No, I do not have the wrong man. I saw your relative and the white woman take him into the building. Now you can either tell me or I will simply shoot you; it is your choice," Hugo said bluntly.

"Shit," Darrell hissed; he needed to buy time. He'd had his cell phone in his hand because he'd been checking for messages when he left the building. He glanced down at the screen; his last call was to Clint. The asshole with the gun was behind him and he was pretty sure he couldn't see his hands or the phone. He tapped the screen and redialed Clint's number, then he put his finger over the ear piece. He didn't want the man to hear Clint's voice when he answered.

Chapter 103

Clint's phone rang. I thought it would be Betty but he said, frowning, "It's Darrell." He answered and listened for a minute; a look of deep concern crossed his face and he told everyone to shut up. He put the phone on speaker and we could hear Darrell's voice, but faintly.

"Man, I'm telling you, I don't know any Dr. Mendoza. I was just in there visiting my girl, and I ain't got any relatives in that building either."

A fainter voice said firmly, "I do not have time for this game. You will tell me where he is or I will shoot you. You have thirty seconds."

Clint and I ran for the door simultaneously. We were out and on the stairs within a matter of seconds. Darrell hadn't been gone long enough to get any further than the parking lot. I remembered seeing his car when we met him here, so that's where I was headed. We burst out the front doors and I indicated for Clint to go to the right while I ran toward the left. I could see Darrell's head above the other cars in the lot, but that also meant that Clint's head would be visible. I tried to wave him off, but I didn't think he saw me. I knew I was faster than Clint; his sheer size slowed him down. I sprinted like my life depended on it, and when I came around the car next to Darrell's, I dove at a man holding a gun to Darrell's back.

As I hit the man with the gun, there was a loud report and I knew the gun had gone off. The man toppled backwards over my head and landed behind me. He'd knocked me to the ground in the process, and before I could get up a huge foot and leg clad in white rushed past my head. I scrambled up. Clint had kicked the guy's hand and the gun he was holding skittered across the blacktop, but the guy was fast, ridiculously fast. He was up and had pulled out a nasty-looking knife. I slammed into him again and felt the knife blade graze my arm. Then suddenly, there were so many dragonflies everywhere I was almost blinded. I waved my hands at them instinctively, like a man trying to rid himself of a swarm of gnats. It took me a second to realize that they were taking me away, and then I wasn't in the parking lot anymore.

The sudden transport through the door knocked me off guard, and I landed on my butt in the middle of the path where I always seemed to arrive. The swarm of dragonflies was still there, and instead of dissipating like usual, they almost seemed to get thicker, more concentrated. It took me a second to realize someone else was coming through. I scrambled to my feet and began to run, turning back once to confirm what I thought. The man, the murderer, was right behind me, and he was gaining on me.

Suddenly there was a loud siren, and bursts of a mechanical voice on a loud speaker seemed to be coming from everywhere. "Alert" and "intruder" came blaring from all directions; red lights were flashing from somewhere overhead. I dug into my pocket, trying to get the comm badge out so I could alert Clarisse. Once I'd finally managed it, I hit the pad and screamed, "Clarisse, he's here, he followed me through!" If she responded I couldn't tell; I couldn't hear anything over the loudspeaker. I ran even faster, with no idea where I was going.

Chapter 104

Blare let Clarisse into his office. Her face held a haggard expression and she sat heavily in the closest guest chair. "The timeline, it's changing again, but I can't tell what is causing it. For now they are little changes; nothing substantial, but we must stop it!" He could tell she was on the verge of tears.

"Yes, I am not surprised, and I agree we must stop this thing now." His comm badge beeped and he said, "Yes," rather sternly to the caller.

"Dr. Blare, this is O'Connell in the transport room. We've received a request to open the door from Director Montgomery at the GSC and...Chief Inspector Blare at Interpol."

"Damn it!" Blare said irritably. "I'll be right there. Tell them they must wait." He turned to Clarisse and said, "They have Director Calibri in custody. He was the traitor at the GSC. My father wants to send agents here to help us, but I don't want them here. They can only do harm. Come, we must go to the transport room."

They left his office, and before they could leave the residential building, the alarms began to go off. He turned to Clarisse. "I reset the system to notify us if anyone but Mr. Mann came through from either the 21st century or from our time. Someone is here." He began to run toward the building's exit when Clarisse's comm badge went off.

"Wait, Dr. Blare, it's Frank." She tried to listen, but the alarms were too loud. She thought Frank said he was there and the murderer was there, too. "Where, Frank, where are you?" she asked through the badge. When there was no answer, Blare grabbed her arm and they ran out of the building. Blare had his UD out. She could see a map of the compound on it and three moving dots on one of the pathways. They ran in that direction.

As they got closer, they saw a huge black man dressed in all white running down the path. He was chasing a smaller man that Blare thought he recognized as the one who'd infiltrated his quarters some time back. As the path straightened out they also saw Frank running in the lead. Then suddenly there were hundreds of dragonflies and Frank disappeared into them. Then the other man went into the swarm, and finally the large black man dove toward it, barely getting there before they disappeared.

Blare stopped suddenly, leaning over a bit to catch his breath, finally saying, "That was him, the man who broke into my quarters. I recognize his build."

Clarisse had gained her breath and composure and said, "Yes, that was Frank in the lead, and his friend Clint was the larger man." She turned to Blare and grabbed his arm. "Dr. Blare, how could they all come through like that? Did you see the swarm? There is not supposed to be a swarm like that. Something is desperately wrong!" Her voice had begun to rise in panic.

The alarm stopped suddenly and Blare looked around. It must have detected that the men had left and shut itself off. His comm badge beeped again; it was O'Connell, "Sir, please come quickly, they want to exercise the emergency door. We were still tied into them when the alarms went off. They want to know what's happened."

"Yes, yes, I'm on my way. Tell them to stay where they are," he said irritably. He and Clarisse jogged to the transport terminal, not paying attention to the concerned looks of their associates as they moved through the compound.

His father's face was framed in the monitor used for communication to his world. His expression was simultaneously angry and concerned. When he saw Blare he said, "What in the hell is happening there, Christian?"

"Chief Inspector, we need to discuss this privately. Please go to Director Montgomery's office and I will contact you shortly." Blare reached down and entered the command to disconnect with his world. Then he turned to O'Connell and said, "No one is to come or go. Put us in lockdown." He turned and walked away. Clarisse had to jog to keep up.

Chapter 105

I was running at top speed when the door opened and I went through. I landed on concrete and stumbled and rolled. I was stopped painfully by hard steel, my head taking the brunt of it. I had no idea where I was, but I was sure I wasn't going to be alone for long. I scrambled up and tried to gain my balance, but I'd hit my head pretty hard and I was little dizzy. In my peripheral vision I saw another man appear from a swarm of dragonflies to my left. I stumbled backwards, knowing it had to be the man who had followed me from the parking lot to the compound, and now wherever I was.

I backed into a railing. I could feel the cold metal as my hands grabbed it. The man was coming at me and still had his knife. I ducked to my right as he hit me, then suddenly a mass of white and black hit him and he went over the railing.

I leaned over and put my hands on my knees, nauseous from running and hitting my head, but also from knowing that Clint had been with me all along and had just saved my life. He put a large hand on my shoulder and said breathlessly, "You okay, man? Shit! You're bleeding!"

He tore open my shirt sleeve and started to poke around. I jerked hard and tried to stifle a scream. "Hold still," he said as he ripped the sleeve completely off my arm and wrapped it around the wound. I remembered now...the guy's knife had grazed me, but I didn't think it had done too much damage.

"It's just a scratch, I'll be fine," I said as I fished in my pocket for my cell phone.

Clint wrapped it tightly and said, "Yeah, you'll be okay." Then he looked around and I looked with him. We were on the USS San Francisco Memorial, a platform on a small outcropping in Lands End that was made up of the damaged bridge wings of the World War II era cruiser. I guessed I'd hit the concrete platform first, and then slammed into one of the wings. Clint was looking over the side, scanning the thick trees and bushes at least a hundred feet below us for the assassin.

"Should we go down and look for him? He might be hurt, and if he ain't, I'd like to be sure he is," he growled.

I smiled. "No, but we do need to get out of here." I dialed Selena's phone and she answered immediately.

"Frank, where are you, are you okay? Is Clint with you?" she said breathlessly.

"I'm fine and Clint's fine. What about Darrell?" I asked.

"He's fine; that guy tried to shoot him, though." She was whispering. "He said you both disappeared. He's asking a lot of questions and he's quite angry."

"Okay, we need you to pick us up, and I think we need to get Jorge and Felipe out of there. The killer knows where you live. I'm not sure if he's alive or not, but we can't risk it. Can you pick us up and ask Kath and Darrell to get the guys out of there?"

She sighed. "Of course, but where should they take them?"

Good question, I thought. The only place I could think of was Clint and Kath's house. I told her that and then told her where we were. She said she'd be there soon.

"Selena, one more thing—please tell Kath and Darrell to be very careful that they're not followed, okay?"

I hung up and looked at Clint. The shock of what had happened should have been wearing off, but he still looked dazed. "You okay?" I asked.

He smiled and said, "That was…amazing. My god, Frankie, is that what happens to you?"

I had to return the smile; he had just made his first and hopefully only journey through the dragonfly door. "Not quite like that. There were way too many of them…usually there's only a few. I think something is very wrong with the door."

Clint's smile faded and he said, "What do you mean?"

"I don't know. We need to talk to Jorge and Felipe. Come on, let's move over to those trees and wait for Selena," I said, pointing to a small forest of trees on the other side of the parking lot.

Chapter 106

Christian contacted Director Montgomery's secure line as soon as he was in his office. Clarisse was sitting in the guest chair in front of his desk. They had discussed what they should say about the alarms and decided the truth was best. Dr. Montgomery was sitting at his desk, with Blare's father leaning over him so that he too could be seen in the communication monitor. Christian explained everything that had happened and that he did not want, or need, outside interference.

Dr. Montgomery responded. "Dr. Blare, we've identified the man who infiltrated your quarters. His identification papers state that he is there under the pretense of being on the grounds-keeping staff. The name they used was Hugo Beletz. But we now know that he is a trained assassin; they've been training him since he was a small child. We have reason to believe he's responsible for many deaths, murders. They've been planning something like this for years."

Christian sighed heavily, then said, "Why wasn't he in the DNA profile for the compound staff?" He thought he knew the answer, though, and Dr. Montgomery confirmed it.

"Someone at Bio-1 altered his records, removed him from your files so that you would not be aware of his coming and going, much as they did with Dr. Dyson's profile."

"I see; that could explain some of the problems with the door," Christian said almost to himself. "We tied the door activity to the compound systems, just additional security to be sure no one could somehow use the doors without authorization. If what Felipe believes is correct, the hybrid doors were picked up by Jorge's dragonfly. It would have been confused at the signals it received, and when it picked up not one, but two similar DNA strands to Jorge's, it became even more corrupted…."

"Christian…son, please understand that this situation is now beyond your control," his father said with an undertone of emotion. His father was the consummate professional, and was always respectful of a person's hard work and accomplishments. The personal reference, as opposed to his professional title, startled Christian and concerned him. Could there be more that his father wasn't telling him? "There is at least one more person at the compound that has been working with these…with the SS. I think we can all agree that you need my help to flush this person out before he does more harm."

Christian was sorely tempted to respond in kind, but he realized his father's concern. Instead, he said, "Director Montgomery, Chief Inspector Blare, I think you need to understand something vital." His voice was firm and confident, and he saw his father flinch ever so slightly. "The door that Frank Mann is using originally began with more than one dragonfly.

As you both know, there should be just one dragonfly per person. We feel that is tied to the fact that his door is a hybrid made up of his DNA and the DNA of both Drs. Mendoza. But Mr. Mann is now experiencing swarms...I saw them myself. Other people are coming through on his door as well, which you know should be impossible. I have sent all the data to Felipe Mendoza, and once we've completed this conversation, I will be contacting him to discuss the necessary solution to return both Jorge and Felipe and to seal the doors."

His father's expression was pained. He said through clenched teeth, "And what do you propose to do about Hugo? Do you know where he is? What about this other person, the one at the compound? How do you propose to find out who that person is? I can send a team now. They are equipped to flush this person out and help you with the return of the Drs. Mendoza and Hugo."

Christian softened his voice. His father was concerned for him and he knew it. "No, Father, that will not work. We cannot risk using any of the doors at this stage. I will assign my own security to find the person on this end. I will be in contact soon regarding your other concerns." Christian terminated the connection before his father or the director could respond.

Clarisse's expression was bordering on shock. Chief Inspector Blare was known for his hardline tactics, and to see even a touch of emotion was...well, a bit surprising. And of course Dr. Blare had basically hung up on both of them.

He smiled warmly at her. "I'm sorry, my father is…well, he's my father. Do you think Frank will contact us soon? I need to speak to Felipe, to confirm what I just told them and to work out a plan."

"I hope so, Dr. Blare," was her only reply.

He nodded and said, "Please go back to your quarters and monitor the timeline. I need to know everything that has changed, regardless of how small it appears. I fear we may need to do some damage control before this is over."

She rose to leave, and as she was approaching the door what he had said sunk in. "Damage control? What do you mean?"

"We may need to tamper with the records of Mr. Mann's time, remove references to Hugo and Dyson. I'm not sure what else."

Chapter 107

Selena arrived ten minutes after I called her. I saw her car pull into the parking lot and Clint stepped away from the trees we were standing in and waved his hand high above his head, which seemed almost as high as the average flag pole. She had no trouble spotting him.

Once we were in and properly seat-belted, she headed toward the Sunset District, all the while firing questions at us about what had happened. She was equally distressed and impressed at our quick thinking, and happily informed us that aside from complete confusion, Darrell was fine. It was a great relief. We had both heard the gun go off, but neither one of us had time to check if Darrell had been shot.

As soon as she hung up with us she had told the others to load up in Clint and Kath's SUV and get to their house. No questions. Just do it; she'd be along soon. I wasn't sure what we were going to tell Darrell, but there was no doubt an explanation of some sort was in order. We owed him that much.

Because it was the middle of the day there was a lot of street parking, so within minutes we were all assembled in Clint and Kath's living room. Darrell was pacing back and forth and you could almost see the steam coming out of his ears. He said immediately, "Where in the hell did you two go?"

I looked at Clint, then at the others. I didn't want to tell him the truth, but I respected him and considered him a friend. I'd also put him in danger. Finally I said, "If I told you that Jorge and Felipe were from another time, that I am the key to getting them home, that the current and future timelines are in danger, and that the guy in the parking lot has killed two people and wants to kill us, would you believe me?"

Everyone was staring at Darrell, their collective breath held, waiting to see what he'd say. Finally he narrowed his eyes and said, "You on drugs, Frankie?"

I laughed. Not much else I could do, because if someone had said all of that to me, I'd think the same of them. "No, but the truth of what is going on is just as ridiculous, and the less you know, the better off you'll be."

Clint said, "I'm sorry Dar; I didn't know that guy followed us."

Kath let out an audible breath. "Of course, he knew Jorge was at the center; he must have been staking the place out and saw us load him into the car!" She looked at Darrell apologetically, like she should have known they were followed, too.

"Look, he's obviously good. He was blatantly following me. He must have been a lot more careful when he followed you from the center. But it doesn't matter; I don't think he'll be bothering us again." I turned to Darrell and said, "Thank you, for everything, but I think you should go home. We should have this all resolved really soon. There isn't much more you can do, and I don't want you to have to explain anything we do to anyone else."

Darrell glanced at Clint and then narrowed his eyes at me again. "What ya mean, Frankie? You guys aren't gonna do nothing illegal are you?" Darrell's past, and repentance from that past, had made him an ardent law-abiding citizen.

I shook my head and said, "I don't think so. I don't want to, but I don't want you involved. It's better that way, please trust us." I was pleading, and I could tell it was working.

He looked around the room and said, "Will you call me if you need me?"

I patted his back and said, "Yeah, we will. Thanks, Darrell."

He left and I filled the others in on what had happened. Jorge was still on the foggy side, but I could tell he understood what I'd said and he definitely understood what Felipe said next.

"Jorge and I looked at the data that Christian sent over. There is no doubt in my mind that the door is extremely unstable. These swarms you are experiencing, we believe they are a result of all the unauthorized and altered doors that have been opening and closing since Jorge's arrival. I do not believe they will remain fully open for long. In fact, I think they are now destabilizing. If we don't get back soon, we may never get back." Felipe had removed the nasal cannula while he spoke. Now his breathing was labored, and when he was done speaking he put the cannula back up to his nose.

"Okay, let me try and open them. I won't go through, but I think we can talk to Clarisse using the comm badge."

Chapter 108

Clarisse went back to her quarters and ran the algorithm to update the timeline. The program took a few minutes and she paced impatiently. When it was done, she reviewed the data and was shocked by what she saw.

Things had changed dramatically. According to the timeline of the very near future, the UD and comm badge found in Jonathan's hotel room had eventually been sent to the FBI for analysis. One of the techs at Quantico realized its potential and managed to clone most of it, eventually selling it to a terrorist group. That group used it against western governments to take control of banking and governmental systems. A man fitting Hugo's description went on a murderous spree, killing many people, and once caught he told all. That also reached the ears of the FBI, who put him together with the devices. Hugo was able to give them enough information to use the devices against the terrorists that had purchased the cloned information.

The entire future was changed. If she were to go to her time now, it would be nothing like what she'd left. The world would be in a perpetual state of technological and physical war that would take billions hostage and kill billions more. These events, combined with the agricultural disaster, would certainly lead to the end of civilization. The only reason she was safe was because she was currently in a time that preceded the 21st and 22nd centuries.

Her chest began to tighten. Panic, anxiety, and sheer terror started to take over. She took several deep breaths and buzzed Dr. Blare. He didn't answer and she tried again. When that didn't work, she activated the trace she'd put on a few days before. Suddenly she heard his voice, and that of another person she thought she recognized.

Chapter 109

Blare's comm badge beeped. It was O'Connell in the transport room. "Sir, I tried to initiate the lockdown procedure, but sir, something is wrong. Someone has already locked us down and I cannot access the system."

"Calm down, O'Connell. What do you mean someone has already locked us down? It can't be done from any other place." Blare sounded much more calm and controlled than he felt.

"Agreed sir, but someone has done it; they have access. I'm trying to trace it now, but… well, they are very good, sir, they've covered themselves well." O'Connell was probably one of the best computer techs of his time. Christian had handpicked him. If he couldn't figure this out, they were in very deep trouble indeed.

There was a knock on his door. As he moved to open it, he said to the visitor on the other side, "One moment," and then to O'Connell, "Keep trying, I'm on my way."

Christian opened his door to find a man who he recognized as another computer tech holding a gun to his chest. The man—he thought his name was Joe—moved forward, causing Christian to back into the room. Joe closed the door behind him and waved the gun toward a guest chair. "Sit, Dr. Blare. I really don't want to use this." The gun was a laser pistol, and Christian knew that if it was fired at him, it would first burn, then disintegrate the flesh and tissue it touched. It would be excruciating for a few short seconds, and then he'd simply die. He wondered momentarily how Joe had managed to get the gun through the scanning protocols.

"Joe, is it? I think you should know that we've arrested everyone involved in this. Dyson and Hugo are dead, we have the sample, and soon there will be Interpol agents here. You simply cannot get away." Of course, he didn't know for sure that Hugo was dead, but Joe didn't know that. He thought he sounded calm and confident, but now he wished he'd taken up his father's offer of outside assistance. His comm badge beeped a few times, but he ignored it.

Joe smiled mischievously. "Dr. Blare, your expression tells me that you are aware that I have control of the lockdown." His smile transformed into a malicious grin and he said, "Imagine my surprise when I hijacked the program to find that you'd altered the lockdown protocol to leave a few doors open. One is Dr. Jorge Mendoza, but the other two…well now, that's certainly interesting, isn't it?" Christian had altered the protocol to keep Jorge's, Felipe's, and Frank's doors open. He didn't think either Jorge or Felipe could use their doors, especially since he was sure Felipe's door was beyond use, but he was sure that combined with Frank's DNA, they could return using his door.

Joe didn't wait for a response. Instead, he said, "So that tells me a few things. First of all, Dr. Mendoza is still in the 21st century. Second, he has the sample with him, and third, of course, is that Felipe Mendoza is alive and well, probably with his brother. But do tell, who does the third door belong to?"

Christian had no intention of telling him. He said, "Why are you doing this? Don't you understand what your actions could mean to our time, our people?"

Joe laughed. This time it wasn't just malicious but condescending, something Blare hated in any person's tone. "Oh, Dr. Blare," he said shaking his head. "You'll find out soon enough, so I'll just tell you now. My great-great-grandfather was an amazing man. I think you'll recognize his name, Silas Gregaria? Of course, I can see it on your face. Yes, yes, you're wondering why that didn't come up in my profile. I'm sure you're aware that so many records were destroyed during the dark decades. For the protection of our family, and to ensure that we would succeed in our ultimate goal, the names of my family members were changed and all records prior to that were destroyed. So of course you would have no way of knowing where I came from. But be assured I am a progeny of *greatness*. Now I must admit, I do believe you when you say Jonathan and Hugo are dead, and that is mostly unfortunate. Jonathan was my cousin, but his death will have little impact on us. Hugo, on the other hand, was quite useful; a man without a conscience or a soul is a truly valuable asset."

Christian's head was spinning. So it came to this; a diabolical and insane man's dreams were coming true almost a hundred years after his death. Christian said, "So what do you plan to do then? Jorge won't come back unless I tell him to, and your plan won't work without the sample."

"Oh, that's simple. You're going to tell him to come back, or I'm going to kill everyone in Bio-1. Then I'm going to convince Dr. Mendoza to come back because his lover is in danger. Don't for a minute think I will not do that, Dr. Blare. It's of no consequence to me either way if the staff here dies." He waved the gun around. "We have plenty of scientists to work the sample into a virucide."

Chapter 110

Clarisse was now feeling a panic so overwhelming she didn't think she could control it. She ran into her small bath and threw up. The sound of her retching had blocked out some of the conversation from Blare's badge, but she had the general idea. They were locked out of their world. Joe, a tech she knew well and had considered a friend, was virtually in control, and Jorge and Felipe were still in the 21st century. If they did what Joe wanted, there was no doubt in her mind that he'd kill everyone anyway. Before she could organize her thoughts, another, even more devastating thing came to mind. Joe could gain full knowledge of the door technology before Jorge and Felipe could destroy it. Of course, what did that matter? They'd all be dead. Her comm badge beeped, interrupting the transmission from Dr. Blare's badge. It was Frank.

Chapter 111

I summoned the dragonflies. The swarm was large, but not as large as the last few times, so I took some comfort in that. I hit the comm badge and it took Clarisse a moment to respond.

"Oh, Frank," she said, taking a deep breath and launching into an explanation of what she had discovered with the timeline and what was now happening in Dr. Blare's office. She was breathless when she finished.

I blew out a huge breath and told her what had happened with Hugo. "We're not sure if he's dead or not, but from what you just said, it seems that he's not. So what now?" I looked at Felipe and Jorge in the hope they had some ideas.

They were conferring quietly with each other and finally Felipe said, "We need to send Jorge and the sample back. Clarisse, when Frank's door is used, is it detected on your end? I assume not, or this man Joe would know you're talking to us now."

"No, Joe can see that it isn't part of the lockdown, but he shouldn't be able to tell if it's in use. But what about you, Felipe? You need to come back, too. We need to get you to our doctors," she said, the panic rising again.

"Clarisse," Jorge said weakly, "Felipe must stay to repair the timeline. With the changes you've detected, we don't even know if the technology we had is there…to heal him."

"What about this dude holding Dr. Blare hostage? What are we going to do about that?"

Clint asked. His expression told me he had some ideas about that, and I wasn't sure I liked them.

"Hon, I know what you're thinking, but you're not a fighter," Kath said, which was what I was thinking he was thinking. On the other hand, what else could we do? They needed help and we'd had the element of surprise on our side, since this Joe guy wouldn't know we were there.

"Clarisse, if Clint and I came with Jorge, do you think we could maybe get the upper hand on this guy? He wouldn't know we were there, so…." I wasn't sure where I was going with that, and before I could say anything Clarisse spoke.

"I see what you mean. Maybe if you and Clint came over, we could surprise Joe, possibly capture him and detain him long enough for us to reverse the lockdown and let the Interpol agents through. Then they could take custody of him. Hopefully, by that time Felipe would be done and could come back. We could seal the door and this nightmare could be over." She was speaking very fast and her voice was rising, showing just how scared she was.

Felipe said, "This would only work if Frank's door cooperates with his commands. The door is so unstable I can't be sure it will do that. I also need something, Clarisse. I need to know the exact configuration of Jonathan's UD and comm badge. I have an idea as to how I can destroy the devices remotely."

Kath asked, "What about this Hugo guy? We don't have any idea where he is."

I turned to Felipe and said, "If we had his fingerprints you could program our law enforcement system with his information. Then we could place an anonymous call to the police. With any luck they'd pick him up and arrest him. If they could tie him to Jonathan's murder and maybe even Eddie's, he'd go away for a long time."

"That's good, Frankie, someone like him would probably get killed in the slammer. Besides, Darrell and I know some guys with connections to lifers. We could ask them to get the word out on this Hugo dude, make sure he doesn't survive his first week." What Clint had just said should have surprised me, suggesting that we solicit a murder contract on someone via the prison system. What surprised me more was that I actually liked the idea, a lot.

Selena was shaking her head, then said quietly, "I don't condone murder, but this man is a killer, and from what Clarisse has said, his future actions could destroy the lives of so many people, I can't object. But how are we going to ensure that he's tied to Jonathan's murder?"

I smiled. "The knife. I bet he's still got it and will hold onto it. It's his only weapon at this point. Speaking of that, did anyone pick the gun up that Clint knocked out of his hand in the parking lot?"

Kath smirked and said, "Darrell brought it up with him. I have it in my purse. He said not to touch it; he used a tissue to pick it up. Do you think we could get a print off it?"

"No need for that," Clarisse said. "Now that we know who Hugo is, I can access his file here. Hold on." We could hear fingers typing rapidly, then she said, "I have them. They might have altered his DNA profile, but they didn't bother with the prints they filed with his documentation. Felipe, is your UD on? I can send it over now."

"Go ahead," Felipe responded. We saw him fiddle with the device and then he said, "Got it. Now get me Jonathan's information quickly; we need to move fast."

The dragonflies had begun to appear, so I quickly said, "Clarisse, the dragonflies are back. I'll get back in touch shortly. Try to find out more about what's happening with Blare."

Chapter 112

We heard a beep as the dragonflies closed the door and the comm badge disconnected. I looked around the room and finally stopped on Selena. "Did you bring it with you?" I didn't have to elaborate and neither did she; she simply nodded and smiled.

Felipe said, "Frank, I have to warn you and Clint, it's possible you won't be able to control the door. You could get stuck there, or it could send you back before you are able to subdue Joe."

"I know, Felipe, but we have no choice. I'm not willing to destroy our futures without at least trying to save them first." I glanced at Clint, who nodded his agreement, and I said, "Besides, you guys said the doors are tied to all three of us, so maybe if we all concentrate hard enough...I don't know, they'll listen."

Jorge smiled weakly. "Yes, I think that will work, but we must be quick."

Kath grabbed her purse and pulled the gun out. "Here, you may need this." Marcus had taught both Clint and me how to shoot when we were teenagers. It wasn't because he thought we should be armed, it was because he had a tidy little collection of guns and wanted us to be aware of the power and responsibility they placed on a person. I still had two of the revolvers, mid-nineteenth century collector's items, in a safe deposit box at my bank. Clint took the revolver from her and checked the cylinder. There were five bullets left. That

would have to be enough. I was hoping we'd
return with all of them.

Chapter 113

The first thing Clarisse did was access the system so that she could modify the intruder alarm that Dr. Blare had programmed. He'd told her it was set to go off if anyone besides Frank came through; she needed that to include Clint as well. She then reactivated her connection to Dr. Blare's comm badge; she also used the program on her computer to determine his whereabouts. He was still in his office, and Joe was talking.

"Let me see if I understand this. You have no way of contacting Dr. Mendoza? I find that hard to believe, Dr. Blare, but if you'd like to play that game, I'm sure with proper persuasion we could get Dr. McClellan to get in touch with him."

"Clarisse McClellan doesn't know anything about the door or its functionality; she's a computer scientist and a systems analyst!" Blare said angrily. "Besides, that was an integral part of Jorge's failsafe program. No one could communicate with someone who'd travelled to the 21st century unless the traveler initiated the communication. It's not set up like the compound system to our world." Christian narrowed his eyes at Joe. "But you know that, don't you? After all, if you could communicate with your co-conspirators, you'd already know how badly they failed you." He wanted to make Joe angry. Anger often clouded judgment, and he needed this man off guard.

Clarisse wished there was a way to warn Dr. Blare about what they were planning. Then she had an idea. She beeped his badge again, and this time Blare answered.

"Yes, Clarisse, what is it? I'm quite busy at the moment," he said, trying to warn her off.

"I know, Dr. Blare, and I'm sorry to interrupt, but it's rather important. Dr. Mendoza has made contact. He plans to come back very soon, but he was adamant that he see you first and privately."

Joe held his hand up and mouthed, "Put her on hold."

"Clarisse, I have another communication coming in. Can you hold on while I address it?"

"Of course, sir." Then she switched over to the reverse function she'd programmed into his badge so she could hear what was said.

"Where does Dr. Mendoza's door drop him when he returns to the compound?" Joe asked.

"His quarters."

"Tell her to have him come here when he arrives and you will wait for him. Also ask her about Felipe Mendoza."

That wasn't good, Clarisse thought. Dr. Blare could monitor every corner of the compound from his office, and the possibility that Joe would see them all arrive would ruin the element of surprise that was needed to make this plan work.

When Blare came back on the comm badge he repeated what Joe had ordered.

Clarisse responded, "Sir, Dr. Mendoza was insistent that you meet in *his* quarters. Besides, the staff is very nervous due to the lockdown. If they see Dr. Mendoza before you do...well, they would certainly overwhelm him in their need for reassurances."

Blare looked at Joe and Joe shrugged, then mouthed, "Felipe."

"Fine, I'll be there within a few minutes. What about his brother? Will he be coming back with him?"

"He didn't say, sir. I was told he was very ill, and my timeline algorithm does not reflect that he ever returns." She allowed a certain amount of emotion to seep through, to show her sadness in Felipe's almost definite demise. She hoped that he understood. He wouldn't know she could hear them, but hopefully, he understood that something was afoot.

***

Christian was taken aback by what she said about Felipe. Could that be true? After everything, he still didn't make it home? Suddenly it occurred to him that she might be aware of what was happening with Joe; but how? It didn't matter, though; he had no choice but to do as Joe said and hope that he could somehow overpower him at some point.

He said, "I see. I'll proceed to his quarters now." He turned to Joe and looked at him coolly. "And what is your plan after Dr. Mendoza returns?"

Joe was equally cool. "That really isn't your concern, Dr. Blare." He waved the hand with the gun toward the door. "Let's go."

***

Clarisse rushed to Jonathan's quarters and hacked into his computer again. She was able to pull his comm badge information from her quarters, but his UD would not be linked to the main system. He would, however, have a link set up on his personal computer. She downloaded all the information onto her UD and then hurried to the path where Frank and the others would arrive and waited for them to contact her.

Chapter 114

We were as ready as we were ever going to be. I was standing near Jorge and Clint was speaking quietly to Kath at the other end of the room. Selena came over to me and took my hand and said, "See you soon." Then she kissed me lightly on the cheek. No warnings to be safe or anything; she seemed confident that we'd succeed. That made me feel a little better, but not entirely comfortable. She turned to Jorge and handed him the small metal case containing the virus sample. He tucked it into the side of the wheelchair and smiled at her. She gently touched his face and said, "Take care of yourself."

When Clint was by my side I summoned the dragonflies. They came quickly, and to my relief, it wasn't a great swarm; just like the first time, a few of them lazily hovering around. I touched the comm badge and waited to hear Clarisse's voice on the other end.

"Frank, I have Dr. Blare and Joe going to Jorge's quarters. I'm monitoring their progress now. Felipe, are you ready for me to transmit the information you requested?"

"Yes," he said, "send it now." He fiddled with his device and after a moment said, "I have it; good luck."

I took hold of Jorge's wheelchair and said, "We're coming now, Clarisse." Then I stepped forward into the dragonflies. Clint was behind me, so close I could feel his breath when he exhaled as we went through the door.

We landed in the usual spot; the wheels of Jorge's chair crunched loudly on the gravel. Clarisse was standing a few feet away, and when she saw Jorge she leapt forward and knelt in front of him, taking his hands and bringing them to her lips, tears of what I thought was joy streaming down her face.

He managed enough energy to kiss the top of her head and said, "I missed you, darling." Just being there seemed to have an immediate effect on him. His color was improving and his eyes were taking on a clarity I'd never seen before.

Clint cleared his throat and said, "Uh, guys, I think we should get this going." He was nervous and I didn't blame him. We were there to capture a bad guy and save the future. I had a moment to wonder how it was that my life had suddenly turned into an action adventure movie.

Clarisse stood. "Yes, come. We need to get Jorge somewhere safe." She looked down at her UD and said, "Dr. Blare is almost at Jorge's quarters." She moved to the back of the chair and pushed it down the path quickly until we reached a small square metal shed with a slightly pitched roof. "We can't let anyone see him, not until this is done and Dr. Blare is safe." She looked at Jorge apologetically, and he nodded that it was okay. She opened the shed door and pushed the chair in. It was clean and organized, and shelving lined all the walls except the one with the door in it. He was a little cramped in there, but at least he'd be safe. She handed him another UD device and said, "It's tied to mine, so you can monitor what we're doing, I'll be back for you as soon as I can." Then she leaned down and kissed him.

She led us around the shed to a narrow path. "This will take us to the back of the residential building. It's not used that often, so we should be able to move undetected."

"Clarisse, what's the situation? Dr. Blare is with this Joe person. Is the guy armed?" I asked.

She nodded, "Yes, I believe so, or Dr. Blare would have tried to overpower him. If he is, it's with a laser gun. It's capable of cutting a man in half in only a few seconds."

I heard Clint hiss "Shit!" under his breath.

"Great," I said. "So what are you thinking?" She was still moving at a fast clip on the path and I reached forward to stop her. She turned and looked at me. "Clarisse, what's the plan?" I said sharply.

She looked from me to Clint, but before she could respond, Clint said, "Look, we have the element of surprise. I think we should shoot first and ask questions later, but I don't wanna shoot this Blare guy by mistake. Tell us what they look like."

"Dr. Blare has blond hair and blue eyes. He'll be wearing white coveralls. I'm not sure what Joe has on, but his hair is quite dark, so it should be easy to differentiate the two. Are you armed?" she asked.

"Yep, but nothing as fancy as a laser gun, so we need to be quick," Clint said with a slight smile. He was the better marksman, so I was glad he had the gun.

"All right, this is what I think we should do. Clarisse, you'll knock on the door and I'll stand to the side, with Frank on the other side. When they answer, I want you to push the door open as hard as you can, then drop to the ground. I'm gonna fire quickly and hopefully I'll have a clear shot," Clint said.

Clarisse said, "The door slides open, but I think that's better because you should have an unobstructed view of the room."

Clint thought for a second, then said, "Okay, same plan, but when the door slides open, I want you to dive to the left and get out of the way."

"Wait; I thought we were going to try to subdue the guy and detain him until the authorities here could take him," I said without much conviction.

Clint said, "Frank, the guy is armed. I'm not taking the chance that he shoots and kills one of us. I don't wanna do it this way either, but we don't have a choice."

Clarisse nodded her agreement. "He's right, Frank, we don't have a choice." They were both right, but I didn't have to like it.

She turned and walked quickly until we reached a large metal building. She led us around it until we came to a glass door that opened into a corridor. "Jorge preferred to have his quarters at this end. It was quieter and easier for him to come and go without being bothered by other personnel. He was quite popular here," she said in offhand manner that seemed detached. Before she opened the door she checked her UD again, and when she was sure Dr. Blare and the other guy were in Jorge's quarters, she opened the door and we went inside. She led us in and stopped at the first door we came to.

Clint and I took up our positions on either side of the door. She knocked and waited for an answer, but none came. We looked at each other with concern and confusion. She touched the comm badge on her lapel and said, "Dr. Blare, it's Clarisse. Are you in Dr. Mendoza's quarters?"

We waited, and when there still was no answer, I motioned for them all to move to the end of the corridor, "Do you think he killed him?"

She shook her head. "No, his badge signal would have changed if his heart stopped beating."

"So he's either not letting him respond or he's knocked him out somehow." I ran my fingers through my hair and said in exasperation, "What now?"

"How do those doors open? Is there a key or something?" Clint asked.

"No key; the pad to the left of the door is a palm reader. Dr. Blare would have overridden it to get in." Suddenly something clicked with her and you could almost see the wheels turning in her head. She did something with her UD and said with a slight smile, "I've done the same. Now I can open the door."

I said, "Try one more time to get him on the comm badge. Tell him you're here. I'd rather this guy open the door expecting you. If he's quick, the sound of the door opening without his permission could give him time to get into a firing position." Clint nodded and we went back and took up our positions.

Clarisse tried again. "Dr. Blare, I'm here, outside in the corridor. Can you let me in? Jorge asked me to join you." She looked at each of us and we waited. A very slight beep sounded and the door began to slide open.

She didn't stick with the plan though; she stood in front of the door while it opened. I could see Blare slumped in a chair, but I couldn't see the other guy. Suddenly Clint's left hand shot out and pushed Clarisse, his right came up, and I was momentarily deafened by the report of the gunshot in such close confines. He fired a second time, but not before the other guy fired too. A burst of light shot through the opening and hit the opposite wall of the corridor. It momentarily flamed before petering out. Clint lowered the gun and stepped in, and I followed. Clarisse was picking herself up off the corridor floor where she'd fallen when Clint pushed her.

The man was lying on his side. Something that looked like a gun, but not quite, was in his hand. Clint kicked it away with his foot and knelt down to feel the guy's pulse. There was a lot of blood and I didn't think he was alive. Clint said, "Clarisse, call a medic or doctor or something. This guy's still breathing, but not for long." She made the call and then moved to Dr. Blare. He was coming around, but very slowly. Clint had pulled the pillow from the bed and stripped the case off, using it to plug the bullet wound in the guy's stomach. He turned to me and said, "Give me your shirt." I was wearing the remnants of my long-sleeved shirt over a t-shirt and I stripped it off and handed it to him. He used it to wrap the other bullet wound in the guy's leg. I was impressed that both of Clint's shots had found home.

Clint went over to check on Dr. Blare. "You got clocked pretty good, Doc, but you should be okay." He had tilted Dr. Blare's head to the side; I could see a rather large lump starting to form at the base of his skull by the hairline. When the medics arrived, Clint explained that he thought they should do an MRI on Dr. Blare to be sure he didn't have a more severe head injury. I wasn't sure what it was—Clint's size, the fact that they had no clue who he was, or if maybe they no longer used the term MRI—but they sure looked perplexed.

Clarisse, Clint, and I took two of the four medics with us and went to collect Jorge. When we got there he was smiling and said, "You did it?" The medics began scanning him with some sort of hand-held device and then started to take him away. As if on command, the dragonflies began to appear, hovering lazily around us, like they were simply playing on a bright spring day. Jorge addressed the medics. "Could you wait a moment, down the path a bit?" They obeyed and Jorge looked up at us with admiration and appreciation. "You saved us, all of us. I can never thank you enough."

I knelt down in front of him and said, "You don't have to thank us, just get better. Save your world and take care of this beautiful woman." I reached over and grabbed Clarisse's hand gently.

His eyes were filling with tears of gratitude, and I realized I would miss this man, who was part of me, a great deal. I squeezed his hand and stood. Clint reached over and squeezed his shoulder. "Take care, my man. I'm better for knowing you." He leaned down and planted a light kiss on Clarisse's cheek. She smiled demurely and turned to me. We hugged fiercely and then Clint and I walked into the dragonflies.

Chapter 115

Selena and Kath looked anxious when we arrived, but when they realized we were unharmed, relief washed over their faces. Felipe was sitting at the desk in the corner that held Kath's laptop; he was also using the nasal cannula again and looked a little green. "Are you ready to go home, Felipe?" I asked, knowing the answer.

"More than ever. I sent a virus to Jonathan's devices. They'll activate and overheat, and it will destroy them. I also accessed your criminal database and entered Hugo's information and fingerprints. You can make the call to your authorities whenever you are ready."

"Great. You'll close the door when you get back?" Deep down inside I realized I didn't want it to close, because once it was closed I'd never see them again.

He nodded and stood up a little shakily, and Selena moved toward him and hugged him. "Take care," she said as she kissed his cheek. Kath and Clint said their goodbyes and retreated to the edge of the room. The dragonflies hadn't left this time; they knew their job wasn't quite done. I grabbed Felipe's elbow and walked him over to them, and then we were gone. Clarisse had remained at the arrival spot and was waiting. Felipe walked to her while I stayed put, surrounded by the dragonflies, and in seconds I was back in Kath and Clint's living room. It was quick, and this time the dragonflies disappeared in the blink of an eye.

Clint pulled his hands down over his face and blew out a massive breath. "Holy shit, man! That was something else! I'm sorry, Frankie, I'm sorry I didn't believe you…you know, before."

I smiled and then just laughed outright. They were all staring at me. "Clint, I would have locked you up in a padded room if you'd come to me with what we all just went through." He laughed long and heartily, and Kath and Selena picked it up and laughed with him.

Kath said, "I need a drink; anyone else?" Selena smiled and they both headed toward the kitchen. I had shoved my hands into my pockets, mainly because they were shaking and I didn't want the others to see. It was out of relief, but still it was embarrassing. My left hand wrapped around something and I realized it was the comm badge that Clarisse had given me. I smiled to myself. It was useless once the door was closed, but I'd always have it to remind me of the importance of the decisions that we make and how they'll impact the future.

Clint looked at me and said, "What?"

I shook my head. "Nothing, just thinking about my future," I looked toward the kitchen and the woman that I'd spend the rest of my life with, "And how great it's going to be."

Chapter 116

Clarisse stood on the catwalk. Jorge's arm was around her, and for the first time in a long time she felt safe. They gazed out at the beauty of the snow-covered plains and the hills beyond. The moon was full and bright, and she realized this would be the last time she'd see them bathed in the iridescent glow that only a full moon could provide.

"I wish we could have warned them about the future," she said quietly.

Jorge tightened his grip and said, "If you had, we wouldn't be here." She knew that, of course, but to know the suffering that was in store for them was hard to bear.

"Will you miss them?" she asked.

"Yes, I suppose I will, but Felipe will miss them more. Will you?"

"Yes." She leaned into him and they stood silently for a few more minutes before heading in for the night.

It had been eight weeks since they'd returned. Interpol had descended on the compound as soon as the lockdown was released. Joe was treated and taken into custody, there were more arrests, and the entire situation caused Interpol to take a closer look at groups they considered "non-threatening." All but the main compound had been dismantled and returned to their time. The cleaners were currently making sure that all traces of their time spent there were erased.

Felipe had received the medical care he needed and recovered quickly. He and Christian had taken up full-time residence at the GSC facility in Toronto, and synthesized the virucide quickly. They'd implemented a worldwide dissemination, and the flora of their time was already responding with the results that they'd all worked so hard for. They'd also moved the healthy agriculture from the compounds to their time. With the virus eradicated, the new flora was thriving. They were only keeping Bio-1 going until they could be sure everything was going as planned. Clarisse would be leaving tomorrow morning to return to her time and her work at the GSC. Jorge would follow in a few weeks when the final removal of Bio-1 was completed.

Epilogue

The sun was slowly sinking into the sea, turning wispy white clouds a pale pink and the horizon into a fiery show of oranges and yellows. We'd arrived at Kyle and Trish's house almost two hours ago. Betty, Clint, and Kath were already there, and Selena and I were the last to arrive for this impromptu cocktail party.

It had been Selena's idea to do this. She'd said that these people were our friends and most likely an integral part of our future. They deserved to know. Clint and I were hesitant…the fewer people that knew of our future the better. But she was right about their importance in our lives, and that was what finally convinced us.

I'd finished telling them everything; Clint, Kath, and Selena had made a few comments or corroborating remarks, but everyone else remained silent through the story. We were sitting on the roof deck of Kyle and Trish's house, looking out over the spectacular view of the Golden Gate Bridge and the bay. With the sun's setting it had begun to get cool. Trish got up and turned on two heat lamps, and within minutes we could feel the warmth emanating from them. Still, no one stirred or made a sound. Finally Kyle got up and took the elevator down one level to the house. While he was gone, Trish refreshed everyone's drink. When he returned he sat heavily and looked at me.

"I just talked to Detective Rice. He was the local detective assisting in the investigation of Eddie's murder at the VA, and because this fellow Jonathan was there, they'd also brought Rice in on his murder in front of your house," Kyle said, as he looked from me to Clint. I started to object and Kyle held his hand up to stop me.

"Don't get all riled up, Frankie. I didn't tell him anything. He called me yesterday and left a message, wanted to know if I knew anything about Jorge. The guy is missing, you know, and he's also AWOL, so Rice is getting some pressure from his fed counterparts and the military. I told him what Betty and I discussed; that as far as I knew, Jorge had walked out of the hospital on his own, that no one has seen him since." He paused to take a drink, swirling the ice in his glass thoughtfully before taking a long pull on his whiskey.

"I wanted to know what he'd tell me regarding this Jonathan guy. We go way back so he gave me a little information. They'd found Jonathan's hotel room key and tracked it to a room at the Holiday Inn on Van Ness. The only things they found in the room were what they thought was a cell phone, or PDA, and a little button-type thing. The tech guys at the PD couldn't make heads or tails of either of them. A day after they retrieved them, the damn things started up and began to fry from the inside out. All they have now are two hunks of plastic and metal."

I smiled and looked around. Kath and Selena were managing to keep their expressions blank, but Clint had a satisfactory grin on his face. I nodded and said, "We know, but it's great to get confirmation. Did he say anything about Hugo?"

Kyle nodded. "He said they'd received an anonymous call from a pay phone in the Civic Center BART station about him, and they picked him up a few days ago. He had a pretty nasty knife on him with some dried blood on it, and they're pretty sure it's the same kind that gutted the lawyer and probably Eddie too." Selena had made the call from a pay phone and was assured they'd look into it. Since Hugo knew where we both lived, I decided neither of us could go home for a while. Clint and Kath offered their guest room, but I could afford to rent a furnished apartment for a few months. Regardless, we were both happy to hear we could go home soon.

I smiled, and before I could speak, Clint said, "Forensics will find out that's Jonathan's blood, probably some of Eddie's, too. He'll go away for a long time. Hopefully, he'll piss someone off in prison and they'll take care of him." Clint didn't hide his desire to see Hugo die a horrible death; he was still hurting from what Hugo had done to Eddie.

"I see," Betty said, a little sarcastically. "That's real Christian of you." She furrowed her brow, then said, "But I understand. Did your little futuristic friend say that's what happened to him?"

Clint, Kath, Selena, and I all exchanged glances. We'd thought of that but we never had a chance to ask Clarisse about it.

Kath had been mostly quiet, but she finally spoke up. "We don't know; we didn't get a chance to ask, but I think they would have come back, or at least communicated with us, if things didn't go as planned."

Betty nodded at Kath's explanation, but I couldn't tell if she was satisfied with it. Then she said, "So this door, it's closed? Forever? Or can they come back again?"

Selena spoke up. "Yes, it's closed, and according to Jorge and Felipe, they vow never to open it again. They said they'd destroy the technology as soon as they closed up the compounds and removed all evidence of ever having been there. I would think that they're nearly done with that now." She finished quietly. I could tell she missed them both, especially Felipe. She'd spent the most time with him, and I knew she was sad that she would probably never meet them again. If all of this hadn't happened, she would never have met them, and neither would I. I took comfort in knowing I had the small amount of time with them that I did.

"Hmm," Betty said. "That's a hell of a story, kids, and honestly, I think you've all gone bat-shit crazy." She nodded toward Kyle. "But based on what we know from Detective Rice, I think we don't have a choice but to believe you all."

***

Detective Rice disconnected the call and now looked at his phone with curiosity. His old friend, Kyle, knew more than he was telling, that was for sure, but he didn't really care. The murdered lawyer wasn't a lawyer; in fact, he wasn't anyone. His identification was stolen and his prints didn't come up on any of their databases. But these gadgets they'd found, now those piqued his curiosity, and he was pissed that they self-destructed, which was essentially what they'd done. The tech guys said they had put them aside to work on a more pressing matter, then they just started up on their own. A light humming sound turned into a buzzing noise, and the next thing they knew, poof! Melted plastic and twisted little pieces of metal.

They'd picked up this Hugo Beletz guy in the Tenderloin; he had been arrested for assaulting a liquor store clerk when the clerk tried to stop him from walking out with some food. The guy was rambling about the future and screaming profanities at the arresting officers. Funny thing, though; when the guy cussed, he sounded like Mr. Spock in *Star Trek IV*, like he'd just recently heard those words and wasn't sure how to use them. The other interesting thing was that he had one of those little buttons on him.

Did You Enjoy The Dragonfly Door?
Let the world know by posting a review. Click this link and it will take you directly to the reviews page: (review url).

Comments? Questions? Feedback? Or Receive Updates On Upcoming Projects.
I would enjoy hearing from you. Please email me at margaret@margaretmillmore.com
I will not share your email address with anyone.

For More Information About My Work (turn the page) or Visit my website at http://margaretmillmore.com or my Amazon page at http://www.amazon.com/Margaret-Millmore/e/B005ME8QTQ.

Doppelganger Experiment

After more than four weeks in a coma, Jane woke up to find several things wrong; she didn't remember the last three years, she was married to a man she didn't know, and frightening dreams were infiltrating her sleep. But were they dreams or memories? As she struggles to recapture a life she doesn't remember she discovers clues that lead to flashes of memories and the discovery of horrific experiments that end in murder... and something worse than murder. A psychological thriller based in San Francisco.

Click here to get your copy:
http://amzn.to/B005MGOX50

The Four - *A Series*

They do exist and they always have. They live, love, and work amongst us and they are part of us. But they are different too, they are stronger and they live longer. They are the topic of many books, movies and myths, but their existence remains a secret, not everyone would accept them. And like us, they have those that are simply evil. Keeping these evil ones under control is the price they must pay to continue the lives they love. They must protect their human brethren from the Dark Ones, those that would rather kill than preserve.

Century after century the good battled the Dark Ones, always prevailing and preserving the lives of their beloved humans. In the 17th century, two powerful Dark leaders emerged, they organized their forces and a bitter war ensued. It was a fight to the death and the good thought they'd won. Four warriors led the battle, four warriors whose strength was beyond anything they knew, four warriors whose legacy had to be protected…

The good formed a consortium and with the help of a powerful sorcerer, a spell was cast; a spell that would follow the warriors' lineage in case their power was needed again. The warriors are long dead, but their heirs are not, and now they must fight. The Dark Ones have re-emerged, they are more powerful, more resourceful and they want to control mankind and the world.

Click here to get your copy:

Book I: http://amzn.to/B008UYO0WC

Book II: http://amzn.to/B009ZE7O24

Book III: http://amzn.to/B00BY8G83U